broken
dreams

WHITL⊙CK
F A R M S

Forbidden Hearts

Broken Dreams

Tempting Promises

Forgotten Desires

broken dreams

NEW YORK TIMES BESTSELLING AUTHOR
CORINNE MICHAELS

Broken Dreams

This book is a work of fiction. Names, characters, places, and incidents either are products of the author's imagination or are used fictitiously. Any resemblance to actual events or locales or persons, living or dead, is entirely coincidental and beyond the intent of the author or publisher.

Cover Design: Sommer Stein, Perfect Pear Creative
Editing: Nancy Smay
Proofreading: Julia Griffis & ReGina Kate
Cover Art drawing: Samaiya Beaumont

dedication

To those who have experienced grief and found a way through it.

Dear Reader,

It is always my goal to write a beautiful love story that will capture your heart and leave a lasting impression. However, I want all readers to be comfortable. Therefore, if you want to be aware of any possible CW please click the link below to take you to the book page where there is a link that will dropdown. If you do not need this, please go forth and I hope you love this book filled with all the pieces of my heart.

https://corinnemichaels.com/books/broken-dreams/

one

GRADY

"Let's go, Jett, you need to get dressed." I huff as I try to convince my three-and-a-half-year-old to put his freaking shirt on.

He stands there, arms crossed, and shakes his head. "No school."

"Yes, school, Daddy has to work."

"No work, Daddy!" He steps back. "Animals!"

It's been a hard transition moving back to Sugarloaf for both of us. For one, I'm living with my sister, Brynlee, in her three-bedroom house with her version of a petting zoo out back. Which Jett wants to be in all the time.

And I'm caring for the new horses Rowan just purchased while I try to get my flight instructor business going.

Third, I'm doing it on my own and doing a bang-up job at it so far. That's to say I'm really fucking horrible at this single father shit.

"After school you can go see them," I negotiate. I never realized toddlers are literally like dealing with a hostage situation. He can argue, pitch a fit, refuse to do what you ask and then, when he hears something he wants, he caves.

Lisa would've handled this perfectly.

The thought of my wife whispers through me like the wind,

1

leaving my chest cold as it exits. It's strange at times when I feel her loss, like now, when our son is being defiant.

"I pet them?"

I sigh. "Yes, Auntie will let you pet them, but only if you get dressed and go to school."

He sways a few times, as though I just asked him to solve a trigonometry problem, and shuffles toward me. I fight back my grin and slip the shirt over his head. Once he's dressed, he leaps forward, wrapping his arms around my neck. I catch him with a laugh and hold him tight. Some days I don't know how I do this, the ones where he's never happy, throwing himself on the floor over a bath, or sick. Then these moments remind me why it's all worth it.

Why giving up the life I worked so hard for the found family I had in the navy, the way it felt to be a hero in some way didn't matter because Jett needed me more.

He needed me to be the man to walk away from it and give him a home.

"Love you, Jett," I say and then kiss his head.

"Love you, Daddy!"

And then he's off, running out of his room, no doubt to try to escape to the barn where Brynlee is feeding her menagerie.

I push up, groaning as my knees creak, and go after him.

There I find him, in my sister's arms, squeezing her cheeks together. "Hello, Grady," she mumbles with her mouth smooshed.

"Morning, Brynn."

She tries to smile but can't. "Jett, you're squishing my face."

He laughs. "Auntie sounds funny."

"She looks funny too," I joke, unable to stop my older-brother instinct to piss her off from rising.

Brynn widens her eyes and puffs her cheeks, forcing him to let go, which causes him to giggle more.

That laugh, so much like his mother's. Lisa laughed with her whole heart. It was goofy and loud, but it was beautiful and free. I wish I could hear it again, even just once, so I could truly memorize it.

"You look funny and smell," Brynn attempts to insult me.

I roll my eyes and grab Jett from her arms. "Good comeback."

She shrugs. "I'm not as quick with the insults, I suppose."

"It would seem not." I put Jett down. "Go get your shoes and your lunch bag."

He runs off, and Brynn hands me my coffee tumbler. "Here. Are you going to Rowan's this morning?"

I nod. "Yeah, I'll drop the menace off and head there, work with the two new horses and then go fly. Easy day."

"I'm sorry I can't drop him off for you today, seems stupid for you to drive there to just drive back here, but I have court today and I won't be able to leave early if you need me either."

I nod. "I'll see if Asher can, if needed. I have a flight today around two, but I should be back to get him before they close."

Every one of my siblings live on the same land. My great-grandparents bought over two hundred acres and farmed here for a long time. Asher, my oldest brother, inherited it when our mother died, and he divided everything equally. The issue is that my acreage is nothing but trees. I did that because both Brynn and Rowan wanted to live here, and that gave them housing options as well. We had a holdup with the permits, something about drainage issues, so what was going to be about six months of living with Brynn is looking much longer.

"Sounds good," Brynn says as she takes a sip. "Any word from the builder?"

"They *believe* they'll have the permits next month. Then I need the builder to get going, but until we have those, everyone's hands are tied."

"You know you can stay here as long as you want. There's no rush for you guys to move out."

I would move into a rental, but so far, my new company has only secured one client and I have no money. I'm trying to get my business off the ground—pun intended—but it's been a hard go so far.

In the meantime, I'm also doing a courier service for the

CORINNE MICHAELS

insanely wealthy or big companies when they require small items within a very short time. Some bigwig in New York City is having me shuffle paperwork that has to be signed and witnessed. It allows them to receive it in minutes versus hours. I think it's crazy, but they pay the money and I need a lot of it since my brother isn't paying me, not that I'd take it anyway.

I smile at my sister and her big heart. "I do. I appreciate that."

"But I'm driving you nuts . . ."

"It's not you, Brynn, it's that I want to get Jett settled. I need to be his father full-time now and that means a home I can raise him in."

The entire reason I gave up my lifelong dream of being a pilot was for him. To give my son the life his mother wanted him to have. One where he can run and play, be around horses, give him a family life like I had growing up. I would do anything for my son and to honor my late wife's memory.

"Well, I love having you both here and you are raising Jett now, Grady. We all need a little help from family."

And really, it's been great having Brynn around too. She's amazing with Jett and he adores her.

My wife died when Jett was four weeks old. It was the worst thing that ever happened and I was lost. I had just under four years left on my commission, which I finished out, but during that time, I was a part-time dad.

Shortly after his birth, the navy was sending me overseas for six months, Lisa and I knew it was coming, we were prepared. What I wasn't prepared for was to be without her and moving Jett to live in Oklahoma with his grandparents. It wasn't ideal, but it was the reality of our situation.

When I got back, he was happy there. He had fun with his nana and pop, playing on the farm his mother grew up on, and we agreed that while I was finishing out my commission, they'd keep him there and we'd have regular visits.

Now I have him, and I want all the time back that I missed.

4

I smile at my sister and nod. "It's not like any of us will be far from each other once I move out."

"True. Don't forget, tomorrow we have dinner with the family to celebrate Rowan's big news."

"The one where we pretend we don't know he just bought another two-hundred acres?"

She grins. "That one."

"Why the hell did he pay that much for it?"

"Because he was in a bidding war with Charlotte Sullivan."

I roll my eyes. "So he paid way over what he should've just to win?"

Brynn laughs softly. "You said the magic words—he won. That's all that matters when it comes to her and that entire family."

My brother is a damn idiot.

"Listen, I was thinking about you."

"This is never good."

"Shut up. Anyway, I was thinking that you should get out and meet people," she says as she shoves some papers in her bag.

I stare at my sister like she just grew horns. "Meet who?"

"People! You need to make friends or date someone."

"I have friends."

She crosses her arms over her chest. "You don't. You have siblings. We're not friends. I'm serious, it's been just under four years and . . . I don't know, you should get out there again."

It's not the first time I've heard this. However, I have no desire. I loved my wife. I lost her, and I would really prefer to keep myself safe from that level of pain again.

Besides, I am focused on Jett and starting a business. Now is not the time to deal with this, and my sister, while coming from a good place, doesn't get that.

"It's not all that easy to find dates when you don't know anyone. Besides, I'm enjoying getting to know the town. I don't have time to go out and . . . deal with that shit."

"So you do want to date again?"

"No. I don't want to date anyone."

She continues as though I didn't say that. "I have this friend, you'd be perfect together."

"I'm not dating your fitness friend." I swear to God.

"Why not? You said you don't have time to meet people, I know people. There you go."

I sigh heavily. "I don't need you to set me up."

"You need someone to step in."

"No. I don't."

"Listen, go out with Margaret. She's sweet, beautiful, has a good job, and likes kids. I have a reservation and everything for you."

"Cancel it," I say through gritted teeth.

Jett comes back in the room. "Daddy, I have shoes!"

I'm so not done with this conversation, but I'm not having it in front of Jett. I turn to look at my son and shake my head. "You do, bud, but you have two different ones on, and they are on the wrong feet." I lift him up into my arms, and he laughs as I roar like a lion. "Come on, let's go find the right ones. See ya later, Brynn. And I mean it, cancel it because I'm not going."

"We'll see! Have a good day, boys! Love you!"

Once I get him fixed, I grab both our bags and get on the road to head to the daycare, leaving my sister's asinine idea at the house. The drive there Jett seems fine, he's watching something on the iPad on our twenty-minute trek. Finding childcare was nothing like I thought it would be. We only have one in town, which had a wait-list, but thankfully, there was an opening in his classroom and we were able to jump the line since Brynlee helped the owner out of a legal issue a few months back.

When we pull up, Jett is looking out the window with a pouty face on.

Please don't let today be like yesterday.

"Let's go, bud," I say as I take his hand and we walk to the building.

It's been an adjustment for all of us. The first few weeks after we got here, it was fun. I showed him around, spent the days going to the park and for ice cream, but now I have to get our lives going.

"No school, Daddy." He pulls on my arm as we reach the front.

I crouch down. "I know it's hard, you miss Nana and Pop, and our home, but this school is fun. Your teachers are nice and . . ." I'm explaining this to a three-year-old who doesn't care, but I don't know what I'm doing, and this seems like the best option. So I go back to my original point in negotiations. "School is fun."

"No fun."

No, it's probably not. I hated school, but alas, he has to go.

"Hey there, Jett," a soft voice says from behind me.

When I turn to look at the speaker, my breath lodges in my throat. This woman is stunning. She has long blond hair that is pulled to her right shoulder, the warmest, most beautiful blue eyes I've ever seen, and she's holding the hand of a little girl who is identical to her.

"You must be Jett's dad, I'm Addison and this is Elodie. They're in class together."

I rise and clear my throat. "I am." I extend my hand. "I'm Grady Whitlock."

"Oh! Oh wow! I never put two and two together. I'm Addison Davis. I moved here a few years ago, I'm not really all that sure about who is who, and I swear people show up and I feel dumb not knowing them . . . and . . . I'm rambling," she says with a laugh. "Let me try this again. I know your brother, Asher, from working at Run to Me."

"Run to Me?"

I don't know what the hell that is.

"Yes, it's the safe haven in town for runaways. I'm one of the founders. My friend, Blakely, is the other owner out in Oregon."

"That's great. Welcome to Sugarloaf. Although, I guess I should be hearing the same since I never really lived here."

"No? I didn't know that."

I shake my head. "My mother moved here when Brynn was young, but I was in college and . . . since then, it was the military for me."

"Thank you for your service."

7

I shake my head. "No thanks needed."

I'm always so uncomfortable when people say that. I did what I did because I wanted to do it. I loved my job, flying, everything about it, and I don't feel I did anything extraordinary. Sure, it's not something everyone does, but it doesn't require my thanks.

"You have it anyway."

Elodie starts to grumble. "I want to paint, Mommy!"

At the same time, Jett starts in. "No. School!"

"Does this get easier?" I ask Addison.

"Not even a little bit, but Elodie hated school at first. She was always with me or family. So, when I had to get her in here, it was a shock. He'll settle in. They're really great here."

I nod, hoping that's true. "If you say so."

She lifts Elodie into her arms. "Stay firm and show no mercy."

"Solid advice."

"Do you want some help?" Addison offers. "They say it takes a village."

Not wanting to feel like a complete loser who can't even get his kid inside a daycare, I flash a grin and shake my head. "I got this. I was a squadron leader and if I could get those infants to listen, I can handle this."

Jett pulls on my arm harder.

Addison watches him try to rip it from the socket and pulls her lips in, fighting a smile. "Okay. Good luck, then. I should get her in, I need to relieve my overnight staff."

"Of course."

"It was great meeting you. I'm sure we'll see each other around."

Not if I can help it. I have no time for friends or women who are beautiful. If I even mention this, my sister will get ideas and God knows she doesn't need more of those.

"Great meeting you too."

She enters the building as Jett tugs my arm, this time I swear something pops as he attempts to move to the car. "Not happening, my man."

And then . . . he throws a fit that I was not prepared for.

He flops to the ground, screaming and kicking his legs. "No school. No school!" Over and over, he yells as I heft him into my arms and try to pin his legs to stop him from kicking me repeatedly. People are staring, watching as I take my inconsolable toddler into daycare.

The front desk doesn't judge, the woman there smiles. "I see Jett isn't excited today?"

"Huh?" I ask, unable to fully hear her over the wailing in my ear.

"Not happy?" she shouts back.

"What was your first clue?" I say with a smile to avoid her thinking I'm being a dick.

She laughs and then walks me down the hall and opens the classroom door. Addison sneaks past me, giving me a tight-lipped smile that's full of understanding.

The teacher walks over, and I put Jett down but hold his arms tenderly. "Jett, enough."

He doesn't agree. He keeps going.

I have been in some pretty intense situations. On a deployment, we were doing routine flight maneuvers and I lost an engine. It was something I'd trained for, but in that moment, it jolts you a bit. I relied on my training, stayed calm, and got us back on deck without issues.

There's no training manual for this.

"Jett, buddy, you gotta stop," I try again as his tears break my heart.

The teacher is beside me, her hand on my shoulder as she tries to reason with him. "Jett, we are going to play with the trucks soon, do you want to come?"

He turns his head away.

"No trucks, huh? Well, Ms. Jamie is coloring, would you like to color?"

He doesn't respond, but the yelling has at least stopped. Now we're just all being ignored.

The teacher fights back a laugh. "I could see how coloring isn't that fun. Your daddy flies planes, right?"

That gets him to meet her gaze.

I answer for him. "I do. Jett loves the planes."

She gasps, which is clearly meant for show, but he eats it up a little more. "I love planes too! Do you know that we also have planes to play with?"

He turns to face her a little more. "Planes?"

"Yes, we have a whole bin right there."

Jett's watery gaze looks to me and then the area where the bin is. I feel his death grip on my hand start to ease, the planes are going to be what gets him to go, I just have to wait him out. The teacher extends her hand, and he lets go of mine and takes hers.

Crisis averted.

I stand here, unsure of what to do when the other teacher comes over. "It gets easier."

"Does it?"

"I've seen the kids who were the worst now run to the building. He'll get there."

I watch my son, who has had his whole life uprooted, push the plane around the rug that has roads printed on it. He has always been a happy kid. Every time I visited or we video called, he smiled the whole time and never misbehaved. Now that he's with me all the time, it feels different.

"What now?" I ask.

She tilts her head to the door. "Now you leave in stealth mode. We have this, Mr. Whitlock."

I'm glad someone does because I definitely don't.

When I get outside, Addison is there, running her hands through her hair as she paces. "I understand that, but I *have* to get to work. I can't wait hours for him to sober up enough."

I walk over and call her name. "Addison? Everything okay?"

She pulls the phone from her ear. "I have a flat and no spare and the tow company can't get here until who knows when."

"Can your husband or someone pick you up?"

"I'm a widow and . . . you know, it's fine. I'll call a friend and just wait a while."

Her words strike through me. She lost her spouse as well and is raising her daughter on her own. Much like me.

By the time someone else gets out here, it'll be a half hour. I'm right here and in no big rush to get to the airport.

"Or I could drive you," I offer.

Her eyes widen. "No, I don't want to inconvenience you by going all the way in the center of town. I'm sure I can find someone."

"I don't mind. I was going your way anyway. Please, let me drive you."

"Are you sure?" she asks hesitantly.

"Of course."

It's not like I can be late since my brother doesn't pay me.

"You're a lifesaver. Thank you."

two

ADDISON

I'm not sure this is really the smartest move, getting in a car with a guy I met five minutes ago, but he's a Whitlock and . . . well, that's all I got.

I fire a text off to my best friend Devney letting her know my plan in case I go missing. She will be the one to assemble a search party for me. Grady had to step in and talk to the tow company after I freaked out and hung up on them because they were talking in circles. So, I'm sitting here as he tries to reason with the owner.

> My car had a flat and the spare, well, it was flat as well. Grady Whitlock is driving me to Run to Me.

DEVNEY

> Interesting morning. I didn't know you met Grady.

> I met him this morning. Hence the texts letting you know.

I share my location.

DEVNEY

> You're a dork. I'll make sure you get to where you're going or at least be able to lead his BROTHER to where your body is.

preciate it.

Grady walks around toward the front of the car, and I try not to notice how attractive he is. He's tall, lean, and has dirty blond hair that looks like he ran his fingers through it, pu   it to the side. There's an air of confidence that surrounds him as he walks, it's really freaking sexy.

And just like that, I shut it down. He may be the best-looking guy in the world, but I don't know him at all.

"All right," Grady says as he gets in the car. "The w company will come out and bring your car to Tired, and they promised to drop it off at your work after it's fixed since they 'caused a great inconvenience,' his words, and there will be no charge for the tow."

"Thank you. You really didn't have to do that."

He shakes his head. "Not a problem."

I let out a huge sigh and then we pull down the drive. Run to Me is in the center of town and it would've taken me another hour to get there, and my new assistant has been there since ten p.m. last night.

"I really appreciate this."

He laughs. "Addison, I'm driving you on my way to work, it's really no big deal."

Right. He said that. I fall silent for a second, looking out the window. I feel as though I need to fill the quietness because I'm awkward.

"So," I say, sucking in a huge breath. "How are you liking Sugarloaf?"

"I'm not sure yet."

I smile, knowing exactly what he means. "I remember that feeling. I grew up in a small town, but each one has its own quirks. Sugarloaf is really a great place, but it takes some getting used to. It must help having your siblings, though."

He nods. "It does, and . . . you said you're a widow?"

I did say that, didn't I? It's not some big secret, just not usually what I lead off with. "My husband was killed a little over three years ago."

And here comes the apology that always follows.

"It sucks, doesn't it? Being a widow with a kid. My wife died around the same time as your husband. She had an aneurysm shortly after she gave birth to Jett."

I turn slightly. "That's really unfair."

"Life seems to be at times," Grady replies. "Anyway, I came here to be closer to family and give Jett the normal life she wanted for us."

"At first, I came here just to run away from my hometown in Oregon. It was too hard, seeing the ghost of my husband, Isaac, everywhere. So, I left, ran to the other side of the country here, because Devney Arrowood is cousins with my husband's best friend. Or should I say late husband? I keep battling with that."

He chuckles a little. "I feel the same. Lisa is still my wife, in a way, but she's not here so do I say wife or dead wife or wife who used to breathe?"

"It's so awkward."

"And trying to talk about it with someone else is even worse." Grady looks over with a smile.

"I was waiting for the apology," I confess. "It always comes."

He nods. "And I get it. People don't know what to say."

"I always wished they'd ask what he was like. I'm sure not everyone feels that way, but I wanted to talk about Isaac, not be sad."

"Tell me about him," Grady encourages.

I lean my head back, smiling as I remember. "He was a nerd. A total football maniac. He taught history in high school just so he could coach football. It was all he ever wanted to do. His smile was warm, and he had the worst jokes I'd ever heard. I miss him, but . . . life goes on, right?"

"It does, even when we feel like it might not."

It's been three years now, and sometimes it feels like yesterday. Other times it feels longer. I forget things, like the sound of his voice, and then I have to listen to an old voicemail to feel close to him again.

"Tell me about your wife," I say, turning to look at him better.

"Lisa was always smiling. It didn't matter what was happening in our lives, she smiled through it. When I was leaving on deployment, she would wink at me, kiss me, and then walk away while the other guys' wives would be crying and sad. It was like she just knew I'd be back and that was enough for her."

"She sounds like an amazing woman," I say as we pull up to Run to Me.

"She was. I miss her every day. I'm sure you understand that, but Isaac sounds like a very lucky man."

I laugh softly. "I told him that often." There's a pause and a part of me doesn't want to get out of the car. "Thanks again. Truly. I need to go relieve my employee."

Grady inclines his head. "I'm sure we'll see each other around."

"I'm sure we will."

And I don't know why that makes my stomach flip.

Thankfully my car was returned to me, without a bill, and now I've accomplished yet another thing on my list—going on with my life.

"Wow, Addy, this is a big step," Chloe, my friend, says while I'm grabbing a cookie from the snack table after our grief support meeting.

I grab the last oatmeal raisin and turn to her. "What else am I going to do? I need a date for this wedding, and the only way that's going to happen is if I start dating again."

At least, I think that I think it's time. It's been three years since my husband died. Three years of being alone and wishing I had something like my friends have. Not to mention, over the last year all I've heard from my sister-in-law is that Isaac would've wanted me to be happy.

So, I'm going to be happy.

I hope.

"Well, I've been back in the dating pool for two years and I'm warning you now, there's a lot of pee in the pool."

I burst out laughing. "Great."

Chloe and I have a lot in common. We each met our husbands when we were young, fell in love, stayed together through college, and then got married. Her husband was killed in a horrible car accident, where my husband was murdered in cold blood. Still, we were young, in love, and had our lives ripped away from us. Only difference is that I have a little piece of Isaac. I have our daughter, Elodie, who helped me continue living after that horrific day.

"Trust me, it's not great," Chloe says with a smirk.

"Aside from that part, I don't even know how to start dating," I admit. "Brielle, my sister-in-law back in Rose Canyon, thinks I need to make an online profile, but . . . she's usually wrong about these things."

"God, the online dating pool is even worse."

I'm starting to regret my announcement today about being ready to date. "How bad can it be?"

"Think of the worst date you've ever imagined."

I try to picture that, but it's not like I have any dating experience. I dated one man and ended up marrying him. However, Brielle had a series of really shitty dates in college. I remember listening to her laugh about the terrible dinners and awkward kisses she had.

"Okay, I got that in my head," I tell Chloe, borrowing Brielle's experience.

"Perfect, now multiply that by one hundred."

I groan. "You are really killing my buzz."

She laughs. "I'm kidding, kind of. Not really. Actually I'm not kidding at all. However, it'll be fun watching you suffer along with me."

In the last few months, I haven't heard her even going on any dates. "Are you seeing someone now?"

"No, after I ended up finding out the last guy was engaged, I decided to take a break from the murky waters I was swimming in. I'll try again once I have the stomach for it."

"You know, you're doing a really good job convincing me it's time," I say with sarcasm.

Maybe I'm not ready for this. I'm okay alone. I have my daughter, she's amazing. I have my friends and I'm a part of the Arrowood family as if I was born into it. Devney saved my life by having me come live here after my husband's death. I'm happy and have a great job that fills my soul by helping runaways find help instead of ending up in a horrific situation. Sure, I'm lonely and miss being held, kissed, loved, but that'll fade more over time.

However, I have a motivating reason, I need a date for Jenna's wedding back home in Oregon.

Chloe rests her hand on my arm. "I'm curious though, why now?"

I let out a soft chuckle. "I need a date for that wedding. I'm tired of being Isaac's widow and living under that cloud when I'm there. It may seem stupid, but it's what's pushing me to put myself back out there, and I don't think he would've wanted me to be alone and sad. So, carpe diem and all that shit."

I needed to say it. To speak the words into existence and let the universe know I'm open to possibilities.

"I think he would too. I tell myself the same thing, I just wish it was as easy as it was to find Chet. He came up to me on the bus, sat beside me and smiled, I did the same and then he held my hand. I don't know, that was that."

"It was easier when we were kids," I agree. It was easy for me too. I liked Isaac, he liked me, and I kissed his cheek one day, then we were together.

"And here we are now, adults and trying to have lightning strike twice."

I nod and take a bite of my cookie. "I'd appreciate if it at least gave me a jolt in the next two months."

Her lips purse. "Wait . . . two months?"

I sigh. "My childhood friend is getting married, and her fiancé is running for senator out in Oregon, so they're going all out. I really, really don't want to go alone, especially because I'm a bridesmaid. I need to have a date. I *need* to be with a man who is hopelessly smitten with me."

I don't have to explain why. She understands how hard it is to be in the place you had your whole life altered. When I go back to Rose Canyon this time, I will not be that girl. I'll be in a different place—a better one.

So here I am, unattached men, I'm ready for love.

"Dating with a time crunch, what could go wrong?"

"Hey, Addy," Phil Davenport says as he comes to stand beside Chloe. "Great meeting today."

"Hey, yeah, it was. I'm glad to hear that you're coping better with your mother's death this session."

Phil's mom died about four years ago. He lived with her his whole life, cared for her through her cancer, and their relationship was always a little strange, according to Chloe. They were partners in the annual dance-a-thon, they played BINGO together at the Rotary Club, and they shared other unconventional moments that the town always scratched their heads at. However, there's no judgment at our meetings. It's a safe place where we can come and work through our emotions.

After the meeting at the diner, though, is a different story.

"I am. I miss her, she was my best friend, but then you understand that. I know you felt the same way about your husband."

I nod, because words are kind of . . . lost on me with that one. Losing a parent is hard, but it's not the same emotions as it is when you lose a spouse.

Chloe smirks and takes a sip of her coffee.

Phil lets out a deep sigh. "Well, I'm really excited for you. To go out and just take what you want. To be unafraid to try to find love again."

"Thank you, Phil."

"You inspired me. So, I was thinking I'll pick you up and we can go out on Friday night."

Chloe chokes on her drink and I stand here with wide eyes. "I'm sorry, what?"

"Friday. I figure since you just announced you're dating again, you're probably free this Friday? It could be Saturday or even Sunday if that's better for you." He leans in. "I think we both feel this attraction and now we can explore it since you're open to love."

Oh Jesus. I look to Chloe for help, but the traitor just laughs silently. I don't know what to say. Phil is a nice guy, but . . . definitely not my type. He is probably about eight years younger than I am, and we have nothing in common.

This seriously can't be happening to me at our grief support group. "You know, I'm not sure I'm ready to start this weekend."

"No? I know that it feels fast, but you even said a few months ago that we have to act when we know it's right."

"I said that, didn't I?" I sigh and look away.

Chloe, the unhelpful asshole, steps in. "She sure did, Phil. Way to take charge." I glare at her, but she continues on. "See a need, fill that need."

What I *need* is for her to go away. "Chloe, didn't you say you had to pick up your mother?"

"Nope. I sure don't."

I'm going to need more than grief counseling after this. I turn back to Phil. "I wish I could, but I don't have anyone to watch Elodie."

I use my three-year-old as the shield I need to get out of this mess.

"I can watch her if Devney can't. I'm free this weekend." If looks could kill, Chloe would be dead. "You guys should go, have a great time. Elodie will have fun with her aunt Chloe."

Phil wastes no time. "Great. So, which day, Friday or Saturday? If I can be honest, Saturday isn't best for me. I have an online tournament where we have to build a castle, a new home, and a barn for my animals within six hours, and I'd rather not miss it. I've been training for it daily the last three months."

"A video game?"

"It's a great one, I'll show you some of my videos online."

"I can't wait . . ." I lie.

Phil grins. "This is going to be the best date ever."

It'll be something.

He walks away, and Chloe can't stop her evil laugh. "Definitely didn't date that one."

I turn to her. "I hate you."

Chloe lifts her cup and grins. "You said you needed someone smitten on a time crunch. Here's to the happy couple."

I groan. "I should've stayed home."

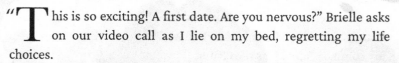

three

ADDISON

"This is so exciting! A first date. Are you nervous?" Brielle asks on our video call as I lie on my bed, regretting my life choices.

"No, I'm not because this is not a real date. It's more like . . . I don't even know what to call it."

"Why?" Her warm blue eyes that look so much like her brother's fill with confusion.

I roll over, propping the phone on the pillow, and go over a few details about Phil, which causes her to laugh. "I mean, you have something in common . . ."

"What?"

"You both go to that grief group."

I roll my eyes. "Totally something to build on."

"Hey, Addy!" Spencer says as he ducks in front of the camera.

"Hey, did your wife tell you I'm dating again and I already got asked out?"

"She mentioned it."

And those three words cause a pang in my chest. I want that. I had that. It was amazing to just share things, stupid things, with Isaac.

23

Is it so wrong to wish for it? I want someone to share daily details with again.

I force my feelings back into the box they escaped from. "Right. He needed to do Friday because he has some world building video game tournament on Saturday he's been training for."

"Cancel on him," he says without any hesitation.

"I can't." Phil is a nice guy and he's also typically shy and reserved. For him to come up to me after that meeting took a lot of guts. If I were to cancel or stand him up, I would never forgive myself.

"You know my stance on this."

Yes, Spencer gives zero fucks, and he would never force himself to do it. I grew up in a tiny town on the Oregon coast where I was surrounded by the four best guys any girl could dream of.

However, Isaac didn't come alone. I also got his three best friends, Spencer, Emmett, and Holden. They were the four points to my compass, and I was the center.

Now we're all on different courses and some days, I feel a little lost.

I smile softly at Spencer, my earlier thoughts escaping again. "I know. I just want to have what you all have, you know? I miss having my person, the one I could talk to about anything."

He looks over at Brielle and then back to me. "I get it."

"So, I need to get back out there."

"Well," Brie cuts in. "I have your online profile up. Devney has the password too and between us, we'll pre-screen and it'll be great."

"No! I never agreed to that!" I protest.

I am not letting them arrange my dates.

"It's all set. Devney will babysit on the days you have a date and . . . we'll find you the perfect guy."

I groan and flop back on the bed. "I can't with you."

"Look, go on this date Friday and then we'll hopefully have some good candidates lined up. This can be like . . . a practice run."

Not a chance in hell. Brielle will never give me the password, but

I'll get it from Devney and stop this train before it goes off the tracks.

The next two days I do everything possible not to think about this date. I work, clean my house, rearrange Elodie's room for optimal space, and even get my receipts in order for tax time—in eight months.

However, today, I can't avoid it.

I'm going on a date tonight and I still don't have the heart to call him and cancel.

There's a knock at my door and when I open it, Devney is there.

"Your babysitter has arrived," she says, holding up a bottle of wine.

"Is that for me?"

Her laugh is loud. "Not a chance. You need all your faculties for tonight."

"I'll probably be home before you can crack it open."

I step back and she enters. I can't begin to explain how much I adore her. We sort of became instant friends when we were kids. She came out to visit her cousin, Emmett, in Rose Canyon, and since I was the only girl cool enough to hang out with them, I got to know her. We were pen pals and when I went through losing Isaac, she had me come stay with her.

It was the best decision I ever made.

Sugarloaf was a fresh start. One that doesn't have the ghosts of the past hovering over me.

"Where's Elodie?"

"She's in the playroom watching a movie. I fed her, gave her a bath, and she's in her pajamas."

"Just in time for me to feed her sugar and soda and stay up all night."

I roll my eyes. "Please, you'd never."

"True, but this is a special occasion and all." Devney places the

25

bottle on the table and looks at me with pursed lips. "Is that what you're wearing?"

"Yes, what's wrong with it?" I look down at my sundress.

"It's . . . well, are you going to church or a date?"

"It's a dress."

"It's not exactly sexy."

I look heavenward. "I'm not *trying* to look sexy."

"Then you're doing a good job," she says with her brows raised. "Look, I know Phil is absolutely not going to be the man you fall for, but this is your first date in like . . . thirty years. You practically came out of the womb and attached yourself to your husband. You have to go into this with a little effort."

I glance at my attire again, feeling a little stupid. "I thought I looked pretty."

Devney steps forward, her hand resting on my arm. "You do! It does, but you look pretty to go to work or the store, not your first date."

"This isn't what I planned, you know?"

She smiles. "I know and while you're pretending to stay mad at Chloe, which I'm really enjoying, you have to hand it to her. This is the best scenario."

Now I wonder if she cracked that bottle before showing up. "Umm, what?"

"Phil is a noncontender. What a perfect practice run."

Again with the practice run.

"I don't want a practice run. I need a real date."

Devney sighs loudly. "You have no idea what you're stepping into. I wouldn't even begin to imagine it. This date is your first time sitting across from a man in a romantic situation since losing Isaac. Think about how hard this would be if it was with a guy you actually thought you might be able to date for real. It would be so hard, Addy. Use this date to test that water before you dive in."

I imagine what it would be like if it was someone else, someone who was tall, commanding, sexy, and made my stomach do little flips. Someone like Grady Whitlock who left a note on my car when it magically showed up at Run to Me.

Shaking my head to dispel that line of thinking, I look at my friend who has a soft smile on her lips. "Maybe you're right."

"I know I am. Come on, let's go up there, find something really sexy to wear, and do your makeup just a touch heavier, so you can really let yourself have this experience."

The whole point of this is so I can keep my promise to myself that I will not go to this wedding the sad widow. I'm ready to be happy again and that means moving on with my life. This date doesn't have to be perfect or with the perfect guy, it just has to happen so I can find that guy who I want to bring.

So, I should try give myself over to the whole idea of dating, and Phil is nice. He isn't going to be creepy or rude, he's just not my type.

Elodie runs in before we head upstairs, leaping into Devney's open arms, and giggles. "Aunt Devney!" she says, which sounds more like "Deb-knee." "Tomorrow Mommy take me to the park!"

"The park!" Devney's voice is laced with excitement. "I love the park! Why didn't you tell me?"

"You tan tome!" Elodie offers.

"I would love that. We should bring Aunt Chloe too."

"Mommy, tan Chloe come too?"

I smile at the ever-kind heart of a three-year-old. "Yes, honey, she can come too."

Elodie claps her hands together. "Park. Park. We go to the park!"

Devney kisses her cheek. "And tonight, you get to hang out with me, does that sound fun?" She nods quickly, squeezing Devney again. "I love this kid."

"I do too."

Devney adjusts her and then moves to the other side of the room. "Now, go upstairs and find something whistle worthy."

When I come back down, I'm in an eggplant-purple dress that falls right to my knees and has a sweetheart neckline. Ironically, I wore it to the last wedding I went to in Sugarloaf. It's cute, flirty, and a good medium for a first date. I paired it with my gold heels and clutch.

"So much better. I can see some boob at least."

I shake my head "All right. I'm going to be late now." I rush over to Elodie and kiss her cheek. "Be good for Aunt Devney."

"I will!" she says with a giggle.

I look to Devney, praying she'll give me some kind of pep talk, but she doesn't. "Have fun. I'll be here."

"That's it?"

"What did you want, a talk about the birds and the bees and how you shouldn't put out on the first date?"

I swear to God. "You're no help."

She shrugs. "Seriously, Addison, relax and try to at least enjoy yourself."

I nod, grab my keys, and head out before I can change my mind.

We're seated at a table close against the window that has amazing views. For the last thirty minutes, Phil has talked nonstop, and I mean . . . Non. Stop. I have tried to pay attention, but I can't take it anymore. So, I've been staring out the window, counting planes as they fly by. Summit View restaurant is high up on the back side of Sugarloaf Mountain, and it's where everyone goes for dates or romantic dinners.

"And then, I found out that my internet was out again, so I spent six hours on the phone with them, getting things fixed. I need internet for my tournament tomorrow," Phil drones on.

"Of course," I murmur and count another plane passing the mountain. That makes thirty-eight. It must be a busy night.

The only thing giving me solace is the conversations around me that I can focus on. The table to the left is on their first date. The girl's voice is extremely high-pitched, making it near impossible to ignore. "Then the girl slammed her hand down." She mimics the behavior, causing me to jump a little. "I said, oh, no lady, you're not going to talk to me that way in my gym."

I smile, and it must be good timing because Phil soldiers on, his face animated as he talks. I try my best to refocus on him, but his voice is like my high school science teacher, and I would fall asleep in each of his classes because his tone was so monotone.

The table behind me is some kind of business dinner. There are two guys, but one has done most of the talking. I hear him mostly because of the Southern accent. It's lyrical and so much better than Phil.

"I'm sorry, son. I want to invest in your company and all, it sounds great, but we're a family business. We like to know our people, their families, their friends, and you just ain't willin' to give us the information we need. Do you have a wife? A fiancée? Someone to accompany you on these dinners?"

Phil reaches his hand forward, snapping me away from that conversation. "I figured for our second date maybe we could do something else."

Well that wakes me up. "I'm sorry, I missed what you were saying?"

"I was just saying that since it's clear our chemistry is off the charts, we should have a second date this Sunday."

"Oh, well, I don't know because I have Elodie and work and . . . you know. I'm not sure about how much time I can devote to dating. You understand how it is with all the time you have to give to your tournaments."

I hear a laugh from behind me that gets covered up by a cough.

"While I understand that, I think you're underestimating how much playing video games has helped me through my grief."

"I completely understand that, and I'm not asking you to stop, but there's more that I would need as a single mother."

Phil leans back. "I work, Addison. I don't make much, but there's real money involved in my World of Warcraft this weekend." He leans in. "The winner takes five hundred dollars."

"Wow."

He nods. "Exactly what we call it. Are you a Worldie too?"

I have no idea what that means. "Can't say that I am."

"I just hate to see us be over before we began. We have something special here."

Another chuckle and then a utensil dropping. I hear a deep voice, but it's too low to distinguish who it is. "Excuse me," he says as he pushes his chair, causing it to hit mine.

When I go to turn, Phil takes my hand in his. "Addison, I like you. I think you like me too."

I stare at him, forgetting what dragged my attention away. "I do like you, but I don't think we have all that much in common."

"Of course we do."

I blink a few times. "Like what?"

He leans back, thinking about it for a while. "I don't know, but we have this chemistry."

Oh boy. I need to walk this down carefully because I really don't want to hurt his feelings. "Chemistry is only part of a relationship. We have to build and create a life from that. You and I have so much to overcome, it would be so hard. I mean, you'd have to sell your video games and move, and you would need to work full-time and become a stepdad."

Phil's face pales. "I don't think that's fair to ask."

"It's not, which is why I think we need to really evaluate what we're doing here."

I'm just making shit up at this point.

"I guess you're right. I can't leave my mother's house. It's all I have left of her." He bobs his head a few times. "I'm sorry, Addison. I should've thought this through."

"It's okay," I say softly. "I'm glad we had dinner and this talk before things got too serious."

"Me too." He lifts his hand for the waiter, who comes over.

"Yes, Monsieur?"

"We need the check please," Phil informs him.

The waiter, Luke, returns a minute later with the black leather holder, placing it down. Phil glances at it and then me. I look at it and then back to him. I guess I'm paying. "I've got this."

He nods. "Thanks, my paycheck didn't get deposited and I didn't win my tournament yet, I planned to pay for the second date. Well, thanks for dinner. I'll see you at the next meeting." Phil stands and walks away, leaving me still pulling my wallet out.

"Bye . . ." I say to no one and slip my card into the folder.

Then I hear that laugh again. I turn in my seat, ready to square off with whoever is laughing at my horrible date, and find Grady there, back to me as his dinner companion is walking away.

Grady shifts, facing me. "So, did you have a nice dinner?"

"Since you were listening, what do you think?"

"I think your date needs you to tuck him in."

I roll my eyes. "I think your business partner thinks you need a life."

"All that Mr. Jeston should care about is my work, the fact that I have a decade of pilot experience, and that I'm discreet. He'll call tomorrow with a change of heart."

Didn't sound much like that, but what do I know?

Grady smiles and looks handsome in his button-up shirt, hair pushed back a little and that smirk on his face. The waiter returns, taking the check and card with a look that clearly says he doesn't approve.

Yeah, me either.

Not only did I get asked out on a date I didn't want to go on, but then I paid for us both. I would've rather gone to Sugarlips Diner, but then the whole town would've seen instead of just Grady.

"What are you trying to get him to do?"

"Give me four million dollars."

If I had a drink, I'd choke on it. "For what?"

"I need to buy a plane that I can fly wealthy businessmen around on. I'm expanding what my company can do."

I nod, as though I have a clue why he would need four million dollars to start a company just flying planes. "And he's not budging?"

"He wants me to be married or dating someone serious, God only fucking knows why."

"Is that legal?"

Grady shrugs. "He's not my employer and he's investing. There aren't really any laws around that."

A part of me aches for him. "Does he know about Lisa?"

He looks over to where Mr. Jeston is on the phone at the bar. "I explained part of my situation. His wife died a year ago and he's already remarried. Doesn't seem to understand my hesitancy to start over."

Well, that's dumb. "I'm sorry."

"Doesn't bother me. I'm not in any place to be dating. I'm perfectly content being a bachelor and being a good father, that's what matters. I need to take care of Jett, not date. I want my company up and running, I want out of my sister's place, and I need this plane so all of those things can happen."

I was like him a year ago. Life was fine and I was alone, there was no need to date anyone because I wasn't ready.

It wasn't until I went back home six months ago to visit Brielle and saw her and Spencer that I realized I ached for what they had. Even then, it took months to get to this point, and now look at me.

"Tell him dating is overrated. Your friend here can attest to it. Because my date, Phil, asked me out at my grief support meeting."

Grady's eyes widen and then he chuckles. "You're kidding."

"Nope."

"Wait, he asked and then made you pay?"

I sigh. "And they say chivalry is dead."

"Maybe I'll tell the story of your bad date is why I have no desire to deal with it."

I finish my glass of wine and stand. "You could, but then he'd really think you were a loser."

Mr. Jeston returns before he can reply and I walk away, leaving my first terrible date behind me, ready to find Mr. Right.

four
GRADY

"What, no chaps? I was ready with my phone," my asshole brother Asher says as he leans against the barn door.

"Sorry to disappoint."

He shrugs and walks toward me. "Ahh, I'll catch you some other time. No one would believe that you, out of all of us, would've found a love of horses."

It wasn't my doing, it was Lisa's. She grew up on a horse farm in Oklahoma and spent her whole life loving these animals. In our time together, I learned everything I could, and we had four horses ourselves. We spent every weekend working with them before she got pregnant, and I sold them six days after she died. I couldn't handle it. However, being here, and around them again, makes me feel like she's with me as I ride.

"And no one would believe you'd end up as a sheriff with two kids from different women, but here we both are."

"Yeah, here we are, but at least that means I get laid."

"I got laid plenty." Before I met my wife, at least.

He chuckles. "Listen, I stopped by to apologize about the other night."

Ahh, yes, the other night, when Brynlee and Phoebe coordinated a possible suitor to randomly show up at our family dinner.

"It's not your fault, it's your sister and fiancée's doing," I remind him as I brush the horse after a good run this morning.

"The two of them thought it was the only way. I got on her ass about it, so she'll back off. Phoebe just wants everyone to be happy, a lot like Brynn does."

The thing is, you can't make someone be happy. I wish everyone would stop trying to fix me. Sure, my life is a mess. Sure, I don't know what end is up right now, but I'll figure it out. I always do.

"I know she meant well. I also know Brynlee was the mastermind behind it all. It's forgiven." I toss the brush in the bucket and walk the horse back to his stall.

"How are things going with Brutus?"

Once he's in, I close the door and pat his neck. "He's a great horse, he just needs a firm hand. A little more training and he'll be there."

Asher walks closer and the horse snaps his teeth at him, causing him to back up. "I swear, they all hate me."

I chuckle. "I think you should avoid animals after your last attempt with the goat." Where Brynlee is like Snow White, Asher is like Squidward, who gets mauled by animals. For some reason he just doesn't vibe with anything but dogs. They love him.

"The fucking goat kicked me! Anyway, I came to see how you were after you were ambushed."

"I'm fine."

"Seriously?" he asks, clearly unconvinced.

"Yeah, I forgive Phoebe. It's our sister who might have retribution heading her way."

Asher grins. "That, I accept. She deserves it. Any trips to New York this week?"

Since my only flying lesson client barely wants to attend, I had to find another way to make some money. I started a courier service for people who want things delivered quickly, discreetly, and are willing to pay a shitload of money for the convenience. What works out great is that I will only do it for flights under three hours.

"No, because the two clients who use me for this don't have

anything happening this week. So much is done electronically that it's usually people doing illegal stuff who don't want anything they send being traced."

Asher shakes his head. "I really didn't want to know that."

"I figured." I slap his chest as I walk past him. "Makes it all the more fun."

Plus, I don't think anything is illegal, it's just sensitive paperwork people don't want any chance of being hacked.

My brother falls into step with me, and we head out to where the new acres Rowan purchased are. Our family had plenty of space, but his plans are to expand his production with the dairy farm as well as take on horses. I think he's insane, but I've always thought that.

"And the investor?"

I shake my head. "Jeston wants me to be married or in a committed relationship. He invests in people who have strong convictions. Fuck if I know what that means."

Asher slaps me on the back. "Sorry. You have other options?"

"I'm meeting with Mr. Kopaskey this week to discuss it. Other than him, no other investor has replied. I can scrap the plan, but that feels like giving up."

"You really want to fly a private plane?"

I tilt my head, wondering if he even listened when I talked about the money I can make. First, the price to rent a private plane, but then I'd make even more if I'm the pilot.

"I want the money so I can build the house and give Jett a safe and steady home."

Asher sighs heavily. "I envy you, Grady. You're out here, fighting for what you want."

I stop walking. "I didn't get out of the navy to live in Brynn's house forever. I have to move on."

"And does that mean meeting someone? Dating?"

"No."

"Why not?" Asher asks.

I don't remember my family being this damn annoying, but here we are anyway. However, if anyone will understand it, it'll be him.

"Let me ask you something. If God forbid something happened to Phoebe, and you lost her, in a tragic way, how quick do you think you'd be to jump back into dating? What is the appropriate time to go by before you'd want to ever endure that shit again? Would you want Olivia to endure having to lose *another* mother figure if something happened to her? Even better, I'll up the ante, you are a single dad, had to leave Olivia in another state because you knew it was the right thing for her to have a stable home, then took her from that, and have no damn clue what end is up. How appealing is that to a woman?"

He lets out a long sigh. "I'll back off."

"Thank you, however, if you want to loan me Phoebe to pretend to be my girlfriend so I can get the money from Mr. Jeston, I'd appreciate it."

My brother's eyes narrow. "Not a fucking chance."

"Worried she'll pick me over you?" I taunt.

"She likes men who aren't losers that live with their sister."

I go to slap him, but he moves, and then, like we're twelve, I chase him around the barn so I can kick his ass.

"You need to stop glaring at me," Brynn says as we take our seats at the town play, which she managed to talk me into attending.

"I will when you stop suckering me into these bullshit town events."

"You are so grumpy!" she huffs. "I swear, you make Asher look like sun shines out of his ass. You don't know anyone here, you won't date, and you're always in a mood. It's really exhausting being your sister."

She's right. I am all those things, but *she's* the damn exhausting one. I modulate my tone so I don't come off hostile. Brynn can be a little sensitive, and while I'm not in the mood for this crap, I love my sister and hate hurting her feelings.

"I'm s_____ ad a meeting with my last potential investor tod_____ Kopaskey, and I just have a lot on my mind."

Bryan shifts in her seat. "What did he say?"

"Didn't say much, just wanted to meet again at a dinner party before deciding one way or the other."

Which then came to me making a huge misstep.

Mateo Kopaskey and the other investors are old money guys. They invest in people, not companies, really. They tend to think of the people they give money to as friends in the end, and the last six deals they made were all with men who were married or in serious relationships.

So, when he asked me about bringing my significant other to their dinner party, I lied and said she would love to come, I just needed to check the dates.

Great plan that was.

I figured I could make up some bullshit about a breakup and there'd be no harm no foul, but then he talked about her coming to another event in a few weeks after that.

Which now means I need to find a date or be prepared to lose the deal completely.

"That doesn't sound all that bad, Grady. I'm sure they'll invest. You're a veteran with combat flying experience, a great dad, an okay brother, and you're the smartest of us all."

All of that is great, but I'm pretty sure I'm missing one title out of that list they care the most about—husband.

"Well, all of that is great coming from you, but it's them I need to sell on it. They like family men. They like guys who are married, with kids, and have a home they need to pay for."

That's the hardest part. It doesn't matter if they walk away because I'm not in a relationship, because they owe me nothing. I need to find someone who doesn't give a shit if I'm married, a widower, divorced, or any of that. I'm a damn good pilot and I know this business. It's the right move, but I need startup capital.

"How are you not a family man, when you literally had a wife and have a kid?"

"I don't actively have one for these parties."

"So, maybe you should find a girlfriend since you have the kid part, and the home is coming."

I glare at her. "No and we discussed this. I have no desire to ever date again. I'm happy finally building a relationship with Jett, and being around my family—most of them, at least."

She rolls her eyes. "I know you, Grady. You've always wanted a family and the childhood we didn't have, more than Asher or Rowan or even me. Mom used to say that you were just like her, searching for that person who made you complete. When Lisa came around, everything felt like it had fallen into place. I'd never seen you so happy."

And I was. I had everything I wanted, it was great, but things didn't work out and I had to pivot. I'm doing that, even if my annoying sister thinks I need to be in a relationship to be happy again.

"Well, happiness is fleeting and I lost her and missed raising Jett as a baby. Right now I'm focused on getting the life I didn't plan on track."

"And what better way than finding someone to *create* that life with you?"

I swear, my sister needs to find a hobby and stop meddling in everyone's lives. "Were you this irritating with Asher?"

"First, I'm not irritating at all. Second, no. He never wanted a relationship. When Sara got pregnant, I remember thinking, oh, great, he'll finally at least date her. He didn't, he just arranged it so they could raise Olivia in harmony. It worked for him, and I think he would still be single if he hadn't met Phoebe."

"Ever think I want that?" I ask, pointing out the obvious.

Brynlee smiles and pats my arm like a child. "You're not Asher. You're not jaded and bitter because of our childhood. Thank God you're nothing like Rowan who is a player and drives everyone nuts with his antics. You are just scared to love again."

I rear back. "I'm not scared."

"It's okay to be afraid. It's why you won't even meet someone because you can't risk being hurt again. You're afraid, Grady."

A part of me knows what she's doing. She's goading me into agreeing to meet her freaking friend who I have zero desire to meet. "I'm not afraid and I'm not falling for it."

She gives me a patronizing smile. "Whatever you say, but just know that I understand. No one judges you for it."

I groan. "I should've stayed in Florida."

"Where you could be alone and afraid? No, this is better. At least you have us here to keep you from falling apart."

I swear to God. "Brynn . . ."

"Addison!" Brynlee says, getting to her feet. "Hey!"

"Hey, guys! Hi, Grady, nice to see you again."

I stand to greet her, schooling my features so they don't show how much I like seeing her. We follow the same schedule in the mornings, and I look forward to meeting her in the parking lot since Jett refuses to enter the damn building without Elodie.

We've become friends of sorts, or at least partners in misery.

"You too, especially because I thought you had another date tonight." I smirk.

She mentioned it this morning and I had to bite my tongue to keep from giving her crap about her shitshow last night.

"I do," she says, tilting her head.

"I figured after last night you'd take a break. How did things end with Mr. Married-With-Two-Kids? Is tonight your second date?" I ask, genuinely curious how she'll explain this one. Rowan and I went to dinner at Sugarlips and Addison was there with yet another disastrous date.

Interesting, since I never thought Addison was the kind of woman to sleep with another woman's husband, but what the fuck do I know? I have seen cheating far too often in the military to be fazed by any of it.

She glowers at me. "No, no second date since his wife probably wouldn't like it."

"That's a shame, he seemed like he had potential," I joke.

Addison rolls her eyes. "I used to think you were charming."

Brynn laughs. "Think again. I didn't realize you guys knew each other so well."

"Elodie and Jett are in the same class. We met and I told you I brought her to work when her car broke down."

My sister gasps. "Oh! That's right! Sorry, I've been in the middle of an arbitration the last two weeks and my brain is a little scattered. Plus, I'm studying for the bar exam."

"Come to think of it, I'd say we're friends. Right, Addison?"

She glances at each of us and nods. "Yeah, I guess so."

"See?" I say, feeling quite triumphant. My sister wanted me to make friends, and I did exactly that. "I have a friend."

Addison tilts her head. "I think I'm missing something."

"Just my asshat brother who refuses to move on with his life, that's all." She waves me off. "Are you here with anyone? If not, you can sit with us."

"I would love to, but my dates are here."

"Dates, as in plural?" I wait for clarification.

She laughs. "Yes, Devney and Chloe."

A date with her friends. I feel stupid now.

Brynn looks around. "Oh, they're here too! I didn't know they were coming this year."

Addison nods. "They're somewhere. This is our favorite thing in the town."

"The play?" Brynn asks with wide eyes.

"It's truly like a train wreck you can't look away from, but they try. So, we come, sit near the front, clap loudly, and do our best to enjoy it."

I turn to my sister. "You said it was good."

"I said it was entertaining," she corrects.

Great, I let her drag me out for a play that is apparently terrible but entertaining.

"You also said moving to Sugarloaf would be a good idea."

Addison grins. "I love it here, but it takes a bit until you find the fun."

Find the fun? What the hell does that even mean? I don't have time to find fun, I need to find four million dollars, that's what I need.

Brynn leans forward. "He's really afraid to open himself up. He's trying to land this investment, but he isn't seeing that if he does what they want and what I want, he'd be killing two birds with one stone."

I'm going to kill her with one stone. "Brynn," I warn. "Seriously, enough."

I don't need to look like some loser in front of anyone here.

"I'll stop. I just want you to be happy, but you need to not let fear rule your life."

Now I'm definitely going to kill her.

"I am not scared. Jesus."

She pats my leg. "Don't be mad, Grady. It's okay. I really get it. I would be terrified like you too."

"I'm not scared. Want me to prove it? I'll let you set me up with that damn girl you keep bugging me about and then you'll see I'm not afraid, I'm just not in the mood to date." And after I say those words, I realize what this little shit just did. She completely manipulated me, and I'm the goddamn idiot who fell for it.

Brynlee grins. "Good, so Saturday night. I'll watch Jett and you can go on a date."

"Can't wait," I mutter, trying not to look like more of an idiot than I already do.

Someone calls Addison's name, and she turns to them and raises a hand before looking back at us. "It was great seeing you both. I have to go take my seat before it starts. Enjoy the show and good luck on your date!"

She already saw a show called the Whitlock family drama, written by Brynlee and starring me.

"See you later," I say, saving face.

Brynlee leans back, her hands folded in her lap. "Maybe you're not so scared after all."

The lights lower and I lean close so no one else hears. "No, but you should be because I may kill you if this date goes badly."

She laughs. "You could never hurt me, I'm your favorite sibling."

"You were once."

"And I will remain after you meet your perfect date on Saturday. I'm really proud of you for being so brave and opening yourself up for love."

five

GRADY

"Would you like another glass while you wait, Grady?" the waitress asks.

"No, I'm fine, thanks. I'll let you know if I need something."

"Okay."

My date is late. Not just fashionably late, either. We're talking twenty-five minutes and counting. I sent her a text, but no response.

I'm on my first date since I lost Lisa, and I got stood up. I feel like there's a lesson in this somewhere.

When the chime rings, I look up at the door, equally hoping it is and isn't my date. Dinner alone tonight sounds just about perfect. And it's not my date, but I wish it was, because instead, it's Addison with some guy, his hand on her lower back. She looks stunning. Her hair is curled in loose waves and she's wearing a blue dress that matches her eyes. Her long legs are on display as her date leads her toward the booth behind me.

I lift the menu to cover my face as they approach, at least I'll have fun getting to watch her date while not having to endure mine.

"Here, I'll take your sweater," the man says.

"Thank you, Dan."

The fake leather seat crumples as she sits, her back to mine, and then he takes his seat. I can't see them, but I get to hear everything.

The man clears his throat. "I'm glad you agreed to go out tonight."

"I'm glad you asked," she says back.

"Well, a beautiful woman such as yourself has to be seen in person."

"Thank you. You look very handsome as well."

Scintillating conversation so far. I see this guy as a real winner . . . not.

"I'm glad you think so. I have never had a woman complain when I show up. I've been told I'm better than handsome."

I roll my eyes because I hadn't heard ego like that in a while.

"Right. So, you said you're in finance?" Addison asks.

"I am, but we don't have to talk about all that mundane shit."

How the hell is finding out what you do for a living mundane? That's called small talk, asshole.

Where the hell is Addison finding these guys to date? Also, if this is what is out there, I'm just fine on my own.

"Oh? What would you rather talk about?"

"I've found most women really don't care about the small stuff. It's more important things that matter. Things that you are really curious about."

I turn my head a bit more. While I've been out of the game a long time, I'm not sure where the hell this is going.

"Things like?"

"Marriage, goals, how many homes I have?"

"You have multiple?" Addison asks.

Dan chuckles. "I do. I have a house in Philly, one in New York, and then I own property in the Keys."

Addison goes silent for a moment. "That seems . . . ambitious."

"Real estate is always a good investment. Anyway, I like nice things and nice-looking things . . ."

The way he trails off has me picturing a complete douchebag who is leering at Addison, clearly stating she's one of those things.

"I . . . yes, I guess most of us do."

"So, Addison, let's talk about the things women always want to know," his voice is low and attempting to be seductive.

Although, to me he sounds more like a stalker.

So yeah, totally winning there, Dannyboy.

"Well, I'm curious what you mean by that."

The guy chuckles. "Are you?"

She just said she was, Dan.

"Please, tell me what women really want to know," Addison suggests, and I can picture her leaning back, hands together on the table or in her lap.

Her date's voice drops a little and I have to strain to hear it. "You want to know if we'll be compatible elsewhere . . . if I can do all the things to make you scream my name." Silence on her part. He continues on. "I can. I'm not boasting, but every girl I've fucked has been satisfied, so you can relax, eat, and then we'll go back to my hotel and I'll prove it."

What the actual fuck?

"I'm sorry, but I think you have the wrong idea. I said I'm looking for a relationship," Addison says with a slight shake to her voice.

"No, you said you wanted to date and have fun."

"Yes, date as in . . . well, date."

"That's what we're doing, and after, we'll have my version of a date."

Oh, fuck this guy. No way in hell is he going anywhere with her. I push out of the booth and stand, walking over to their table. "Addison? There you are!"

"Grady?" She looks to me, with a mix of confusion and grate-fulness.

"Hey, I tried to call you a few times. I thought we had a date tonight, but I guess I was wrong."

"We did? Tonight?"

I nod, turning my back to her date. "Yes, I came here, hoping I'd find you. I was worried I had the wrong date and time."

She looks to her date and then me. "I, well, didn't think it was tonight. I'm sorry." Then she turns her gaze back to him. "Dan, I really didn't mean for this to happen, but you know, this probably is for the best."

"We had plans. I had plans for tonight."

He sounds like a petulant child.

She moves out of the booth. "I'm sorry. I'll call you if . . . well, I probably won't. Good luck in the future and finding your next conquest."

I grab her sweater off the hook and place my hand on the small of her back, guiding her away from the dickhead of the year.

We exit the diner, walking towards the cars, and she exhales loudly before beginning to laugh. "Oh, I'm so done with this."

"He sounded like a winner."

She clasps her hand over her mouth as she fights back her laughter. "I can't even. Did you hear him talk about himself in the bedroom?"

"I did."

"Who *says* that?"

Clearly, Dan, but it was still just insanity. To come out, before you even get drinks, and state how you're going to have sex—good sex, according to him—is not normal.

At least not any kind of normal I would want to be around.

"I'm sorry, Addison."

"Please, call me Addy. And what about you? Where is your date?"

I nod my head slowly. "Ahh, she no-showed."

She starts to laugh again. "We are a pair, aren't we?"

"We are."

She leans against my car with a sigh. "I . . . I need a drink after that."

"Come on, let's go."

"Go where?"

"To get a drink," I say, starting to walk toward Peakness, which is three blocks down. "We both need one."

Addison catches up to me, neither of us saying anything, just enjoying the cool breeze. I glance over at her, she smiles, and then we keep going, still not speaking.

It's nice not to have to fill the silence.

I'm sure she's still processing what the hell that was back there.

We get to the front of Peakness, the only bar around here, and I pull the door open. I've only been here once when I came home to see my siblings. It's a quintessential dive bar, with neon lights on the wall and the bar stools filled with single people.

"Maybe this is where you should've started the dating search."

She smiles. "Probably, but I was never the bar kind of girl."

"What kind of girl were you?"

Her eyes twinkle in the neon lights. "I bet you'd like to know."

I would, because she's the one person in this town I really like being around. She's funny and smart. She is great with Jett and gets what it's like to lose the person you were meant to spend the rest of your life with.

I spot a few open seats at the bar. "Want to sit there?"

"Perfect."

We take the two seats together at the end and the bartender comes over. "Addison! Haven't seen you around here before. And who is this?"

"Carmen, meet Grady Whitlock," Addison says over the music.

Carmen is a short woman with curly brown hair and a smile that you can't look away from.

"Nice to meet another Whitlock. I know your brother well."

"Which one?"

"Both," Carmen says with a laugh. "What can I get for you?"

"I'll take an Aviator on the rocks."

Carmen bobs her head with a smirk. "Gin man, I like it. And for you?"

"I'll have a vodka cranberry."

Carmen heads off to make our drinks and Addison turns to me.

"You drink Aviator? For real? Is that like a pilot requirement?"

I laugh. "I like gin and I happen to like that brand."

Addison rolls her eyes. "Naval. Aviator. Such a dork, but I owe you. Seriously, thank you for stepping in. I would've left, but I think I was stunned and slightly afraid. He picked me up, I didn't have a car, but you saved me—again."

"I didn't save you either time. I figured you would've told me to fuck off if you were fine with it or come with me if not."

She sighs heavily. "I was definitely leaving."

"I wouldn't have judged you either way," I tease her.

"Oh? You would've supported my sexfest with Dan?"

I laugh, feeling a lightness I haven't in a long time. "To each their own, but I'm just saying, I get it. You know, we all have that itch."

"Well, he sure as hell wasn't scratching it."

Carmen returns, placing our drinks on the bar. Addison lifts hers and I do the same. "To bad dates."

"To the end of bad dates," I reply. "You're cut off."

"I'll drink to that."

Her blue eyes fill with emotion, and I reach out, resting my hand on hers. "Hey, what's wrong?"

"This wasn't supposed to be how this went."

"What do you mean?"

"I had a plan, you know? I was going to start dating again, and I thought I would meet a nice guy who would want to at least be a friend to start. Someone I could share things with and who wasn't unwilling to grow up, married, or a total creep who probably would've . . ." She shudders. "Well, it's been a very interesting ride so far, and not a good one."

"At least you wanted this," I say with a laugh. "I was totally fine being single, but my sister insisted on pushing me to date."

"What do you mean?" Addison asks.

"The investors I'm meeting with, they do a lot of schmoozing, and it requires dinners and parties. They have made it very clear they like to give money to men who are in committed relationships. They invest in families, and the significant others play a large role in their inner sanctum."

"How so?"

"Mainly, they have a lot of parties where the spouses attend and it's highly frowned upon to fly solo. I've yet to find a single guy at any of the meetings I've gone to. I've also been turned down by pretty much everyone I met with."

She sits back, shaking her head. "Wow. So no date, no money?"

"Basically. So, while you're ready to move on and get out there, I'm not. I don't want a girlfriend or date or any of this shit. I just want to start my company and give Jett a stable life."

I have said more to this woman than I have even said to my family about this. Which is freaking insane. I don't know why I'm telling her any of it, but she's so fucking easy to talk to.

"Is it because of Lisa?"

I sigh, hating that once again, I want to tell her the truth. "Yes and no. It's been over three years, and I still miss her. I think about how she would know what to do with Jett's daycare meltdowns or she'd never screw up by buying the wrong big boy underwear. She'd have known. She'd have . . . gotten it right. She'd want me to move on, but it's not about what she wants since she left me alone to figure it out."

Addison leans forward, her hand resting on my forearm. "She didn't leave you willingly, Grady."

"Maybe not, but she's not here."

"I was really angry with Isaac, too, who was shot saving his sister. For a while, I grappled with the fact that, had he not stepped in, we would've lost Brielle, who he loved with his whole heart. His sister was his best friend after me."

I understand that completely. I would die for Brynlee—any of us would. "He was a good brother."

"But he was my husband, and I needed him. I also understand it, because if he hadn't stepped in and Brielle was killed, he never would've been able to live with himself. But I was still mad for a period of time. It took me this long to finally be ready to consider another man touching me." We both take a sip and she leans back, one hand resting on the bar. "I just thought it might be better than this."

"I'm sorry. There's no reason you can't find the right guy."

"Thank you, Grady. I appreciate that."

"You're welcome. Why did you want to start dating again?"

Addison runs her finger along the top of her glass before meeting my eyes, and I have to remind myself to breathe when she does. "I have a wedding in Oregon that I'm in. I refuse to go back home without a date. I have spent three years getting over the loss of my husband, and I finally feel ready. The wedding was just the catalyst because I don't want to be the widow anymore. I want to be Addison to them, and whenever I'm in Rose Canyon, I'm not. I'm Isaac's wife, the one who lost everything, and it's pity everywhere. So much that it's stifling. I love them all, and they mean well, but I have learned to move forward, and they're stuck in the past."

"You thought bringing home a date would change that?" I ask.

She shakes her head. "No, but I hoped they'd see me as a person again. It's stupid, and it seems I'm going to have to hire an escort."

We both laugh. "I don't think it'll come to that."

She shrugs. "A girl can hope, but at this rate, the prospects aren't looking so good."

"Come on, surely we can find someone here," I say, joking but also not.

I scan the crowd of people, dancing, laughing, having a good time. A group is line dancing in the center, there are wannabe cowboys leaning against the bar that goes around the dance floor, and women hanging on them as they pretend we're in Montana, not Pennsylvania.

This area is weird. We're two-and-a-half hours to New York City, but it feels like an eternity away with the open land, dairy farms, and the smell of cowpie everywhere.

"What about him?" I say pointing out the guy in the black cowboy hat.

She laughs. "No."

"No cowboys?"

"I didn't say that, but that's Micah, a very well-known player. He's offered, I declined."

"Is he related to Dan?" I ask and get a chuckle from her. "Okay, no Micah, what about . . . that guy?"

This time I point to a man in a suit. He's decent looking, a little older, but that might not be a bad thing.

"That's the mayor's brother, whose wife I'm very good friends with."

"Okay, not a match."

Addison's eyes meet mine and she smiles. "It's fine. There's no one here and I'll have to go back to that awful app and endure more horrible dates."

I shudder. "I'd rather you not."

We both take another sip and she stares at me. "I'm surprised about one thing."

"What's that?"

"Why didn't Brynlee ever think to set us up?"

I nearly choke on my drink. "What?"

"I'm serious. We've both lost our spouses at practically the same time, have kids the same age, and we are both relatively attractive."

"Relatively?" I ask with a quirked brow. "Are you saying one of us is lacking?"

She shrugs with a grin. "You know you're hot."

"I am?"

Addison rolls her eyes and takes a drink, trying to hide her smile. "Whatever."

"Well, I know it's not you who you were referring to."

She places her glass on the bar. "You think I'm relatively attractive?"

"Relatively."

I'm lying, she's fucking gorgeous, but I won't say that.

"And it's a wonder your date stood you up."

"Yes, well, I'm a wonder."

I laugh as she shakes her head. "I'm serious. We're kind of an obvious matchup. We practically live the same life, so maybe that's why?"

"Well, Brynlee is certifiable and knows I don't want a relationship. She wouldn't do that to you."

Addy tucks her blond hair behind her ear. "That's nice of her then."

I sigh, hating all of this. My date standing me up means that I can't even fake this with the investors. I can tell them I went on a date, but what? If only this girl showed, I could have feigned interest and . . .

My God, I have the answer.

I turn to Addison, feeling hopeful for the first time. "I have the answer to our problems."

"What's that?"

"We date."

six

"I'm sorry, *what?*"

Of all the things, I never expected that to be his solution.

"You said it yourself. We're an obvious match. And we don't *actually* date, we just tell our family and friends we're together, go out a few times, and make it look real."

I literally don't know what to say, not because I haven't thought about it before, though I haven't. I mean, dreams aren't thoughts. They're . . . dreams.

So what if I woke up this morning after a beautiful dream where Grady picked me up, we kissed in the car, and went to a fancy dinner where I led him up to my room?

None of it was real because I know that Grady doesn't *actually* want to date anyone.

"Yeah, but I want to date for real. I want to move on. You don't."

He shrugs. "You want to keep going on these dates?"

That's a big fat negative. "No. I'm honestly scarred for life after the last two."

"Exactly. Look, you need a date for the wedding in a month or so, right?"

I nod.

"Okay, and I need a girlfriend for these investor meetings and

59

dinners. It works out perfectly." He's so enthusiastic, I almost forget he's talking about the two of us lying to our friends and family about being together. "We'll go out for the next few months to keep up appearances, and you can come with me to my dinner meetings and I'll go with you to Oregon for the wedding. No more blind dates with assholes or losers. It gives you time to actually find someone you want to bring home for real."

I lean back, wondering if I've lost my damn mind for considering this, but he has a point. I only have a little over a month to find someone I would even want to bring back to Rose Canyon, and so far, my prospects have sucked. This would give me time to regroup, get through the wedding, and then we can break up when we get back.

"It's a lot of lying to our friends and your family."

"We go out on the weekends and have playdates for the kids that they all think are us spending time together. It's not a lie if we're doing it. We just don't tell them the motivation behind it."

I chew on my thumbnail. "I don't know, what if you meet someone?"

"Not happening."

"What if we realize we hate each other? Or I meet someone? Things can get complicated really quickly."

I don't think the first one will happen since I think he's funny, attractive, and apparently is my personal savior lately, but still. My worry is, what if he is all those things and I start to like him more than just as my fake boyfriend?

He doesn't hesitate. "Then we call it off. I don't want to trap you. I just want to fake date you. That way, we can both get what we want, at least for a few months."

Come on, Addison, say no. This is a bad idea. You want love, not a fake relationship. You also want a date to that wedding . . .

Instead of telling him how stupid this is, I say something else. "Okay, but no one, and I mean no one can know this is our plan. If one person finds out, the whole damn town will know. And when we get back from Rose Canyon, we say the trip was bad and we end the agreement if your business deal is all set."

"Good because we have to really sell this relationship to everyone, especially because the investors live around here and would hear about us."

"Meaning what, exactly?"

"You're going to have to pretend you really like me."

Yeah, that was my fear. We're going to have to look like a real couple. One that holds hands, kisses, dates . . .

I groan and swallow the rest of my drink in one gulp. "I need one reassurance."

"Name it."

"No matter if we break up here or this doesn't work because people figure it out, whatever it is, you agree to go with me to Oregon for the three days and be doting and completely in love with me."

If I'm doing this, I want to know it wasn't just for his benefit.

He holds out his hand. "Deal."

I shake it and then Grady rubs his thumb across my hand. "Dance with me?"

"What?"

"Dance with me. We need to get the town talking . . . unless you want me to kiss you in front of everyone."

"Dancing is good," I say immediately.

He chuckles and then helps me down, guiding me out to the dance floor. Sometime during our conversation, the lights dimmed and the music changed to a slow song. Grady guides me to a spot where we can be seen by anyone and pulls me into his arms.

His arms are around me, and mine rest on his chest, feeling the steady beat of his heart as my mind is jumbled.

This is crazy, right?

I can't decide if this is brilliant or just stupid. I'm not sure yet. On one hand, this is great, I can stop dating these really awful guys and start up again once the weight of this wedding is over. Plus, it's helping Grady and also myself. On the other hand, this could all fall apart and I walk away with egg on my face and hurt my friends by lying.

Then I think . . . they'd understand.

"Hey," his voice is deep and raspy against my ear. I lean back to meet his eyes. "You're trembling."

I am. "I'm just nervous about all this."

He pulls me tighter. "We're not doing anything wrong, Addy. We're two friends, stuck in shitty situations, and we found a temporary solution."

"I know, and honestly, this works well for me too. I just suck at acting."

"I'm not excited either, but we will be dating. I'm going to take you to dinner, we'll hang out, see each other in the mornings, we just will be . . . pretending like it's more than just our growing friendship. Now, put your head on my chest and relax."

I sigh and do that, letting the music and Grady move me. His hands move up my back as he keeps me close and I really hope I remember that he doesn't want more than a pretend girlfriend, no matter how real it feels.

"Holy fucking shit, tell me it's true!" Chloe says as she enters Run to Me, wide eyed and practically screaming. "You're dating Grady Whitlock? And you didn't tell me!"

I get up and walk toward her, grateful we didn't have anyone here needing help.

"Please do not come in here like that again." I sigh. "You would've scared any people seeking refuge away."

"Well, please don't keep secrets like that again! You're dating Grady? Say it ain't so."

Here is my first test. "It's so."

"Oh my God. How? What? Details!"

"Will you stop shouting if I tell you?" I ask with a brow raised.

She nods, hand over her mouth.

After our dance, we sat at the bar, talking about what we thought this first week should look like and how to proceed. We both have kids, and while they're toddlers and would never remember this, he and I agreed that we needed to act with their best interests in mind. So, the first week will really be just like if we started dating for real. A weekend dinner, a movie, maybe a surprise lunch, but nothing with the kids unless it's about school or something.

Also, we agreed we didn't need some elaborate lie, we just stick to the truth, minus the fake-dating agreement.

"You know I had a date on Saturday?"

"Yes, with Dan, right?"

"He was a total creep. Grady's date stood him up, he heard the things Dan said, stepped in, and we ended up getting a drink at the bar. One thing led to another, we danced, laughed, and then he asked me out again."

Chloe's cheeks are going to hurt from how hard she's smiling. "And you said yes!"

"To a date, Chloe, not marriage." Sheesh. She wasn't this excited about anyone else. "Why are you beaming?"

"Because Grady is hot! Like super hot. Not only that, he's one of us. He gets you and what you've been through. I don't know, it just seems perfect."

At this rate she's going to be picking out invitations.

"Nothing is perfect. We know that."

She waves me off. "Yeah, yeah, but I don't know, this has potential."

I rest my hand on hers. "Potential to go either way so . . . reel it in."

"It's reeled."

I laugh once. "It's so not."

"I'm working on it."

"Okay."

That wasn't so hard. It's all true, and he did ask me out for Friday and then if I'd like to go to his brother's for a barbeque. He assured me it wouldn't be a thing, but the sooner we went around his family, the better.

Therefore, technically, we are dating.

At least that's my story.

"So you danced?"

I nod. "I'm shocked you haven't heard all the details. I already got a text from Devney about it."

"I'm low on the gossip line. It's always the Arrowoods who get it first. So, you danced, how many times?"

"Two."

"Did he cop a feel?"

I roll my eyes. "Did you hit your head? What is wrong with you?"

Chloe has always been excitable, but this is next level, even for her.

"Nothing, I'm just hopeful, that's all. I'm also really proud of you for putting yourself out there."

"I won't lie, after that last date, I was ready to call it quits."

She gives me a sad smile. "I get it. I had more Dans and Phils than I care to admit. It's why I just can't do it anymo—"

The door chime pings and I look up to see Grady walking into my office with a handful of flowers. "Hey." His voice is smooth and causes my stomach to flip.

"Hey," I say breathlessly, forgetting Chloe is next to me.

I wish I could say I'm acting, but I'm not.

We just saw each other a few hours ago when we dropped our kids off at the school, but there's something about seeing him here, like this. I swear I can feel the way his heartbeat thumped beneath my palm.

He steps in and smiles at Chloe before walking to me. "These are for you. I was going to see if you were busy for lunch, but it seems someone beat me to it."

Chloe nearly trips on herself. "Not me! I have plans already. Just stopped in." She walks in front of Grady and extends her hand. "I'm Chloe, by the way."

"Nice to meet you, Chloe." He looks to me with a grin. "If I remember correctly, you're the one who set her up with Phil?"

She pales, and I want to kiss him for that comment.

"Not really. Phil asked, I just . . . accepted for her."

He laughs once. "I'm sure she appreciated it."

"I didn't," I respond when she glances at me.

"If it weren't for all your bad dates, Phil included, you wouldn't have spent all this time together and now look, you're going out."

"We are having dinner," I clarify. One of the things I told Grady was that we had to be strategic and go slow. No way would I be jumping into anything, no matter how good looking he is. No one would have believed it for a second if we tried to sell that idea.

Grady's eyes twinkle with mischief. "I was hoping lunch, too."

I work hard not to let my heart get too excited by this.

This is going to be the hardest part for me.

"I could eat."

"Yeah?" he asks.

I nod. "Let me see if one of the girls can cover the front. I'll be right back." I point to Chloe. "Reel it."

"I know, I know."

I go back to where my assistant is working on inventory and let her know to keep an eye on the front while I run out.

When I get into the reception area, Chloe is talking with Grady who is being incredibly charming. I clear my throat, drawing both of their attention.

"Ready?" I ask.

"Just waiting on you."

"Have fun, you two," Chloe's mischievous voice follows us out the door.

"That was smooth," I say to him as he walks with his hand on my back toward the diner. "A lunch before our date."

"Well, darling, I couldn't stop thinking of you."

I laugh, again reminding myself of the game we're playing. "Please, your sister made you come, didn't she?"

"Guilty. You know she works for Sydney Arrowood . . ."

"Who is my best friend's sister." This town needs a hobby and yet they played right into our hands. "That moved a bit faster than I thought. I sort of forgot Brynlee works with Sydney."

Grady guides me away from a puddle. "I didn't put it together either, but when you told Devney, she told Sydney, who then went to my sister."

"So here you are."

"Here we are."

He opens the door to Sugarlips and I swear, the entire diner freezes. The eyes of every single customer turn to me, and Grady and I stand here, not sure what to do.

I force a smile, wondering if I forgot pants or something by the way they're all staring. "Do we go all the way in?" I ask him through my teeth.

"Is this normal?"

"Nope."

He waves dramatically. "Hi, everyone."

A chair scrapes and Sydney stands. "Go about your business, people, it's not like we haven't seen residents eat before." She stares at them until they start to do as she says and then gives me a wink.

He leads me over to an open table against the window. People keep eyeing us, but I do my best to ignore them and focus on Grady. "That was eventful."

"I had no idea it would be that intense."

"Me either," I admit.

I definitely didn't think the town would be this invested in a budding relationship. Many people have dated. Sure, they all know my struggle and the hell I went through after Isaac, but I've settled here and done well.

"Although, maybe I should've since Brynlee almost tackled me when I got to the barn this morning."

I laugh once and then Magnolia is at the table. "Can I get you two anything to eat?"

We place our orders and then return to the conversation. "Why did she tackle you?"

66

He shakes his head with a grin. "Because she heard it from Sydney."

"Ahhh, you didn't tell her?"

Grady leans closer so no one can hear. "I didn't want to be obvious. If I told her, it would've been inviting her into my love life, which is the opposite of what I've been doing. Like you said, we'd proceed with caution."

"And we wouldn't tell people," I say just as quietly as he spoke. "We'd just let them find out."

"Like we are now."

I nod once. "Exactly."

Nothing about this, other than the friendship we have formed, is real. Still, it's working like we hoped. They definitely believe there's something going on.

Grady's smile widens and then he leans back. "Are we still on for dinner Friday night?"

"Yeah, I have Chloe babysitting, so it works out. Where are you taking me?"

"I figure our first official date should be a nice dinner."

I let out a giggle because the only nice place around here is Summit View. And I've already had a disastrous date there. "Well, at least this time we can openly laugh at each other."

"Also, I'm paying, just so we're clear."

"You don't have to—" I stop talking when I see the look on his face. It's obvious that he doesn't approve of the way Phil proceeded. "Did you win a tournament lately?"

"Yes, it was called, I need a girlfriend for money."

"And your prize?" I ask, playing along.

"The best fake girlfriend of the year."

seven

GRADY

Today was an eventful.

First, Addison wasn't at the daycare to help me get Jett in, which was not the crisis it would have been a few weeks ago, but he didn't go in willingly.

Second, I had to fly to New York City to drop off paperwork to some billionaire who wasn't even there when I arrived and I had to wait three fucking hours for his assistant to finally show up because he was at lunch. My agreements are hand-to-hand delivery, it's all part of the contract, so I was stuck.

And I was pissed.

That delay caused me to miss a meeting with a potential investor and picking up Jett. Since Brynn is in court, and Asher is on duty, it means that Rowan is watching Jett.

I knock on the door to my brother's small farmhouse and there is no answer. This is off to a good start.

"Rowan?" I call.

No answer.

"Jett?" It's more likely that my son ended up watching his uncle. "Buddy, are you here?"

Nothing.

As I walk around to the barn area, I hear his laugh. That effortless, from the pit of his belly laugh that always makes me smile. There's nothing like it and I swear I wish I could bottle up that sound and save it.

I turn the corner to find him on the back of Matilda, Brynn's childhood horse. She's old and unrideable, but Brynn loves her and she is spending her days being pampered and grazing her favorite field.

Jett leans down, squeezing her neck, and gives her a kiss. "I love this horsey!"

Matilda swishes her tail and turns her head. "She likes you too," I say from the door.

"Daddy!"

Seeming to forget he's on a horse, he tries to lunge toward me, but Rowan catches him, setting him on his feet.

I crouch down as he rushes to me, arms wide, and I scoop him up. "I missed you."

"You were in the plane?"

I nod and kiss the top of his head. "I was."

"I rode the horsey," he tells me.

"I saw."

Rowan chuckles. "He didn't want to do anything but be with the horses."

"He's his mother's son." Sometimes I look at him and see Lisa in his eyes or his smile. It should be her teaching him to ride.

"And I'm sure he misses his horse in Oklahoma."

I nod. "I'm sure he does."

I put Jett down and he runs off, getting to live a life I wouldn't have been able to give him if I stayed in the military. Small towns are just different. There's a community that is built in, land he can run free on, animals to chase.

That wouldn't have been our reality. My job was exhilarating and something I dreamed of doing since I was a kid. Being in the air fills my soul, but being a fighter pilot was who I was.

I exhale, letting go of that thought, and see my brother's shit-eating grin. "I hear you got yourself a hot date tomorrow."

"Not you too."

He raises both hands. "I'm not judging or giving you shit, just saying that I work with cows all day and I heard about it."

"Where?"

"Ranch hands are like old women, they talk so much shit, I swear I'm in high school. Also, it's not like you're being quiet about it. Dancing at Peakness and then the diner, what the hell did you expect?"

Exactly what it achieved. People are talking, which means they believe it, which means that hopefully Mr. Kopaskey, who is the investor I was talking to last week, will hear about it soon. All of it leading to the credibility I need to make them think I'm worth giving money to.

All of this is perfect, I have a girlfriend without any complications or expectations.

"I forget privacy is a luxury."

"Because the navy was any better?" he asks.

No, it was even worse. "Not better, just different."

Rowan clasps his hand on my shoulder. "Well, brother, better get used to it."

"Is that why you don't date?"

He laughs. "I don't date because bitches be crazy."

"Or the fact you call them bitches," I toss back.

"I have too much shit to worry about with the farm, the new land, and the horses. Plus, since you came back, Brynn has been preoccupied with making you happy and not lonely, so I've had a break from the nagging."

This plan is almost too perfect if I get the added benefit of annoying Rowan since he'll be off my back. "Happy to help."

"I gotta say, I'm shocked that it's Addison Davis of all the people." He grins with one brow quirked.

I don't know why everyone is so hung up on this. Addison is a beautiful, single woman who is intelligent and kind. Why wouldn't anyone be attracted to her? If I wasn't so busy getting my life together, I would consider wanting to date her.

71

Maybe.

If I was open to it, which I'm not.

"Why does that surprise everyone?"

"It doesn't really. Just didn't know she was ready to date again until I heard about Phil. I mean, I get why you'd go after her, she's hot."

"Is that the most important part?"

Rowan shrugs. "Tell me it doesn't matter and I'll call you a liar."

"Of course attraction matters." And I'm attracted to her, which makes this fake relationship easier to believe.

"Exactly my point. It's just that she came here years ago, dealing with a lot. She was just . . . I don't know, sad."

I want to slap him upside the head. Of course she was sad, she lost her fucking husband.

"Could be because her husband died . . ."

Rowan rolls his eyes. "I know that, dickface. I'm just saying it was more than that. Like, she smiled, but it was never real. She laughed, but it sounded dead. When she opened Run to Me with her friend, things really looked up for her."

When she finally had something worth doing. I didn't have that initial crash after Lisa. The navy still needed me to take an assignment to fly and when I was up there, I was hyper-focused on my job. I couldn't let myself go down that path.

"It's called grieving."

"And you would know what that looks like, which brings me around to this next question, why the change of heart?"

I blink, surprised this is coming from him. "What?"

"You know what, literally two weeks ago Brynn and Phoebe teamed up and you were a fucking dick about it. Not that they didn't deserve it for ambushing you, but you went on and on and on about being single and never wanting Jett to have to worry about losing a mother, and now you're dating Addison Davis?"

Fuck. I did say all that, and I meant it. I'll do anything, and I mean anything to protect Jett. He lost his mother, growing up with a father every day, coming home and running to me. All of it was ripped away and somehow I endured that hell, but the idea of him actually knowing, loving someone like a mother and then her dying or leaving...

Nope.

Not on my watch.

While that may be my truth, there's no way I can say that now. I have to backtrack.

"I'm dating her, Rowan, not marrying her. I don't think that'll change for me."

I know it won't.

"So when a few months go by, your big plan is...?"

"None of your business," I snap back. "What's your big plan for Charlotte? Have you gotten her to stop telling everyone you're a bastard who cheated on her sister?"

He flips me off. "No, and she can keep saying whatever bullshit she wants. I didn't do it. I have never cheated on a woman because I've never been in a serious relationship where that's possible."

Ah, Rowan, the eternal bachelor.

"Have you told her this?"

Rowan laughs once. "Of course I have. But the rumors live on. Anyway, are you bringing Addy over for the cookout?"

Crisis averted.

"If this date goes well, I'll bring her around you assholes and see if she can handle you in large doses."

He laughs. "Hey, Phoebe was able to withstand this family."

"I'm not sure if that says more about her or us."

We start walking toward the house, which is more like a cottage, and sit in the lawn chairs he has out, watching Jett run around in the sunset. A lightning bug flies past him, flashing right where he can see, and he yells.

We watch him chase them and I remember my childhood, doing this same thing in the backyard with my brothers.

"Boys?" Brynn's voice calls out from the side of the house.

"We're back here," Rowan answers and she comes around wearing a pencil skirt, button-up shirt, jacket and heels.

73

"Jesus I'm going to break an ankle."

"Maybe don't wear those shoes," Rowan suggests.

She glares. "You think I planned it, dummy? I just left the office and came to make sure you didn't need help with Jett since you're not known for your babysitting skills."

"I did just fine with Olivia."

Brynn laughs once. "Please, Olivia takes care of you." My sister turns her attention to me. "And I'm mad at you."

"Me?" I ask incredulously. "What the hell did I do?"

Her hand rests on her hip. "Once again, I have to hear all this gossip from Sydney! She said you guys had lunch today?"

"I don't run my schedule and love life through you, Brynn."

"You should!"

"Yes, you did a bang-up job setting me up on that blind date who didn't show," I scoff.

"You're going to pay for that one," Rowan warns.

Brynn huffs. "I like Addison, so I'll let that one pass."

"Aunt Brynn!" Jett spots his favorite person and heads towards her. She makes an oof sound as he plows into her legs. "I sat on your horsey!"

"You did?" she asks him, her eyes wide as love emanates from her. "You are so brave to sit on a horse. I wish I was brave like you."

"Come on!" He tries to pull her. "I show you how!"

I laugh and head over, saving my sister, as he doesn't really understand women's fashion. "Not today, big guy. Aunt Brynn had a long day and it's getting late."

His lower lip juts out. "Pwease, Daddy!"

Before he can beg more, a firefly blinks in front of his face. He laughs and tries to catch it, but Brynn is right there and does it for him. She leans down, showing him what's in her hand, and he's completely captivated by it.

"See how it glows?" My sister's voice is soft.

"It's so bright."

She nods. "Even in the dark, there is light, and where there is light, there is hope. Hold on to it."

I hope I'm not making a mistake with this hoax, because if Brynn finds out, I'm going to hope I never did it.

There shouldn't be nerves on a fake date, but here I am, palms sweaty, heart racing, and that pit in my stomach that's growing with each step to her front door.

I push through it, telling myself that the nerves are because I have it on good authority Mr. Kopaskey will be at the same restaurant with his wife, and I don't want to screw this up.

I need for us to have a good date, keep this pretense up, and get the damn money.

I go to knock on the door, but it opens before I can.

"Hi, sorry," Addison whispers. "Elodie is asleep and we had a tantrum the size of California an hour ago, I'd rather not wake her."

I step back. "Of course. That's daily for Jett, only you get to experience it firsthand."

She laughs. "Please, he's not bad, he's just finding his footing at a place he really doesn't like."

"Yeah, hates is more like it, unless he has Elodie."

We start to walk to the car.

She smiles. "You look handsome."

"You stole my line. I'm supposed to tell you how beautiful you look."

And she does. She really is one of the most stunning women I've seen. Her long blond hair is pulled to the side and she's wearing a short maroon dress. All of that pales in comparison to her long legs in those fucking heels.

"Well, you can tell me now."

I clear my throat. "You really do look beautiful."

"Thank you. I figured if we were going out again, we should give them something to talk about." I open the passenger door for her, and she stands there, hand resting on the roof. "Are you sure about this, Grady? We can back out and I'll just go to the wedding alone."

75

While I had been considering the same thing, when she says it, I don't like the idea at all. "Why do you say that?"

She sighs, looking out the window, and waves. I turn back to see Chloe there, watching us. "Because the people who love us seem to really love the idea of us."

I think back to when I was leaving and Brynlee giving me a million tips on how not to fuck this up. She couldn't be more supportive of the idea of me and Addison, no matter how many times I told her this was only our first date.

"They'll be fine. They'll love us no matter what. Our friends and family might be pissed, but they'll come around."

"You're right. I can stand to go out with you a few times—I guess." She slides into her seat, and I close the door with a laugh.

The ride to Summit View takes about thirty minutes. Getting up the mountain is slow thanks to the winding road. She asks about my day, the new client I got who actually wants to be a pilot, and the delivery I had to make two days ago.

"So you literally fly paperwork to New York City instead of someone emailing it?"

"Yeah, it's always an envelope, so I know it's not drugs or something, plus I scan everything beforehand."

She laughs once. "That is probably smart."

I nod. "They pay me well for it."

"And it's legal?"

"There's nothing illegal about using a courier. Whatever it is, they don't want it to be sent electronically and this ensures hand-to-hand delivery."

"Oh. That makes total sense. I'm sure it's contracts no one wants lost or legal paperwork."

"Exactly, but out here, it would take someone hours to do what I can in just under an hour. It's ease and convenience."

We arrive at the restaurant and are seated at the same table she was at with Phil. Thanks to my generous tip to the host.

I thought it would be equally funny and also sort of sweet.

We're going to have a much nicer date than she had with that douche, and I'm erasing that from this location.

Also, it's hilarious.

"You did this," she accuses.

"What?"

Addison's eyes narrow. "Don't play innocent with me, Grady Whitlock. You sat us here on purpose."

"I did."

The side of her lip quirks up as though she wants to smile but won't. "Because?"

"Because this date will be nothing like the last, so we might as well pretend that never happened."

"Well." She sits back in her seat. "That was unexpected."

Now it's my turn to ask. "Because?"

Addison's smile grows and she shrugs softly. "It was very sweet."

"And also because I thought it would be fun to irritate you," I tack on because I don't want to be sweet. This isn't real and while we have to sell it to the people we're fooling, we don't have to try to fool each other.

Addison is a friend who is doing me a solid. I don't want a relationship. I don't want complications in my life because I have enough of those.

"And then you ruin it."

"It was entertaining," I remind her.

"It was."

I glance around the restaurant and spot him. "Do you see the man six tables over?" I ask.

Addison nods when she sees it. "Mateo and Lily Kopaskey?"

"You know them?"

She tilts her head with her lips pursed. "Duh. Everyone knows them. They're big investors in Run to Me. Their oldest daughter had issues when she was seventeen and they were very generous to help get our location up and running."

This is freaking perfect. "I seriously didn't think I could like you more, and then you go and surprise me."

"Why?"

"Mr. Kopaskey is debating on investing in my company. We'd buy the plane and he'd get all the perks of flights and a pilot on standby while I use it during certain times for lessons. He wants to know me better and have me attend a few events before he makes his decision."

"Lily loves parties and throws them monthly."

"Which is where you come in," I tell her.

Addison smiles. "Date for hire."

The way she says it makes me feel like a dick. "You also get the same for the wedding," I remind her.

"I know. It's totally fine. I know them both well."

"Good. He's the only one who called me back and said he wanted to discuss it more. I could always go back to the others, but say what? Hi, I have someone now?"

Addison pulls her lower lip between her teeth. "It would probably come off as desperate. Does the first investor know Mateo at all? Like I said, they throw a ton of parties, usually at the country club, and they're always huge. People fly in from all over on their private . . ." She trails off and I sit here with a smile.

"Planes."

"So you want to have the plane for many options."

I nod. "I can do my courier stuff now because it's decent pay. The plane I use is small, and honestly works perfectly for that, but I can't escort people around. All I could do is skydiving because most would want to jump out of it."

Addison laughs. "That's a mental image."

"I want something I can do more with. Being a pilot isn't as lucrative as many think, but there are ways to really earn more. One is doing both commercial and private flights. We would be able to have a plane at the ready where they pay a premium for the flight crew." She has this glazed look on her face, which causes me to chuckle. "I just want to offer a service that makes sense in an area that doesn't have it. As Sugarloaf becomes more of a destination with skiing and some of the things I heard about in the planning meetings, it just would be the right time."

"Then I'm here to help. One fake girlfriend at your service."

I can't help the smile that forms on my lips. She's so freaking cute sometimes.

The same waiter she had last time comes over, saving me from saying something stupid. He looks to her and then to me. "Well played. Hopefully you are a better companion than the last," he says with his thick French accent.

Addison laughs and covers it with a cough.

"I'm glad you approve," I say to him.

"We'll see if I do by the end."

I look to Addy to say something, but she just smiles.

The waiter clears his throat. "I welcome you both back to Summit View. I am your waiter, Luke." The way he says it is almost like nuke. "Tonight we have some beautiful specials, they are on the back of the menu. What would you like to drink while you look it over?"

"We'll have a bottle of pinot noir."

"Which one, Monsieur? We have many to choose from."

"Do you have one you recommend?"

"But of course, do you want one from California or maybe my personal favorite from France?"

I have no fucking clue. I just wanted to order a bottle. I actually don't drink wine, I'm a beer guy, but ordering a beer at a fancy place always makes me slightly uncomfortable. So, for tonight, I'm going with wine.

"I'm not sure it matters." His eyes widen as though I just said something heinous. I do my best to recover. "I mean, either is fine, how about you bring us what you think we'll like."

"Very good, I'll bring you two choices . . . and . . . you can decide which tastes better with your very delicate palate." He grins and I have a feeling that was a mistake, but my choices are to call after him and look stupid.

He leaves and Addison leans in. "You're in so much trouble."

"I have a feeling I am."

"He's in training to be a wine sommelier and you insulted him with your 'doesn't matter' comment."

"You know this how?" I ask her.

"This is the only decent restaurant in the area, we all come here for birthdays, engagements, whatever you can think of. Luke is always our waiter and he's a wine snob."

Great, I pissed off the waiter who already likes Addison after the last asshole left her with the check.

"I'll pay his price if it means he'll be nice."

She grins. "He'll appreciate if you go with the French bottle. No matter which you actually like better. Also, be sure to swirl the glass and smell. He really likes that."

"Am I trying to impress him or you?"

"Both."

Of course. Who doesn't have to woo their waiter? "Got it."

Luke returns with two glasses on his tray. "For you, two of my best choices. One is from Italy, it is a bit bolder, reminded me a bit of your first business meeting here, sort of nutty with a punch at the end."

She snickers and I try not to laugh as well. "Accurate." I take the glass, swirl it like I was instructed, sniff, although I have no idea what the hell I'm smelling, and then sip.

Dear God that tastes like battery acid. People like this shit? I force a smile and nod. "And the other?"

Anything has to be better than this.

"The next is my personal favorite. It is from the Burgundy region of France, which is where I come from as well. It is a little smoother, has a sweeter note that I quite prefer."

He hands me the next glass and I repeat the same motions. I slightly hesitate, not sure I want to endure this again, but I'm a man and I can take it. So, I take a sip and force a grin. It's better than the last one, which wasn't hard to do, but how I'm going to choke down a glass is beyond me.

"I agree on this one." I look to Addison. "Would you like to try it?"

She shakes her head. "No thank you, Luke has already sold me on that wine before."

"We'll have two glasses please."

"No bottle?"

I shake my head. "We'll start with the glass."

I doubt they give a to-go cup and there's no way I'm finishing more than one.

"Of course, a *glass*." The way he says it tells me I just insulted him again.

Addison's attempt to hide her grin says I did as well.

He returns a minute later, placing them down in front of us and then taking our orders. Once he is gone, I grab mine, lifting it in the air.

"What do we toast to?" she asks, raising hers.

"To the beginning of a very beneficial relationship."

1.

eight
ADDISON

"I 'm going to go over and say hi to them."

"Who?" Grady asks.

"The Kopaskeys. You need them to see us, don't you?" I ask. There's no point in this whole fake dating thing if we aren't going to make every minute count, right?

He glances over at their table. They've finished their meal and Luke is handing them the dessert menu.

Grady looks back to me. "I think I should go."

"I'm going to use the ladies' room, and on my way back, I'll pretend to have just spotted them. You need to act like you don't know they're here. Otherwise, you should've gone over earlier. Besides, we're on a date, how rude would it look if you left me to see a business associate? Trust me."

He lets out a long sigh and nods. "I trust you."

I do as I said, heading to the bathroom, checking my makeup, and reapplying my lipstick. Dinner was great, and so much better than my last three dates. Grady and I laughed, talked about the kids, and I really explained what Run to Me is and why it started and how Blakely, who is also Emmett's wife, and I needed to do something to help kids in need.

If I didn't remind myself every ten minutes that this is all for show, I would be having the perfect date.

But this is a *fake* date.

I head out, purposely walking around the other side, and then stop as though I just saw them for the first time.

"Lily! Mateo!" I exclaim as I make my way to their table. "I didn't see you guys here."

"Addison. Hey!" They both stand, and Mateo leans in to kiss my cheek. As soon as he steps back, Lily takes me in her arms. "Oh, you look amazing. Are you out with the girls?" She looks around.

I don't have to work hard to make myself blush. "Oh, umm, no, actually. I'm on a date."

Her eyes widen. "A date? Really?" Now she really scans the restaurant. Grady is doing an excellent job at not looking this way.

I pull my lips into a tight line and point low. "See the guy against the window?"

She tilts her head and her brows raise. "I do now."

"That's Grady Whitlock, my . . . date."

Mateo makes a low noise in his throat. "You know Grady, huh?"

"I do. Our kids are in the same daycare class. We've been talking the last few weeks and . . . I don't know, he asked me out. Actually, it's a little more complicated than that."

"How so?" he asks skeptically.

I need to make sure I sell this and really talk up how great he is. Mateo likes men of character. People who do the right thing, no matter what.

I look to Lily. "A few weeks ago, I decided it was time to get back out there. Isaac has been gone three years, and I'm ready, you know? So, I went on one really bad date, which was actually here, and then got set up on another one with someone who turned out to be married." I let that hang for a second and look to Mateo. "The last one I went on was the worst. We were at the diner, and he was just being really aggressive. Grady happened to be there, overheard some of what the guy was saying, and stepped in, getting me out of there. We ended up going for a drink, talking more, dancing . . . and now we're here."

Lily sighs, clutching her hand to her chest. "Oh, how sweet! Addy, that's wonderful."

I nod, and at that exact moment, he looks over, blinks, and then smiles.

I wave and he does the same back.

Then, as though we wrote this as a script, he acts as though he sees who I'm talking to and walks toward me.

"Mateo, it's great to see you," Grady says smoothly, extending his hand.

"You as well. I didn't know you were acquainted with Addison."

Grady smiles as he stares at me. "I am—thankfully. I wasn't aware you were, though."

"We've known her for a few years. This is my wife, Lily."

"It's wonderful to meet you," Grady says, bowing slightly.

"You too. Addison was just catching us up a bit."

He looks to me again and then to the Kopaskeys. "It was great seeing you, but our dessert is arriving at our table. I hope you don't mind if I steal my date back?"

"Not at all," Lily says quickly. "I'm sending invites for a party in two weeks, you both must attend."

"I'll check my calendar," I say with a smile.

"Perfect. It was great to see you again, Addy, and meet you, Grady."

"You both as well."

I walk around the table to where he is and he immediately places his hand on the small of my back as we move to our seats. "Don't look back at them no matter what," I say.

"I had no plans to, but what did you say?"

He pulls my chair out and then takes his own seat. "I told them how we met, and that you saved me. Mateo loves a hero and Lily is a hopeless romantic. All of that is right up their alley."

"You're diabolical and brilliant," he says, admiration clear in his eyes.

"Well, if you're going to get this investment, we need to be strategic. Plus, the more the town sees us and hears about how perfect you are, the more it'll help when we go to Rose Canyon."

"Well, if I land this investment, I'll do anything you need in Rose Canyon."

I laugh and lean forward. "Be careful what you promise."

Because it's going to make us dating here look like a cakewalk.

The rest of my date with Grady went great. After we had dessert, we left and he brought me home, where he walked me to the porch and out of view of my nosey neighbors' prying eyes. Then he kissed my cheek, and that was that. He mentioned a BBQ, but we agreed to wait a week and give the appearance of going slow.

Since then, we've seen each other each morning, where the other parents stare as we bring the kids into school and then pretend they're not watching.

In a few minutes, Elodie and I are heading to Brynlee's house for their weekly cookout. I'm more nervous about this than anything.

I like the Whitlocks, they're great, but they're a bit intimidating. Asher is the Sheriff and I work with him often with Run to Me. Brynlee helps with legal things that Sydney thinks she can handle. I really don't know much about Rowan besides that he runs his dairy farm, and I am just . . . freaked out.

Elodie rushes into the room wearing her leggings and sweatshirt. "Mommy, we go see Jett?"

"Yes, you're going to get to play with Jett at his house."

"Yay!" Elodie spins around in circles.

At least she's not the least bit nervous.

I squat down, taking her hands in mine. "You'll be a good girl when we're at Ms. Brynn's, right?"

She nods, but we all know a promise from a three-year-old isn't worth shit. "And you'll listen to Mommy?"

"Yes."

"And you'll eat whatever they make?"

At that she pauses. Yeah, I knew it was a long shot. Elodie would live on fish sticks and tater tots if I let her. Everything I give her—pork, beef, macaroni—are all called fish sticks. If I say that, she'll eat it.

So, the fight continues. "They'll have fish sticks there."

Her eyes alight. "Okay!"

I knew it.

I kiss her nose, grab the salad I made, and then get in the side by side. The Whitlock farm isn't too far from us, so I thought we could offroad instead of driving. Elodie loves going for rides in the fields and we cut across the Arrowood farm to get there. She loves that we ride through the creek, splashing water as we get bounced around the rocks.

"Again!" she yells after we get through the other side.

"On our way home."

We cut down the path, passing the infamous Arrowood tree-house that Connor built, and then we arrive at the Whitlock farm entrance. I pull out my phone and send a text to Grady.

> Almost there.

GRADY
> I'll meet you out front so you don't walk back here alone.

> Okay. Heading your way now.

I ride down the drive, taking the second left, which heads to Brynlee's house. A few minutes later her cute home comes into view and Grady is there waiting.

My stomach does a little flip when I see him, like it always does, and I remind myself I'm an idiot because he is not my actual boyfriend.

We pull up and he opens my door. "Hey, girls."

"Jett!" Elodie yells and he chuckles.

"He's here, don't worry."

"She's been really excited about today," I tell him.

"Jett too, and me. I'm glad you came."

I smile at that. "Oh? And why is that?"

"So my sister will finally shut up."

I figured it was that. I laugh and we walk toward the back. "So today you want very low PDA, right?"

We sort of covered this when we brought the kids to school yesterday. At this point, we wouldn't really be comfortable around others, especially with the kids around.

"I think so, but I may take your hand a few times. Asher is very observant when he wants to be and with the way they were grilling me this week, I think they'll be watching."

I grab the salad I made and nod. "Okay. I'm ready."

At first I really thought this was unnecessary, but he made a point that if his family doesn't believe we're together, then we can never convince anyone else. Besides, I like a good barbeque and it has the bonus of getting Elodie and Jett together.

We walk around to the backyard where Asher is standing by the grill with Rowan, they're both pointing at whatever is cooking and arguing. Off to the left is Brynlee and Phoebe, who are watching them with wide grins.

Brynn looks over first. "Addison! Elodie!" She rushes toward us. "I'm so glad you came."

"Thank you for having us. I made this," I say, lifting the bowl.

"You didn't have to, but I'm sure it's amazing. Grady can take it and put it inside." The way she says it almost makes me laugh, it's more of an order than suggestion. Then she looks to Elodie. "Are you looking for Jett?"

Elodie sways back and forth, nodding.

"Would you like to go see him?"

"Animals?" Grady asks.

Brynlee glances up. "Of course, Olivia is watching him."

She is the sweetest thing and just turned ten. Grady was telling me how in just a few months of being here, he has learned a lot of ASL to communicate better with her and even Jett is picking it up.

"I love pigs," Elodie informs us.

"Me too, and donkeys and goats and ducks and chickens. Would you like to come with me, and we can find Jett and see the animals?" Brynn asks.

Elodie looks up at me, apprehension in her blue eyes. "Go ahead. Miss Brynlee even has a goat."

"I do! Her name is Baaabs and she's very sweet."

That does it, she takes her hand and they walk off. "You are doing great," Grady says against my ear.

"You, not so much."

"My game is a little rusty."

I grin. "Thank goodness your sister has no issues telling you how to fix that."

"I need to put this inside before Brynn scolds me. Do you want to see the house?"

"Sure."

In all my time living here, I've never been to Brynn's home. I had this idea in my head of white painted furniture with bits of grays and pinks and seeing that it fit the vision perfectly, I smile.

Grady puts the salad in the fridge, and I walk over to a small sofa table where there are family photos. I see the one of the four siblings and smile. Brynn is laughing with her head thrown back as her three brothers lift her in the air. There is one of Phoebe and Asher and he's down on one knee. Olivia's school picture, and then one of Grady and a very beautiful woman holding a baby.

"That's Lisa," he says at my back as I hold the frame.

"She was beautiful."

"She was." I feel that familiar pang in my chest when I remember why our home has photos too. "We have a lot of photos around the house. We also work hard to honor her memory."

I place the frame back down. "How so?"

Grady looks at the photo and then me. "Every night, I read Lisa's favorite story with Jett. It was all she talked about. How when he was born, each night she'd read *Goodnight Moon* to him, until he could recite it without the story. It's important that I carry that on in her memory."

I nod. "Does he know the words?"

"He does."

I loved that book too. It was one of Elodie's favorites but now it's something else. She loves to run in her room, pick a book from her library, and then she sits in the bed, waiting for me to come in.

"I remember some of it, but not all."

Grady smiles and this time that knot in my stomach tightens for a different reason. Because he's so damn cute.

"I need to run upstairs for a second, you can wait here or if you want to go out and see Phoebe . . ."

"Oh! Yeah, of course. I'll go out and wait for you there."

He lifts his hand to my cheek, brushes the skin there, and drops his hand. "Okay."

I remember to breathe and then walk outside. Asher and Rowan are in a very heated debate, and I make my way over to where Phoebe is resting. Her legs are up, hand resting on her belly.

"Do you need anything to drink or eat?" I ask.

"No, no, I'm good. Just expanding by the second."

I sit beside her, remembering how that was with Elodie. "Well, you look radiant."

"That's what I tell her daily!" Asher calls out from the grill.

"Focus on your meat, you both burned the burgers last time!" Phoebe snaps back and then sighs. "I swear, the two of them are competitive in everything they do. Last week they destroyed any chances of eating the ribs because they had to debate for an hour on if they should be in foil or not. This time we gave them burgers, and they decided they needed to give us an authentic taste with charcoal. Do you think either of them have ever cooked on charcoal before? No."

I snort. "Well, I have plenty of burgers at home if we need more."

"We won't because my fiancé knows better than to mess around and not feed me, right, Ash?"

"Of course, my love."

She reaches out and taps my hand. "How are you? How are things at Run to Me? I miss being able to stop in and help."

Phoebe volunteered with us once a week, up until about a month ago when she started feeling sick. I miss having her there. She was such a bright light to those who came in for help. She has a very comforting nature that everyone took to.

"It's been good, we just got another grant so I can do some improvements I was hoping for. Oh, and we're opening another branch in Florida."

She smiles wide. "That's amazing! I know you and Blakely really hoped to have that happen."

We did. Blakely and I were both struggling after all that happened with the crimes against these runaways, so we formed Run to Me as a way to work through our emotions and help others avoid similar situations.

My husband died because he learned about the trafficking happening to runaways, and this is how I carry his legacy.

"How are you feeling, really?"

She rubs her belly. "Tired of being sick from this baby, that's for sure."

"You only have a few months left, right?"

"Yeah, I'm due end of December, but I swear, summer is the worst. I'm so hot and my ankles hate me."

"Are you excited?" I ask, remembering when I was pregnant with Elodie. I couldn't wait.

"I am. Asher is a maniac, worrying over every little thing. Olivia is probably more anxious than anyone. She asked to give the baby a middle name, plus she gets to give her a name sign."

"That's sweet," I say, looking toward the barn area where I can just barely hear the kids laughing.

Phoebe looks toward the giggles and sighs. "I wish I could be out there, I'm sure they're having a ton of fun. However, if I move too much, I puke. It's super fun being me. But since we're on the topic of fun . . . what about you?"

Here we go. "What about me?"

"Are you and Grady moving along well?"

"We're taking this moderately slow."

She grins. "Smart. Be careful, though. Those Whitlock men tend to snatch your heart without you even knowing it."

"That's right, sweetheart!" Asher, with some kind of super hearing power, responds.

"They also should be focusing on the food."

He ignores that one and then Grady arrives, handing me a glass of lemonade and sitting beside us.

"You're not going to help with the food?" I ask.

"Hell no. I sit with Phoebs and watch the shitshow of my brothers. Less chance of injury by either party."

Rowan turns and flips him off.

This, right here, reminds me of home. Before everyone went off and began living their lives all over the country, we were just like this. Isaac and his friends would have barbeques just like this. I would be inside, cooking the side dishes with Brielle, and the guys were attempting to grill something.

I'd always have a backup in the fridge because they lit the entire grill on fire once. After that I was prepared.

The way Grady interacts with his brothers is just like it was between the guys. They were brothers in every way, other than blood. The four of them were a unit growing up, and I loved that they welcomed me into the fold.

Well, Isaac probably demanded it.

Still, I miss them. It's why I go back to Oregon several times a year. All three moved back to Rose Canyon, finding love and starting their lives after Isaac died. Where I lost mine and left because it was too hard to stay.

Now, my heart aches because once this arrangement is over, I'll go back to not having these kinds of nights.

This, right here, is what I wanted when I started back on my dating search. A man who loves his family, has random dinners with them, banters and bickers with the people around him. All of it is right here. And all of it will end—again.

Grady grabs my hand. "Hey, you okay?"

I smile. "Yeah, sorry. I was thinking of some stuff I need to do at work. A few supplies I didn't order."

Not about how I wish I had found someone exactly like him and this was all real.

nine

ADDISON

We're walking back toward the barn as the other Whitlock siblings are engaged in a cornhole tournament. Grady was voted out for Phoebe after he made Brynn lose two games in a row. So, the two kids run in front of us, stopping to see and talk to each animal.

"Elodie, don't put your fingers in the pen!" I remind her as I see her hand going that way.

"She loves the animals," Grady notes.

"She does, she loves everything for about five minutes."

"Jett too, I swear, his attention moves faster than a plane. I can't keep up with him. One day it's airplanes, then trucks, then it's coloring, then coloring is not fun."

I feel him on that. "The minds of three-year-olds."

"They're something, all right."

"I wouldn't trade this time for anything, though. I sometimes can't believe how old she is. It feels like she was just a baby and her father and I were bringing her home."

Maybe for that time again I would trade it. Then I could've loved just a little deeper, let him have held her just a little longer at night instead of forcing him to put her in the crib. If I had known his days were limited, I would've allowed him anything he wanted.

I guess that's why we're not meant to know.

"Daddy, we see chickens?" Jett asks, practically bouncing.

"Go ahead, just don't chase them." Then under his breath he mutters, "Fat chance of that."

The kids run toward the coop that's just to the right of the barn.

We go after them and Jett opens the door for Elodie, who rushes in. As soon as they enter, the chickens scatter to different places, some trying to hide, others approaching them.

"He loves the chickens." Elodie's eyes are full of delight, and she squeals when Jett lifts one in his arms. "Easy, buddy. Don't squeeze. Do you want to go in?" Grady warns.

I exhale through my nose, not really excited about it. "I'm not really a fan of chickens."

He nudges me. "I'll protect you."

I laugh once. "Now I feel better."

"You should. I can be deadly."

"To chickens or others?"

"Test me and find out."

Oh, he's a mess. I sigh dramatically, as though this is such a big feat. "Fine, but if one chicken poops on me, we're done."

"Deal."

Grady opens the door and we enter. The kids are smiling so big as Jett pets the one in his arms. "I gentle, Daddy."

"Good." Grady squats down and one chicken comes to him immediately. He lifts it up and runs his fingers from the top of her head to her neck where he scratches. "Do you want to see, Elodie?"

She looks wary so I give her a big smile. "It's okay, baby."

Elodie heads to him, stopping just a bit from Grady. "Tan I touch it?"

"Do you want to hold her like Jett?" She shakes her head so fast. Grady chuckles and it warms my heart. "I won't let it hurt you, I promise."

Hesitantly, she reaches her hand out, touching just the top of its head, when the chicken moves toward her, she pulls it back.

I smile and then pet the chicken. "See, it won't hurt us. Mr. Grady is making sure we're safe."

She follows my lead and touches the chicken a bit more. "It's soft!"

"It is," I agree.

"I lub this chicken, Mommy."

"It loves you too," Grady tells her.

Jett calls Elodie over as he's now holding a chicken in each arm. "I got you a chicken, Elowdie!"

She squeals and Grady sighs. "That kid already has game. He got her a chicken."

"Well, Elodie adores him so he could've given her a weed and she would be happy."

The one chicken in his arm has had enough and starts flapping her wings and squalling, forcing Jett to release her. "All right, Jett, let's go back to the barn. The chickens have had enough torture."

They run back to the barn, the two of us following again, Grady's hand resting on the small of my back as we exit the coop area.

I fight back the shiver his touch causes and force myself to keep walking. "Do you think your family believes us?" I ask, wanting to remember that this is not a date. This is not the two of us spending time together as we're embarking on this new and budding relationship.

This is an arrangement.

His hand drops. "I do. Like I said, we're friends and it's not hard to sell that I like you. You're funny, beautiful, and smart. There's no reason any guy wouldn't like you."

"Ah, you say that, but we remember why I entered into this agreement."

He laughs. "That last one."

"Was a doozy, I know."

"Although the first guy had potential."

He gives me a hip check and I shake my head. "Not a chance. I

CORINNE MICHAELS

can't even imagine bringing Phil back to Rose Canyon. My friends would eat him alive."

"And you're not worried about me with them?"

"Worried? Kind of. However, if you can handle your brothers and Brynn, I'm sure you'll be fine. Plus, you'll have me to protect you," I say with a laugh.

"Oh, well, in that case, I'm definitely not worried now. You're terrifying."

"Clearly."

I love that we are this way. We can be friends under this whole thing. He makes me laugh and I want to be around him. Also, there's no pressure. I know that he doesn't want a relationship and it gives me some time to get through the wedding and then focus on finding someone I want to build something with.

We stop in front of the fence where a large horse is kept. "This is Brutus," he tells me. "Brutus, this is Addison."

"Wow, he's beautiful," I note as he walks toward us. "Nice to meet you, Brutus."

Brutus walks over, his head held high, and then he touches the palm of Grady's hand. "When I first got here, he wouldn't come near me. I spent a week just sitting on the top of this fence for hours as he pretended I wasn't here."

"Seems he likes you now."

"He does. He likes Jett too. I make Jett come daily with me. Brutus will tolerate Rowan. He absolutely hates Asher, but Asher's got issues with animals." He laughs.

"What about your sister?"

"Brynn, forget it, she's the living version of Snow White. No animal can resist her."

"Why is that?"

"She has a pure heart. At least that's what they say about animals. They can sense your character."

Brutus turns his head to me, nodding, and then nudges my arm that's resting on the top of the fence.

Grady smiles. "He likes you too."

98

"Does that mean I'm pure of heart?"

"Or you smell like apples."

I playfully slap his chest. "Ass."

Elodie comes up behind us. "Tan I see da horsey?"

"Sure can. Come here." Grady scoops her up, putting her feet on the railing as he stands behind her. "Now, put your hand out. Good." He adjusts it so her palm is up. "Now let him come to you."

Brutus doesn't hesitate, his nose touches her palm, and she giggles. The horse makes a snort sound, which makes her laugh again.

"He's silly!"

"He is, but he likes you," Grady tells her as Brutus comes back, repeating the action. "Okay, slowly we're going to touch his face." His hand is around her wrist, guiding her to the white line on the horse's nose. He teaches her how to pet him and Brutus stays, allowing it.

When the horse steps back, Elodie's smile is so wide, it makes my heart happy. "I did it, Mommy!"

"You did."

She turns to Grady, wrapping her arms around his neck. "Tank you!"

Grady hugs her back. "Anytime, Elodie. Anytime."

And this is why I really want to find a man again.

ten

GRADY

"Hey there, sailor, looking for a good time?" A sultry voice causes my head to lift as I'm sitting at the diner to find the most beautiful woman smiling at me.

"For you, I might just be."

"Is this seat taken?"

I shake my head. "I was waiting for you."

Addison takes her seat with a grin. "Sorry I missed you this morning, Elodie was on a video call with Brielle and I couldn't get the two of them to shut up."

"No worries, I was able to get Jett in without incident, thank you very much."

She leans back, looking impressed. "Look at you."

"I'm growing up."

"Did you bribe him?"

I roll my eyes. "Did I bribe him? Of course I did."

That earns me a laugh. "Well, whatever works sometimes. That's my motto."

She really is breathtaking. There are times when we're together that I forget we're not really together. At the barbeque, we sat next to each other, bumping one another when someone said something, and then she took my burger, laughing as she ate it, and I sat there with my jaw open.

We acted exactly how you'd expect a new couple to be. Playful, laughing, and . . . happy.

I wasn't working all that hard to keep appearances up.

I walked her and Elodie back to the side by side and fought every muscle that wanted to lean in and kiss her pouty lips.

Instead, she kissed my cheek and said she'd see me this morning.

Only she didn't, so I texted her asking her to meet for lunch.

"So did you tell your friends about us?"

Addison and her sister-in-law have remained very close. They talk pretty much every day and she knows about us, which I'm assuming means her husband, Spencer, knows as well. However, Addison has been reluctant to tell her business partner, Blakely, or her husband, Emmett.

"I'm planning to talk to Blakely today about it. It feels weird keeping it from them and then showing up to a wedding with you. I had originally responded with a plus one, but I have to tell Jenna a name by today. But, Blakely and Emmett are who scare me, so it's best to break the news to them myself."

"Why do they scare you?"

Addy sighs with a shrug. "They are walking lie detectors. We're going to spend three days there and that's a long time around those two. Blakely was a PI and Emmett is the Sheriff. Both were military. Then there's Spencer, who is a world-renowned investigative journalist. It's like we're going into the lion's den with steak strapped to our bodies."

Well, there's an image worth laughing at. "I wonder, though, if they'll believe it when we show up if you've never mentioned me before. Besides, by the time we go out there, we'll be good at this."

I hope.

I have yet to kiss her, which I need to fix soon. There's been something holding me back. Not because I feel guilt, but because I don't want to feel it. Kissing Addison won't be a punishment, not by a long shot, but she deserves her first kiss after losing Isaac to mean something. To be with a guy who will give her everything she wants and needs.

I'm not that guy and that makes me feel like a piece of shit.

"You're right. I need to tell them so they have time to get used to the idea and maybe won't be complete assholes."

I laugh. "Oh, they will be, and I'll deserve that. I'll be coming onto their turf with a girl who they are very protective of. I promise, they'll be ready to fight. Just like my brothers and I are when it comes to Brynn. They'll want to honor his memory and take care of what he can't."

"Are you all morons?" she asks, shaking her head. "Do you not think we, the women in your lives, have our situations in hand? I don't need them to protect me."

"It isn't about you needing us or not, it's about us wanting to protect you from being hurt. I always want to defend the people I care about, like I do with my sister. It's just the big brother in me, and from what you've explained of Isaac's friends, you're that for them."

Addison leans back, her mouth parted just slightly. "You know, at your sister's house, I thought the same thing. How much you and your brothers were just like the guys."

"Then we'll be fine."

"How so?"

"I understand those guys. If they're anything like my brothers, we'll have our pissing match in the beginning, which I'll win, and they'll be like lambs afterwards."

She eyes me dubiously. "You'll win?"

"Of course I will. Do you doubt my skills?"

"I doubt you'll fool them."

I lean in, placing my hands palm up. She looks at them, then me, and I lift my head just the slightest. Addison takes my cue and places her hands in mine. "I won't have any issues with this, Addison. If it were another time and we weren't on a clock, I wouldn't be pretending anything. I don't have to feign attraction."

I watch as a small tremor runs through her and then she almost collects herself. "At least neither of us have to worry about that."

"So you like me?"

"I didn't say that."

"You think I'm good looking?"

"I didn't say that either," she teases.

"No, you said you wouldn't have to feign attraction, which means you think one of those."

Addison leans forward, her hands still in mine. "No, *you* said that, I just said I wouldn't have to worry about that."

I chuckle softly. "Got me there."

"So you think I'm hot?"

"I do," I say immediately, because she's incredibly attractive and if after all of this, she comes out knowing that, it's a win. I don't like using people and that's sort of what we're both doing, but what if this gives her confidence to find the right guy?

I can give her a chance to put herself out there without getting hurt.

"At least I have that."

"You have more than that, Addy. So much more. Don't sell yourself short because you've met a bunch of asshats who didn't see you for what you are."

Her lips part and she sucks in a soft breath. "And what is that?"

"A woman better than any of us deserve."

"Daddy, I fly?" Jett asks as he runs around the plane. My buddy had this one stored in New Jersey and never flew it. When I mentioned I was getting out and starting a business, he gave it to me for next to nothing.

It's a nice-looking plane, a bit older, lacking some of the new features, but I'm using it for lessons or deliveries, not people, which is why I need something fancier if I want to start my other business venture. This is a 2017 and no millionaire wants to fly in a plane that's past five years if it's not still luxurious, and this . . . isn't.

Still, it works, and did I mention it was cheap?

"Not today, my man."

Today I just needed to do some maintenance since I have to deliver in Virginia Beach in two days. I don't normally agree to go, but this was a personal favor from Connor Arrowood. He works for a security company and needs to deliver this himself by hand, and the drive would be over eight hours, but by plane, it's two. He wants to be back home the same day for some reason.

He sweetened the deal when he said he'd like to introduce me to the owner, who might be a great investor or a possible new client to do courier projects with.

"Pwease! I go in the sky!" He puts his arms out like a plane, moving around the hangar.

I was so like him with planes. I loved them, even as a kid.

"Do you want to fly it?"

He nods vigorously. "Well, I need a co-pilot, can you do it?"

"I fly the plane!"

I open the door and heft him up. He gets in the seat, and I laugh because he can't even see over the yoke.

I walk around, climbing in beside him. "Okay, get your headset."

He looks around and grabs it, pulling it on to rest at his chin.

"Good job," I say as I fight back laughter. He looks so damn cute. I grab my phone and he looks at me with a wide smile. After snapping a photo, I send it off to my siblings in our annoying group chat (which I keep silenced), and then to Addy.

The red notification pops up from the chat.

BRYNLEE

Oh. My. God. I want to squish his little face!

ASHER

Thank God he looks like his mother.

> **ROWAN**
>
> Why are you sending photos in here? This is where we say dirty jokes and make Brynn uncomfortable. However, my nephew probably can fly better than you.

> Brynn is the only one I like.

> **ASHER**
>
> Shocking. She's the only one any of us like.

That's not true, but it works in our never-ending text chain of sarcasm and assholery.

> **ROWAN**
>
> I like you, Asher. Will you be my best brother?

> **BRYNLEE**
>
> I hate this chat. I'm going back into court. Kiss my nephew for me!

"Daddy, we go!"

"Sorry, of course."

I grab my headset, putting it over my ears, and turn the coms on. "Jett, do you copy?"

His eyes widen as he looks around. "I hear, Daddy! I hear you!"

"Are you ready to fly today?"

He nods, the headset falling off. "Grab them and keep them on," I instruct.

Jett grabs them and puts them back on. "I ready!"

My phone pings with a text, which means it's not my stupid siblings.

> **ADDISON**
>
> Please print that photo and put it everywhere. He is adorable.

> Like his father?

ADDISON

No, remember, his father is super hot. Like, oh, baby. Oh, baby.

Then it's a good thing you snagged me and I'm off the market.

ADDISON

If I recall it was you who snagged me.

Semantics.

ADDISON

It counts here. Also, I told my friends about us.

I know she was really nervous about doing that.

How did it go?

ADDISON

As expected.

That sounds ominous.

Jett huffs. "Daddy, we ready to fly now?"

I gotta go, my co-pilot is antsy. We'll talk tonight. Maybe after I get Jett down, I can swing by and you can fill me in?

ADDISON

I'll text later.

I slip my phone back into my pocket. "Sorry, sir. I'm ready for you now."

He stands on the seat so he can see outside. "We go out there?"

"Not this time. The plane has to stay inside."

I can see the disappointment.

"Well, before you can fly in the sky, you have to be able to fly on the ground," I make some bullshit up. Although, it's not completely untrue. And then I get an idea. "You know what, I have another plane you can fly."

"Another one?" he asks with disbelief.

I climb out and walk around so I can grab him. We walk into the simulator that looks a lot like the plane we were in. There are two pilot chairs and then two seats behind. Only the screen emulates the outside. I love this damn thing. It's so real and will definitely give Jett the feeling of being up there.

I get him strapped in before securing myself in the captain chair and disconnecting the co-pilot controls from the simulator. I get everything loaded and his eyes go wide when the windows become the outside.

"Ready?"

"I ready!"

I fly the fake plane out to the runway and go through the motions as though we're really going to fly. I have to talk to air traffic control, check all my gauges, and set a flight plan. I mark that we are only going in a small circle since he has the attention span of a gnat.

Once the light in the middle is green, we're clear to go.

I point to it and explain to Jett that his job is to tell me when it's on.

A minute later, it lights up. "Go, Daddy! We fly."

I should've thought of this sooner. He's so happy, he's nearly vibrating.

We get up in the air and with the way a three-year-old steers, it's a good thing his side is disconnected, or we'd be dead by now.

"All right, Captain Jett, what do you want to see?"

"We go to see Mommy!"

I look over, my heart instantly falling. "Where is Mommy?"

"In the sky."

My chest is tight, and I look over, now wishing we weren't in the simulator so I could pull him in my lap. "Is that where she is for you?"

"She is up there." He points up.

It's not that I don't want to talk to him about Lisa, it's that I don't know how. He's never asked about her and I haven't brought it up. Someone has, though.

"She's in heaven, which is even higher than the sky."

"Nana says she's there."

Fuck the simulation. I turn it off and pull him into my lap. "She's here too." I press my hand over his heart.

"In me?"

I smile. "In your heart. She's with us always and she loved you so much."

Brynn put photos of Lisa up before we came. She said it was important that he know his mother was with him, even though Jett never really knew her. He was just a few weeks old when she died.

"Did you love Mommy?"

"I did, very much."

I loved her more than I knew I could. More than anything, until Jett was born. She was my best friend, and there are times now when I want nothing more than to see her smile or listen to her laugh as I explain something funny.

Over the years, that's faded some, but right now, I would give anything for her to be here and hug this kid. To let him rest his head on her chest instead of mine.

He was robbed of that, but I thank God he was an infant and never had to know her, lose her, and learn to move on, wishing he had a mother.

This is better.

"I love Mommy too."

I kiss the top of his head. "She loved you too, bud. She loved you too, and so do I."

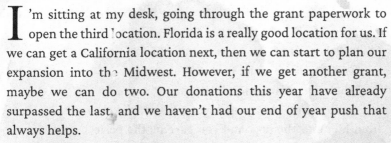

eleven

ADDISON

I'm sitting at my desk, going through the grant paperwork to open the third location. Florida is a really good location for us. If we can get a California location next, then we can start to plan our expansion into the Midwest. However, if we get another grant, maybe we can do two. Our donations this year have already surpassed the last, and we haven't had our end of year push that always helps.

All of this is encouraging.

"Addison, can you come out front?" my assistant calls, sounding almost nervous.

I get up quickly, concerned at whatever has her calling for me.

When I enter the waiting area, I find her facing two people worth fearing.

Blakely Maxwell and Brielle Cross.

"Blakely? Brielle?" I ask, feeling so many emotions at once. Joy because I miss them so much. Confusion because neither of them mentioned this visit when I talked to them yesterday, and fear because I'm pretty sure I know what spurred this surprise visit.

"Hey!" Brielle rushes to me with open arms. "I missed you and needed to lay eyes on you." She pulls me in for a hug and whispers in my ear. "And I had to protect you from her."

I pull back, smiling at her and thanking God I have the best sister-in-law ever.

"I missed you too!"

Blakely walks over, her smile wide, but I know her too well to trust it. "I figured we needed to sign paperwork this week, so why not do it together?"

Yeah, my ass that's why. I hug her as well because I missed my friend. I miss all of them.

That doesn't stop me from calling her out on her blatant lie though. "Or is it because I told you I was dating someone and you needed to assess the situation?"

She doesn't even attempt to deny it. "That's exactly why. Also, you're lucky it's Brielle and me out here and not our overprotective husbands."

I guess that's a relief. But I don't see her son. "And the baby? Did you bring him?"

Blakely scoffs. "Hell no we didn't. This is a work trip."

"Oh? Brielle works for us now?"

"She's my assistant for the weekend."

Brielle gives me an apologetic look. "Blakely needed a break from him and the dog, and you gave us the perfect excuse to run away."

I grin and hug them both again. No matter the reason or the hell I'm going to pay, I have my girls here and I can't be upset about that. "I'm just so happy you're here."

We split apart and they fill me in about the town and everyone there. They tell me all about the six old ladies who have named themselves, The Six Who Knit, and how they are still up to no good.

Everything is as it should be in Rose Canyon.

"How's the football team?" I ask, always wanting to know about the boys there.

This would be the last group of kids who had Isaac as their coach, which is sad to think about. No one else will know how great it was to have him on their sideline, yelling, screaming, and cheering louder than anyone else.

"Horrible. Seriously, I don't know if we can call what they play football," Blakely says without pause. "Every Friday night though, we all pack into those stands and pray for a miracle."

I laugh. "They're that bad?"

Brielle nods. "So bad, but they try, and I think Emmett is actually going to coach next season."

My eyes widen. "Really?" Emmett was a freaking beast at football.

"He thinks Isaac would've approved," Blakely says. "Also, it gets him out of the house and away from me and the kid."

That sounds like a more plausible reason.

"Well, how long do I have you both?"

"Just tonight and tomorrow. We're taking the last flight back to Oregon."

Blakely flops down on the sofa and sighs. "Long enough for you to call your boyfriend and tell him to come meet us."

"He's kind of busy," I say, really hating this.

"He can't spare ten minutes to come meet your sister and best friend?" she tosses back.

I sigh. "He's a single dad, he's working on the plane today with his son. I can't just call him up and be like, come over and see my uninvited guests from Oregon."

"Why not?" Blakely pushes. Well, I don't know why not, but I'm not going to admit that to her. "Is there a reason you don't want us to get to know him?"

"Of course not!"

Which is a big fat lie. Of course I don't want them to meet him. They're crazy and incredibly observant. At least at a wedding there's a million things I could do or say to get the attention off of him. I know everyone there so I could just shuffle him around so no one spends significant time with him.

All of this would've worked. An inquisition from these two is *not* part of my plan.

"Then call him up, tell him your sister and business partner are in town, and they want to meet him."

The more I push back, the more they'll think there's a reason I don't want them to meet him, which is true, but I can't really say that.

"Fine, stay out here and let me call him—in private. Nosey assholes. Both of you."

I walk back to my office, pull my phone out of my purse, and sink to the floor in the corner.

This is a nightmare. A complete nightmare.

I have weeks to prepare for Oregon. On their turf I could handle it, but here, with just two of them . . . I'm going to die.

Am I being dramatic? Maybe.

However, I hover over Grady's name, take a deep breath, and call. No way am I sending it through text with those two snooping women. I wouldn't be shocked if Blakely has my phone tapped.

He answers on the third ring.

"Hey, Addy."

"Grady, my sister and best friend are here," I whisper-yell. "*In Sugarloaf. In my office. Here!*"

He pauses. "From Oregon?"

"*Yes! From fucking Oregon.* I told them about us yesterday, and today . . ." I practically screech. "Today, they're here!"

"Easy, relax. It's fine. I'm assuming they came because they want to meet me?" He laughs as though there's anything about this that is remotely funny.

I roll my eyes. "What do you think?"

"Okay, so I'll come over tonight like we planned."

My eyes widen, I look down at the phone, and then bring it back to my ear. "Are you crazy? You can't come here. I need an excuse. A good one. Jett is sick? No, that is too easy. You're sick? Too coincidental. How about you are stuck in Virginia? Wait, that won't work because Blakely is *friends* with the guys at Cole. Okay, we go dramatic, you were in a plane crash and lost the use of your arms, which means you can't drive, but you'll make a full recovery by the wedding."

Might be the best idea I've had so far.

Grady laughs. "I'm coming over, Addison. I'll bring Jett and it'll be great."

Great is absolutely *not* the adjective I would use, and his calm demeanor has me concerned. "Why aren't you nervous?"

"Because they love you and want you to be happy. They came here to make sure I'm worthy of your time, and if they leave without getting that chance, that'll be worse."

"You say worse, I say necessary." He doesn't understand because Blakely is a freaking super sleuth. She is scarier than any of the guys —I can handle them. I've known them since grade school and with one look I can make all three of them cower. But Blakely, she's not like that.

She assesses, studies, and I can't control her at all.

Brielle, I think I could take, but not Blakely.

"We've managed to fool the entire town, what makes you think we can't handle this?"

I look at the door, waiting for one of them to pop in. "She's terrifying."

"And my sister isn't?"

"Okay, you have a point, but why aren't you . . . nervous?"

Grady sighs and says something to Jett before returning to me. "I don't get nervous when it comes to situations like this. I'm trained to control my emotions and think rationally."

Well, that's annoying. "Okay."

"So, we remain calm, we act like we do around Sugarloaf, and I'll meet your sister and your friend. You weren't nervous with my family the other night."

He has no fucking clue just how nervous I was. I wanted to puke. Still, it went great. Brynn and Phoebe made me super comfortable. His brothers were funny and didn't seem to care too much about either of us dating, and Jett is the sweetest boy who loves me since I come equipped with Elodie.

Maybe this will be totally fine.

"If you think so."

"I do."

I let out a long breath through my nose, working on this calm thing he seems to have down. "So tonight?"

"I'll be there in about two hours with Jett, and if it goes well, we can decide if you want me to come back over after he's asleep to hang with them more."

"I really hope your training includes how to manage two maniacs."

Grady chuckles. "I was trained to handle being captured and tortured by the enemy. I can handle your friend and sister."

"Famous last words."

He sent a text a few minutes ago that he was about ten minutes away, and I've been pacing by my front door ever since.

"Why are you so nervous?" Blakely asks. My eyes meet hers and I swear the look on my face must be priceless because she bursts out laughing. "Okay, I guess you're worried about me?"

"What was the first clue?"

"Oh, I don't know, you're pacing for one."

Brielle walks over, Elodie in her arms, and her kind eyes meet mine. "Is it me? Are you worried about me meeting him?"

That's part of it, but I really didn't think about that as much as I should've. If I'm honest, it didn't even cross my mind, I've been so focused on Blakely that I didn't consider my sister-in-law.

I turn to face her, seeing so much of her brother in Elodie. While she has my coloring, she has his nose and smile. Looking at Brielle holding a part of him, my heart aches a little. "Brie . . ."

She shakes her head. "My brother would never want you to be alone, to spend your life mourning him. He loved you so much and I'm just so happy you found someone. So if it's me, please put that to rest. If it's Blake, well, she's an asshole so just chalk it up to that."

I laugh and the nerves I've been struggling with settle just a bit. "Thank you for saying that."

"I mean it," Brielle says softly. "I want nothing more than for you to have someone who loves you."

That jars me. "No one said love."

"I know that, I was just saying in the future. No matter who it is."

"I love you, Mommy." Elodie's sweet voice fills the room.

"I love you most." I tap Elodie's nose and then Brielle puts her down. I look to my sister-in-law, who is one of my best friends. She's always been there for me, kind, understanding, and supportive. We don't need to say anything to know what the other is thinking, it's in her eyes and I love her for it. I pull her in for a hug and kiss her cheek just as I hear a car door close.

Damn it. He's here.

It's okay, Addison, this will be fine. You'll keep it together, and no matter what, you'll survive.

At least I hope so.

Blakely is at the window, pulling the curtain back. She laughs softly. "I definitely see the appeal."

Jesus Lord. "Blakely!" I hiss. "Get away from the window."

She rolls her eyes. "Shut up, I'm getting a first look."

I pull her back and then command them both to go to the couch and wait. Elodie climbs up in her aunt's lap and giggles. I walk to the door, open it, and wait for Grady and Jett to come up the steps.

"Hey, guys!"

It's clear I'm nervous since my voice cracks at the end. Jett rips his hand out of Grady's and rushes to the door.

"Elodie!" he yells and she's running to him too. The two kids hug with huge smiles and then run to the play area.

"Well, that's the cutest thing ever," Blakely says and then I refocus.

"Grady, this is my friend and business partner, Blakely Maxwell, married to one of my best friends from Oregon. And this is my sister-in-law, Brielle."

Brielle is the first to move. "It's so nice to meet you."

Grady gives her a smile that would have any girl ready to swoon. "You too, I've heard a lot about you."

"All good things I hope?" Brielle actually flutters her lashes.

Oh Lord.

"Of course, I don't think I've ever heard Addy say anything bad about anyone." His eyes find mine and I wonder if I'm still standing, or if I'm a puddle on the ground. The way he stares at me, like I'm the sun or maybe even the world. It's . . .

Fake, Addy. It's fake. Remember it's fake.

Okay, I can do this. I work to give him the same look back. "You aren't going to fool them. Trust me, they know me too well. I'm definitely not that nice."

"You forget I was there when you went on that date with the video game guy. You are that nice and so much more."

I blush, damn it, I blush because he's being so sweet.

"All right. Enough embarrassing me." I duck my head, not wanting to see anyone's reactions.

"I'm happy to meet you as well." Blakely extends her hand.

"Likewise. What you both do is extremely admirable with your organization."

The way to Blake's heart is flattery. Maybe he will pull this off without issues.

"Thank you. We think so too."

"Do you want anything to drink?" I ask, ushering him into the interrogation—I mean, living room.

"No, I'm good. I was just stopping by since you asked me to."

I sigh. "I'm sorry. I know you're *busy.*" The last word is a bit biting as I glare at my sister and friend. I loathe them both for showing up unannounced with demands.

"It's no problem, Jett is more than happy to see Elodie since he misses her."

The two of us sit on the couch.

"So the kids are friends? Is that how you met?" Blakely asks.

Grady turns to her. "Sort of . . . I mean, it's a small town so we would've met anyway, but I met her for the first time when my son was throwing a tantrum about going into daycare. Addy was nice enough to help."

Brie grins and I swear she's about to bounce out of her skin.

"And then Grady helped me when my car had a flat."

"Is that when this started?" Blakely follows up.

"Not completely," he cuts in. "We kept running into each other when she was on those terrible dates. On the last one, when she was out with that real piece of shit, I was fortunate to be there and intervene. After that, we sat at the bar, drank, laughed, talked, and . . . I asked her out." His hand moves to mine and he laces our fingers together. "You know, she's pretty easy to like."

There go my damn cheeks again. All he's doing is holding my hand, but there's something so much more to it. His touch is soft, but he's strong at the same time. I want to stay like this, his warm eyes studying my face, strong hand entwined with mine.

Yeah, I'm a fool.

I clear my throat and tuck my hair behind my ear. Not really needing to feign embarrassment. "You're not so bad yourself."

Jett and Elodie come running in and both of us drop our hands quickly. "Daddy, I fly with Ewodie in da pwane. Can we go *now*?"

I smile and Grady does too. "Not today, but maybe we can take her soon. We have to go see Uncle Asher."

Elodie's lower lip juts out. "Pwease!"

I shake my head. "We have Aunt Brielle and Blakely here, we can't go, sweetheart."

She looks to the couch where they both sit and her shoulders drop just a touch. "Okay."

Grady looks at his watch. "We have to get going. Jett and I are having dinner with my brother. I'm sorry I can't stay longer." He stands and walks over, hefting Jett into his arms.

"Don't apologize. We all appreciate you stopping by on such short notice. Tell Asher we said hello."

"I will." He looks to the girls. "It was great meeting you both. I look forward to getting to know you better when we're in Oregon."

Blakely and Brielle both wave. "Us too!"

They walk to the door and I follow, opening it for him. When he's over the threshold he turns, winks, and gives me a killer smile, and I sigh, like the girlfriend watching her man walk away.

Yup, I'm a fool.

twelve

GRADY

Today couldn't have gone any better if I wanted it to and I have to tell Addison about it. So here I am, way too fucking late at night, knocking on her door because she's the first person I want to share the news with.

The light flicks on in the hall and I see the curtain move on the side. "Grady?" Addison says, clutching a robe closed as she opens the door. "Are you okay?"

"Addy, today was . . . so . . . I can't even tell you."

"Come in and find your words."

I walk past her, my excitement growing as the best freaking possibilities are coming to light. I pace the living room and assemble my thoughts. "Okay, you know how I was going to Virginia Beach with Connor today?"

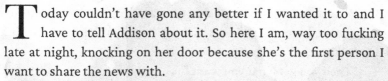

"Yeah."

I nod. "When I was there, he set me up a meeting with the co-owner of Cole Securities."

"I remember . . . I've met them."

"Well, the meeting went great. All of them are former military, so immediately I was welcomed into the fold." I smile and then what she said hits me. "Wait, you know those guys?"

She laughs with a shake of her head. "Yeah, they're friends with Spencer and . . . ended up helping Brielle when she was recovering."

Talk about coincidences.

"Small world. Anyway, so he knows these guys, he served with two other guys that work for them, anyway, a lot of times they need to go places quickly and have two company jets, but are debating adding another one—and a pilot—on standby. Which they'd pay very handsomely to have."

Addison smiles. "That means you?"

"Maybe. They're not sure about adding the expense, but it was a great meeting, and I'm really hopeful."

"Oh! Grady! That's amazing!" She rushes forward, jumping into my arms.

I spin her around, feeling so much excitement.

When I put her down, I don't release her, we stand with her arms looped around my neck and my hands on her hips. "If they invest, then . . ."

"Then you get what you want."

I want to kiss her.

The thought is screaming at me and suddenly, that's all I can think about.

Her eyes are soft as she looks at me, hands falling to my chest. She wants this too, and I don't have the strength to resist.

I lean down as she lifts up, and our lips touch, tentatively at first, and then it changes. As though the two of us broke the barrier and now are tumbling forward. My fingers move up her back, molding her to my chest as she parts her lips just enough for me to slip my tongue in.

The taste of her is intoxicating, mint and sweetness mixed together that makes me want more. Her tongue meets mine, no longer being kissed but kissing me as well. Her hands move up to the back of my neck, keeping me where she wants me.

I hold onto her, loving the feel of her and praying that this kiss never fucking ends.

She moans as my hands move down, pulling her hips closer, and

I'm sure she can feel how hard I am. It's been so fucking long since I've had this.

I feel just the slightest push against my chest and I pull back, resting my forehead against hers. The two of us work to catch our breaths as we stand here. "Addy," I say softly.

"That was . . ." Her voice is low with a slight rasp to it.

I need to see her eyes, to see if she's angry or upset. I thought she wanted this too, but maybe I misread it. I wait for her to look up. There's no anger there, a little embarrassment maybe, but mostly desire.

"Fantastic." I finish the statement.

She smiles. "It was."

Wanting to do it again, I bring my hands to her face, gently cupping her cheeks. I keep eye contact, so she knows what's coming. Her eyelids flutter closed, and I kiss her nose first, then one cheek, the other, savoring her slight gasp before bringing my lips back to hers.

This kiss isn't overly passionate. It's soft, gentle, and probably what our first should've been.

That hazy look in her eyes causes me to smile.

"I didn't come over with this plan."

"I didn't think so."

"Are you okay?" I ask, concerned that I fucked up.

She sighs, placing her hands on my chest. "Yes, I'm okay. I'm glad my first kiss was this way, and with you."

"You're my first since Lisa too."

"Really?"

I chuckle. "You're surprised?"

"I mean, you're a guy and ridiculously good looking, so I assumed you'd at least . . . you know. Get it somewhere."

Many probably do assume it, but I just never had the time. I was so busy trying to be a good father, pilot, friend, and anything else I could be to keep my mind off of being a widower. It was a word I never wanted to claim, so I did whatever I could to avoid it. Not to mention, any free time I had I was going to Oklahoma.

I brush my thumb against her lips. "For many of the same reasons you haven't, I haven't either. Mostly I didn't because I was so fucking busy I didn't have the time to find someone else. My focus was on Jett and that didn't really leave time to get it anywhere."

"I wasn't ready for a long time, and like you, I was busy. Being this single mom, moving out here, and then starting Run to Me. Time got away from me, until it felt like it was running and I had to catch it."

Guilt floods me. "And then I forced you to agree to this."

She shakes her head. "No, that's not it. I agreed to date you because it was honestly what I needed. I wanted to bring someone back to Rose Canyon who wasn't a creep or married or unemployed." She laughs at that last one. "I needed to bring someone home to them, to at least get them to see that I'm not the fragile widow they all see me as, and you're the exact man I want to bring. And now that you've won over my sister and Blake, I know you're the right choice."

Pride swells that she thinks of me that way, but there is that hint of guilt still hanging around because when this is over, Addison will be alone. I'll get to move on in this town as the guy who broke her heart, which I'll be forgiven for since I have no damn desire to date, but she'll have to start over.

"And when we break up, what then?"

She steps out of my grasp, running her hands through her long blond hair. "Then we break up. I go back to dating and you'll have gotten your investment."

"And us?"

I don't know why it's important, but I want to know what becomes of us.

"What about us?"

I step closer. "Will we be friends? Will you pretend to hate me?"

She smiles. "Of course we'll be friends. We just say it wasn't our time or we were better off as friends. I won't make you out to be a villain."

I guess that's one thing going for me. "If it were another time..."

"Grady, stop. I'm fully aware of our arrangement. We don't struggle with attraction, and I didn't mind kissing you, but it is what it is."

"I didn't mind it either."

"So, we're grown-ups, we like each other, there are zero expectations on my part, and we're going to be affectionate around people. At least we had our first kiss here and not at the bar. If it was bad, that would've been awkward."

I don't think it could've been bad, but I guess she has a point. "It wasn't bad."

"No, it wasn't." Addison wraps her robe tighter around her, almost as though she's holding more than just her clothing tight. "Thank you."

"For what?"

"For our kiss being . . . not pity or . . . fake. I can't tell you how long I wondered how that first kiss post Isaac would be, and I'm glad it was like this."

The fact that she's thanking me for kissing her makes me want to again. "Saying 'you're welcome' feels like it was a chore and not what I wanted to do." There is a silence between us and I realize it's almost midnight. I soften my tone, not wanting to upset her. "I should go, it's late and I need to get home."

We walk to the door, and I keep trying to think of what to say. How do I explain things I can't even understand? Do I like her more than I'm admitting to? Why did I rush here to tell her about possibly partnering with Cole instead of going home or over to my brother's?

I know why.

It was Addison I wanted to tell. It wasn't even a thought, I just came here because that's who I wanted to share my news with.

Not because of the fake dating, but because it was her joy I wanted to see.

"Well, congrats on this possibility. It sounds great."

I nod. "Thanks. I think it could be, but . . . we're still on for dinner with the Kopaskeys on Friday, right?"

"Of course. Even if you land a contract with Cole, we still have to keep up pretenses here before the wedding."

Right. "I know, I'm sorry."

"Grady, it's fine. Go home, hug Jett, and I'll see you in the morning when we drop the kids off."

I lean in and kiss her cheek. "Good night, Addison."

"Good night."

I step out into the cool air and walk down her steps, when I turn back the door is shut, and I wonder if she's just as fucked in the head as I am.

The water is cascading down my back, my hand wrapped around my cock, needing to fucking come so bad.

Every muscle in my body is tense as I pump faster.

Her face is all I see.

Blue eyes. Blond hair. And that smile.

God, I feel my cock get even harder.

My hand tightens, and I close my eyes, imagining how hot she'd feel if I was inside her. Wondering how sweet she'd taste as I'd lick her pussy until she screams my name. I can see her now, legs over my shoulders, hands in my hair as I play with her, making her climb higher before easing her back down, her release tasting even better after I've toyed with her.

A shiver runs down my spine as pressure builds in my cock.

I focus on Addison. How much I want her, how her skin will feel beneath my fingers. How her soft scent, a mix of pears and flowers, will be stronger when I'm inside of her. Then I remember the kiss and the way she arched into me.

"Fuck," I moan, inching closer to release. She's in my head. All the time. Every day I stand here, jerking off to thoughts of her. Always her.

If she was in here right now, I'd pin her to the wall and drive my cock into her pussy until she begged for me to let her come again. I'd suck on those perfect tits I barely got a glimpse of and then bite down.

Although, she d look so goddamn perfect in front of me right now, bent over, ass in the air as I drove in deep while my finger teased her tight little ass. She'd like that, my dick in her pussy, finger in her ass, filling her while her hands press against the wall, bracing against how hard I'd fuck her.

That does it.

My orgasm rocks through me so fast, I couldn't stop it if I tried. I come hard, and I still don't feel sated.

I lean against the wall, spent, and yet I know if she was here right now, I'd be ready to go again.

This is a whole new level of bad. I can't be thinking of Addison as I jerk off. I have four million reasons why I need to stay focused, but the most important one is two doors down.

Jett already loves her. He doesn't even want to go into daycare without her and Elodie. For him, I need to remember why I can't consider anything more with her.

He needs me.

He needs a father who will sacrifice everything to keep him from ever feeling hurt again.

I can take it. I can handle the pain, but my son . . . no, my son can't.

And that is why I have to keep my heart out of this.

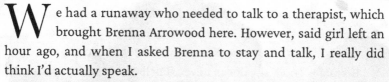

thirteen

ADDISON

We had a runaway who needed to talk to a therapist, which brought Brenna Arrowood here. However, said girl left an hour ago, and when I asked Brenna to stay and talk, I really did think I'd actually speak.

But it's been ten minutes of her here, not saying a word, while I try to get the courage to open my mouth.

Why?

Because I'm fucked in the head after that kiss and need to tell someone who isn't judgmental.

Also, Brenna is a widow and understands this more than anyone else might.

Another minute passes and still she says nothing.

Her patience is admirable, but I'm now feeling like I have to say something.

"You're not going to ask why I asked you to stay?"

She smiles. "Why did you ask me to stay?"

I let out a long sigh. "You're doing some weird voodoo therapist shit."

Brenna places her hands on her lap. "I'm doing nothing but letting you get your thoughts in order. When you want to talk, I'm here to listen."

"Does this fall under patient doctor confidentiality?"

"Do you want to be my patient or just my friend?"

"Is there a difference?" I ask.

"No. I would never speak to anyone about what we talk about. No one."

I may have already known that, but it's still a relief to hear her say it. I can't tell Devney about my fake dating Grady because she is already picking out China patterns. Plus, the agreement was to tell no one so there was zero chance of it getting out, but Brenna doesn't feel like someone.

She's a therapist. A trusted member of the community. She took an oath, or I think she did. Whatever. She won't blab it. It's . . . medical reasons.

Because I'm going off the rails at a speed I can't control.

"I kissed Grady last night. Our first kiss. A real kiss." I add that on because it's the closest I can admit to having anything fake.

Okay, it's out there now. Yeah, can't take that back.

Brenna is good, she doesn't even flinch. She just slowly nods her head. "A real kiss as opposed to a pretend one?"

"Yes, a real one—with tongue."

She smiles at that. "Was it good?"

"Very."

"And the issue is?"

"We kissed!"

Boy, for a very highly trained and respected therapist, I'm starting to doubt her skills.

Brenna leans back in her chair. "You said that, this is a good thing, isn't it?"

"Yes, it is, but it's terrifying and all of it's scary because I needed a boyfriend, but now that I have one . . ."—albeit a fake one—". . . I'm not sure what I'm doing."

Her face pinches. "Why did you need a boyfriend?"

Of course she'd pick up on that.

"It's been three years. Three very long and exhausting years. Three years of going back to Rose Canyon and listening to how sad it is that I'm still alone, mourning Isaac. I can't do it anymore. I have to go home this time on the arm of a man who adores me."

Her posture and expression don't change other than the slight narrowing of her eyes. "Does Grady adore you?"

"He kissed me like he liked me at least, but what if it's not real? What if none of it is?" This is getting close to the confession I can't make.

"I'm just going to ask this, but why would you even think it wasn't real?"

I sigh, the weight of that question boring down on me. "Because a few days before we started this relationship, he said how he doesn't want to be in one."

"I'd say it's clear he does."

No, it's not clear, but I'm not going to tell her that. "Maybe he changed his mind, but I don't know that he wants what I do."

"Do you know what you want?"

"No." I answer much too quickly.

"But yet you asked me to stay here and stare at you for ten minutes because you . . . aren't sure that the kiss you had is what you want?"

I'm starting to regret telling her. Maybe I should've told someone else, anyone else, because she has that eye that sees through the bullshit.

"I don't know what I want."

And that's the truth.

"That's okay. You don't have to know now. Also, Grady may or may not want something more, but that isn't what you two need to decide. To your initial point of it being three years since your husband died, there's no timeline for dating after loss. You and I both know a number of people who decided to never date again. Then there are people like me who struggled with how fast they developed feelings for someone else after loss. There is guilt on all sides of the puzzle and plenty of it to go around."

I know that she's right on the one part—there is no timeline, but I'm not getting any younger.

"I want more kids. Isaac and I wanted at least four. I think that man would've gone for a baseball team if I would've agreed. I'm an only child and I hated it. I was always jealous of Isaac and his sister. They were best friends. Elodie already is without her father and I want her to have a sibling too, preferably before she's ten."

Brenna laughs. "Well, there's nothing saying you won't find someone, but you want to find the right someone. A man who will love Elodie like she's his and be there for you when you need him. I wasn't ready for Jacob when he came crashing into my world and I definitely had no intentions of a relationship. I'm not saying it'll happen with Grady, but I'm also not saying it won't. Until then, enjoy whatever this is, because we know better than anyone that life is short."

Yeah, we really do.

She continues on. "And wants and desires change, even when we think they won't."

Today is the town's fall chili competition.

It's one of my favorite events, other than the dance-off, mostly because I like watching Connor pout after he loses to Phoebe, but this one is special to me.

I love food. I'm also the judge, which is a huge honor and a coveted one. The year I moved here, I was named judge, as I would be the most impartial as the newbie.

For the last week all the town's people have been preparing and perfecting their recipes, as well as attempting to bribe me, which . . . well, it's not really allowed, but it's also widely done.

This year, Devney and I will walk around, try not to pass out from the intense amount of spices used, drink enough milk to stop the burning in our mouths, and see which town person we've pissed off when we crown the winner.

Last year, Lynn Parker won. Which made me her favorite and

I've gotten cookies and casseroles once a month as a thank you to my impressive tastebuds.

I'm pretty sure I picked her because I'd lost the ability to taste by then, but my co-judge, Albert, said it was definitely the best. I stopped at the corner store to get a candy bar before I lose my sense of taste from the chili.

"Hello, Addison, darling. You're simply glowing today," Mrs. Cooke says as I place my KitKat on the counter.

"You are as well, Mrs. Cooke."

"Oh!" She waves me off. "Hodgepodge. If I'm glowing it's because the light is nearing me and I'm avoiding walking to it."

"Nonsense. You aren't a day over twenty." She's actually probably not far off on that light theory, but she's the sweetest woman and a town icon. She and Jimmy have run this store since they married when they were nineteen years old. It's a staple in this town and also where the old ladies hang out for the gossip.

"Addison, is that you?" Mrs. Symonds comes out from the back. "It is. Hello, dear."

"Mrs. Symonds," I say, worried because if one more lady pops out, I'm a goner. I look to Mrs. Cooke, wanting to pay so I can get out to the chili set up and make sure someone hasn't tampered with the judges' cards. It happened last year. "Is it two dollars?" I ask.

"What? Oh, yes," she says as she rings it up.

"Are you all ready to judge?" Mrs. Symonds asks with a little lilt in her voice.

"I am."

She nods. "That's nice. I wish you luck."

The way she says it and the weird look in her eyes makes me wonder if she really does wish me luck or she's informing me of something.

Come to think of it, this group is really more of a trio. A trio of retired women who love to sit around here, watch the comings and goings of the town, and inform everyone of what little piece of information we should know.

"Where's Mrs. Parker?" I ask, noticing one is missing.

"Lynn?" Mrs. Cooke asks.

As though we have more than one. "Yes, she's usually here with you both."

Mrs. Symonds looks away. "Oh, I'm sure she'll be here soon."

"Where is she?"

"You know, she didn't mention it."

I very much doubt that. These three are up to something and I would bet it has to do with today. I wouldn't put sabotage past any of them.

"Really?" I turn to Mrs. Cooke. "You don't know either?"

She shakes her head just a little. "Nope."

"You both aren't very good liars," I tell them.

The two of them glance at each other and then back to me. "Us?"

Oh, now I'm sure of it. "Yes, you two. What's going on? Did you guys swap her spices or something else to make sure she doesn't win?"

"No, no, it's not that at all," Mrs. Cooke says with a smile. "Lynn is just delivering some very important news regarding the competition today."

"Ha!" I clap my hands. "I knew it. You three did something again, didn't you?"

Mrs. Symonds's head pulls back and her mouth opens. "Now, Addison, why would you think that?"

I don't know, because they're devious. "What news is Mrs. Parker delivering?"

"We had an emergency meeting last night."

My eyes widen when Mrs. Cooke at least has the decency to duck her head a little. "An. Emergency. Meeting? About what?"

There was no emergency meeting because Devney would've been notified. If Devney was notified, she would've called me.

Mrs. Symonds grins, clearly enjoying this. "Well, my dear, we told you to join the board last year, but you weren't sure you had the time and all. Anyway, we met. We voted. The rules will be announced prior to the start." She glances at her watch. "Oh, we should lock up so we can get there for the opening ceremonies and make sure the men have the ingredients set up correctly."

I breathe deeply, telling myself that this is really stupid and not worth being upset about, but also, I'm slightly terrified as to what the hell they could've met about. Mrs. Parker won. What could she possibly be upset about? The rules are really fair.

This could be their plan though, to get in my head, like some Jedi mind game for the old and bored crew. We really need to come up with a name for them.

The three gossipitos. Or maybe nosey nursing homebound. I'll think more on that once I find out what's going on.

I grab my KitKat and force a sweet smile. "I can't wait to see you all there and give my love to your husbands." Lord knows they need it.

"We will and you be sure to tell Grady we said hello. I know he was over late last night . . ."

I freeze for just a second and then weigh my words carefully. "What did you say?"

Mrs. Cooke speaks over her. "It's all over town, sweetheart. He came home from whatever he was doing with Connor and rushed to your place. I heard it was around two a.m. A very late visit indeed."

"It wasn't two a.m.," I correct and then realize my mistake because I just admitted that he did come over.

Shit.

"No? Jimmy must've misheard Albert. He's a little hard of hearing," Mrs. Cooke says conspiratorially.

That's an understatement. All she does is shout at him.

"It wasn't like that. He stopped by and then went home."

Mrs. Symonds leans her elbows on the counter. "I heard he stayed for a good hour. A lot can be done in an hour."

Oh Lord. "It wasn't an hour. And we didn't do anything. He needed to . . . check on something," I say with a smile. I should be happy about this since our plan is to have the town believing it, which they seem to now, but I still don't like the fact that Albert somehow saw this. "How did Albert know this?"

"He was checking on the chickens. We've had an increase of foxes lately. One can never be too careful. He was out front, saw Grady pull in, go inside . . . for an *hour* . . . and come out smiling."

I sigh heavily. "If he saw him smiling, he had binoculars." Considering I live a good eight hundred feet off the main road, and there are trees between our properties.

The two of them look to one another. "He didn't mention that."

"Shocking." I need to nip this in the bud before the town starts saying he slept over. "Well, Grady did come by, told me some news he'd been waiting on, and that was it. It was maybe ten minutes." I lift my hand when Mrs. Cooke goes to speak. "I know a lot can be done in just ten minutes, but it didn't. We're taking things slow and I would truly appreciate you keeping this little piece of gossip between us girls. Okay?"

The look in their eyes tells me that appreciation isn't going to happen. "I *might* have mentioned it to one person." Mrs. Symonds voice sounds a little apologetic at least.

"Might?"

Mrs. Cooke nudges her. "Tell her."

"Fine, we told a few people. Just four. But then we told Mildred Stevenson and you know that woman can't hold a secret to save her life."

I slap my palm on my forehead. There's no walking this back. All I can do is let Grady know this is going to spread far and wide now, and hope we can do our best to keep the truth from becoming some ridiculous story that grows in size.

Which won't happen, but I can hope. While we want Sugarloaf to believe our fake dating, we don't need the rumor mill to be out of control to a point that when we break up in a few weeks, everyone feels the need to pick sides.

And it has happened.

"I wish you had asked me," I say softly.

Mrs. Cooke looks clearly affronted by that suggestion. "Albert is usually a reliable source."

I raise a brow at that. "Didn't he tell you that he saw Jimmy riding a horse three weeks ago only to find out it was one of the Arrowood boys?"

She tsks. "Anyone could've confused that."

Right. Austin is a twenty-five-year-old and Jimmy Cooke is nearing eighty-five. Totally confusing.

Arguing with them is futile so I won't. "Since you owe me, what exactly happened at this emergency meeting last night?" I ask.

Both Mrs. Cooke and Symonds look to different areas of the store before meeting my eyes. "You know," Mrs. Symonds says innocently. "I can't say I recall. My memory isn't what it once was."

Lord save me from these nutty women. "I guess I'll find out when I get there."

Mrs. Symonds smiles innocently. "I'm sure you will, and then you can remind me what happened."

I walk the three blocks over to the town square where there are at least fifteen tents set up with all kinds of cooking apparatus. The cooking begins in about ten minutes, then they cook for three hours before they plate and we taste.

As I pass the last tent, I see Devney rushing toward me.

"I called you five times!"

I blink. "Good morning to you, too."

She snaps her fingers. "Called. Because we have a big problem. Big."

I'm going to assume this has to do with the little old ladies in the store. "Is it about today?"

"Yes."

"Do Mrs. Cooke, Parker, and Symonds have anything to do with it?" I ask, already knowing the answer.

"Yup."

I sigh. "Great."

"Yeah, not great. They called an emergency meeting. Who the fuck even knew that was a thing? I digress. They call me at like eleven at night, stating they have some big issue regarding the chili cookoff and I need to get to them right away. I, of course, think it's something incredibly important like someone stole all the tents or we're going to have some horrendous storm. I get out of bed, where my husband was waiting—if you know what I mean—and rush over. I'm irritated because I had to get out of said bed with my very sexy man who I haven't seen in three weeks since he's been on the road, and . . . find the three scheming women with their arms crossed."

I love my best friend, but she really needs to get to the point. "What is the big problem?"

"I hate them. That's one. Second, they have *voted* that no member of the board can judge in the cookoff if their family is competing to ensure absolute honesty."

I feel the air deflate from my lungs. "But this is our thing! I love judging with you."

"Not anymore, pumpkin. It's why I called you. They tried to have you removed as well because they said you'll pick either Jacob or Connor since they're participating this year, but I threatened to tell everyone I saw Mrs. Cooke kiss Mr. Symonds and spread it all over town. Even though it's not true, that was enough to upset them. I'm sorry. I know we do this each year and it's our fun thing." I look to Devney, wondering if I'm going to spread that rumor for her, but she reaches her hand out before I can say a word. "Never fear, though, I fixed it."

Now I'm scared. "Fixed it?"

"Your boyfriend isn't on the board, lives here full-time, his family isn't cooking, and will step in. I only had to threaten him that I would spread the rumor *he* was kissing Mrs. Symonds."

I laugh, my hand covering my mouth. "You're insane."

"Well, it's better than the rumor that a certain man you're dating was seen leaving your house at two a.m."

Jesus Lord. "That spread fast."

"It's Sugarloaf."

"And you believe it?"

Devney smirks. "Hell no. I told them all to shut up, but then it was confirmed when he told me himself it was around midnight . . ."

I'm in trouble. "I was going to tell you."

"Tell me what?"

I roll my eyes at the fake innocence in her voice. "He came over to tell me some exciting news and that was it."

"Uh huh."

I loop my arm in hers as we walk away from where Grady is standing. "I need you to control yourself and not react. Can you do that?"

She nods.

"We kissed."

Devney intakes a breath and her eyes find mine. "A good one?"

"Yes."

"And you're okay?"

"I think so."

She smiles brightly. "That's better than a no."

I can feel her excitement, but bless her, she's controlling it. "I was going to tell you later, when we weren't in the middle of the town where anyone can hear."

"All understandable. So, you kissed and what now?"

I look over her shoulder to see him there, tall, broad shoulders and muscles tensing as he lifts the heavy pot for one of the competitors. Grady turns a little so I catch his profile and I pull my lower lip beneath my teeth, remembering how his face felt in my hands, lips against mine. It was a great kiss. A kiss that I dreamed of having. A kiss I haven't been able to stop thinking about.

His eyes turn to mine and he flashes a wide smile, my belly flipping.

"Oh shit," I hear Devney and turn my gaze to her.

"What?"

"You really like him."

"I barely know him," I say, deflecting her original point. I do like him. I don't want to, but he's sweet, really freaking good looking, and he makes me feel special.

She lets out a long breath. "Addy, it's been three years of you living here and I've never seen you look at a man like that. I've paraded a bunch around you too. Some of Sean's really hot baseball player friends and not once did you undress them like you just did to Grady Whitlock."

I knew that's what she was doing. She is really not subtle. "I wasn't ready."

"I know."

"I don't know that I am even now."

"I don't think it's up to you at this point. I think you like him. I think he likes you. Are you taking him to Rose Canyon?" she asks.

Here is my out. Here is the chance to tell her the truth and not lie to my best friend. The thing is, it's not a lie to me, not all the time. I do like him, and I want to bring him to the wedding. I want to go out with him, kiss him again, and help him get the funding. The only lie is from his end.

I open my mouth to tell her something, but Grady comes up behind her. My eyes widen for a second before I smile. "Hey."

"Hey," he says with a grin. "I thought you'd come over and say hi."

Devney turns. "She wanted to, but I whisked her away to inform her that you, with an unskilled palate for chili, have the privilege of deciding the single most important blue ribbon this town has."

Grady blinks. "This is a privilege?"

"You're being handed an extreme honor," she informs him. "I expect you to be fair and don't worry about the aftereffects of the chili, you'll survive. Also, you should remember that my brothers-in-law are influential in this town and Connor helped you make a connection."

With that, she pats his chest and walks away. He watches her go, brows furrowed when he returns his gaze to mine. "I swear, small towns are a whole other world."

"This town is very competitive, but the Arrowoods are a whole other level."

"I heard all about it as Phoebe explained that it is my sworn duty to not choose an Arrowood. I thought I'm so confused, but she's slightly terrifying the closer she gets to delivering the baby, so I didn't ask more."

I try to picture tiny Phoebe Bettencourt terrifying this man, but then I remember how I was around that time, and I was not a nice person.

"That was probably smart."

"I learn where I can. So this judging thing . . . am I going to have to choose a winner between all these people?"

"Yup. You just can't pick Rowan. It's pretty much impossible for him to win."

"That's fine. I like seeing him lose," Grady says with a laugh.

I smile as we start to walk toward our friends, taking our very sweet time. Nerves hit me because I want to say something about the kiss. I want to ask if he regrets it or tell him I don't, but that I don't think it's a good idea we do it again. I don't want to like him more than I do. I keep having to remind myself of it because I'll absolutely let my heart get away from me.

Still, I don't think it's the right thing to say. If I play it off like I'm totally fine, no feelings, I've practically forgotten it, that might be the better idea.

I go with that.

"Did you hear anything more from Connor's company in Virginia?"

His eyes meet mine. "No, but I doubt I will for a week or so. In the meantime, you're still good to go to dinner with the Kopaskeys tomorrow?"

"Yup."

"Good, we'll call it a victory dinner after we survive this."

I grin. "I hope you're prepared because by the end of this, you won't be able to feel your tongue." And that's putting it mildly. "Do you need some antiacids? We find it's better to prepare your stomach before because things can get a little spicy."

I also usually do it mid-contest just to sort of use a layered effect.

Grady shrugs. "Pffft. I don't need to do that. I ate military food for years, I can handle a little chili."

Oh, he has no idea the plan this town has, and I'm going to enjoy watching him try to keep it together.

fourteen

GRADY

When she said spicy, she was so wrong. Like legions wrong. This is not spice, this is an inferno.

My mouth is burning. I'm pretty sure I'm going to shit fire tonight.

There is not enough milk in all of Pennsylvania to make my tongue stop throbbing.

"You doing okay?" Addison asks with a brow raised.

"Great," I say, or at least I think it's what I say because the ringing in my ears and the swelling in my tongue are making it impossible to tell.

"Good, only have five more. I save the last four people for the end because they are the heaviest on the heat."

Oh my God. It gets worse?

I blink, at least grateful I have use of my eyeballs, although I'm sure those'll be next to go because I'm being eaten alive by pepper.

"Do you want the milkshake? It really helps." Addison extends the cup and I eye it. I really didn't want to look like a pussy, but there's no way I can do another five and have it get worse.

"Thank you," I say, taking a sip. Jesus, I can't even feel the coldness. "Why exactly are all these recipes so hot?"

She smiles while tilting her head. "Did you look at the categories on your score card?"

Of course I did—not. I haven't been able to focus on much as my eyes teared after the first freaking tasting. The rule on judging is that you can't just have one taste of it, no, you have to eat at least three spoonfuls to get the full effect.

I look down at my card and if I had the ability to laugh, I would. It's rated on four categories: presentation, smell, texture, and spice. Then there's a comment section which is really what I've been using.

But now that I see they are graded on the heat level, I see why they're trying to kill us.

"So the spicier the better?" I ask.

"Yes, but it's also overall taste, so they have to balance it. How have you judged the previous ones?" Addison grabs my scorecard and laughs, trying to make herself stop until she gets to the fourth one.

She nods. "They get our cards at the end. Does this say what I think it does?" she asks as she holds up the last card.

I read it again, "I might have to have my stomach pumped after this to avoid an ulcer," and then nod. "Yup."

"Oh, they're going to die when they see this."

"See it?" Fuck. "I didn't know this was the point."

"Well, Mr. I-ate-military-food, you have more of this fun."

I drain the rest of her milkshake, praying it's magical or something because the idea of eating more makes me want to cry. Which I won't do because I'm not a pussy, but I'm wondering if a judge has been able to recuse himself.

Because I might just fake an emergency if not.

"You said this gets worse?" I say as I grab an ice cube and suck on it.

"Well, Mrs. Parker is notorious for her heat. She won last year and I'm pretty sure she's upping her game." Addison places both hands on my chest. "You will get through this. You'll endure. You'll help determine the winner and be loved and hated at the same time." She turns me to face the stand. "Now, let's go out there and pick a winner."

I want to laugh, but she's slightly terrifying so I keep it together. Instead, I give her a sly grin. Since that kiss, all I've thought about was doing it again. I wonder if while we're in this fake relationship, we can move things in another direction.

It's been a long time for both of us. We're friends. We trust each other and have very clear expectations regarding our relationship. It could work. We can test the waters together without any risk of getting hurt. "I need some incentive."

"What kind of incentive?" she asks with a slight hitch in her breath.

"A good one."

Addison tilts her head. "How about . . . you get to have me go to dinner tomorrow and help you get the investment."

I grin. "That's already promised."

She leans in, her hand resting on my chest. "Do you have some secret skills that you've been holding back?"

"Maybe."

I always have skills, and I'm wondering if I don't die from pepper poisoning if I'll be able to use them on her.

"Then maybe we'll see about a reward."

Not really what I was hoping for, but I also can feel the town watching. "All right, let's see what I can do."

We head to the next tent. I choke it down, writing some crap about balance and wondering if they put gasoline in, because my insides are surely about to combust.

Addison laughs and then we get to the three little old ladies who Brynn and Asher warned me about keeping happy.

I force a smile and Mrs. Cooke looks at me with a hint of concern. "Are you okay, honey?"

"I'm great."

"Are you sure?" she asks again.

"Can't wait to try your chili," I lie. I would rather do anything else, but I really want a reward.

149

She smiles, giving both Addison and me bowls. Her presentation is great, and I mark that box with a four out of five. I scratch my cheek, as it itches just a bit, and take a bite.

Fucking hell. That's what it is . . . hell. It's the depths of hell. The place where fire and brimstone were created and it's in this bowl.

I force a smile, but my lips feel a bit hard to move. Well, I need to get the next two bites in.

I turn my head side to side and try to open my lips, preparing myself for what's to come, but I put the spoon down to scratch my neck again.

Jesus, I'm itching.

"Grady, honey, are you sure you're okay?" Mrs. Cooke asks again. "You don't look so good."

"I'm great." I turn to face Addison. "I'm hot out here. Are you hot?"

Her eyes are like saucers. "I think you should sit."

"Why? We have four more," I say, my mouth dry, and I rub my arms as the itching moves there. "Man, it's hot."

"Grady, sit, please." She takes two steps to me and then looks around. "Devney! Come here. And hurry!"

Devney comes over, takes one look at me, and then yells, "Someone get Dr. Schwartz."

Doctor. Why do we need a doctor?

Addison helps me to a chair. "Do you have any allergies?"

I shake my head. "Penicillin and peanuts. Did someone put penicillin in the chili?"

"No, I doubt that."

A few seconds later, Dr. Schwartz is in front of me, her smile is comforting but her eyes tell me otherwise. "When did the symptoms start?"

"What symptoms?"

Addison's brows lift. "Well, ummm, you're kind of swelling. Like a lot."

"What?" I try to say but my lips don't feel like they're parting. I

150

move my hand to my face, feeling the puffiness. Oh fucking hell. My lips weren't swollen from the spicy food, but something else.

She moves behind me, cradling my head in her lap. "It's fine. You look great. Honestly, I was exaggerating."

"Liar," I manage to get out.

Dr. Schwartz leans in. "Are you having any problems breathing?"

"No." I'm not, it's just I'm itching like fucking crazy and I worry my face looks like I went ten rounds in a boxing ring.

"Good. Someone grab my bag," the doctor says. A person beside her does and the doctor gets medication and a needle.

I look up at Addison. "I hate needles."

She smiles. "I'll get you a sticker if you don't cry."

"Terrible reward," I tell her.

"What would you rather?"

"A kiss."

Addison shakes her head with a soft laugh. "Fine, no tears and I'll kiss you. Once your lips . . . you know, go back to normal."

There wasn't a chance in hell I was crying anyway, so I'm kind of looking forward to this.

"Grady?" I hear my brother Asher's voice. I look up and he is trying to hide a smile, but doing a shit job at it. "Oh! Fuck. You look like shit . . ." He laughs again. "Is he going to be okay?" the dickhead finally asks as he crouches next to the doctor.

"Yes, he's just having an allergic reaction. I'm going to give you some epinephrin and that should help."

"Oh, I need a photo of this." He pulls his phone out, snaps a picture, and then slips it back in.

She jams the needle in my leg and pushes down on the syringe. I wince and Addison strokes my hair.

I look up and grin. "No tears."

Addy laughs and rolls her eyes. "My hero."

I feel my body relax after a bit. She cradles me, watching my face with a soft smile. "All for chili," she says, pushing my hair back.

"More for you."

"I'm so sorry. I hate that you ate something that made you this sick."

"It was worth it for this," I tell her, my lips finally feeling more like I have control of them.

Addison laughs softly. "The swelling is already ten times better."

"I want my reward."

"Now?"

I nod. "I was promised . . ."

Then, in front of the entire town, she kisses me, and I don't give a damn what my face looks like or the fact the chili truly did try to kill me.

We're walking through the festival as the sun is going down, the kids are with my sister at the playground.

"So glad you're okay," a person who I have never met says as we walk.

"Thanks!"

Another person approaches. "You guys are the best judges. I mean, you almost died for Sugarloaf."

"He's selfless," Addy says with a continual smile.

I glance down at her. "You seem happy."

"I am, you're a hero and a legend now."

I bump her hip. "Because I got the girl?"

"You didn't."

"Do I need to remind you that you kissed me in front of everyone?"

Her eyes find mine. "I did that."

"You did."

Addison hooks her arm around mine. "I blame it on the chili and fear you might die from Jacob Arrowood putting peanut butter in the chili."

"Uh huh," I toss back.

She playfully slaps my arm with her other hand. "Don't embarrass me."

"I'm innocent here. I was sick and then a very pretty girl mauled me in front of everyone."

"Mauled?" she huffs. "It was a peck."

This is too fun.

"A peck? I don't know, I think we may have to play back the tape."

At that her eyes flash. "Oh my God. Do you think someone filmed it?"

"Are you worried about going viral?" I ask with a chuckle.

"No! But . . . I wouldn't doubt that Blakely has spies watching me or some alert set up on her freaking phone." She smiles as we pass someone else who checks on me.

"Is this going to happen all day?"

Addy grins. "Yes. The people of Sugarloaf will want to make sure you're okay. Also, don't be surprised if Mrs. Parker pitches a fit stating Jacob did this to rig the cookoff and you were in on it."

"What?" I ask, genuinely confused. "How the hell would I be in on having an allergy attack and needing medical help?"

"You didn't die. That's how. And you, my very charming fake boyfriend, stopped the competition and made the three women very upset. Now, you'll be a hero to some and to others, you're the outsider who destroyed their master plan."

And here I thought moving here would give Jett and me a tranquil life. "They have a master plan?" I ask, regretting it immediately.

"It's all very complex, just keep up and hide from them whenever you see them."

I laugh at that and pull her close, releasing her hand and wrapping my arm around her shoulder. She fits there so perfectly, against my side.

We get to the food area and I'm honestly shocked. For as small as this town is, they really do these festivals right. The food area is filled with different food trucks as well as a boozy ice cream, which sounds like a brilliant idea if I've ever heard of one. Part of Jacob's apology was lunch from any of the trucks.

"What are you in the mood for?" I ask.

Addison purses her lips, studying all the options. "Seafood isn't really my thing, growing up on the Oregon coast, I've had so much I'm too picky. The dumplings look good, but . . ." She tilts her head and then looks at me from over her shoulder. "You know what? You were the one who got stabbed with a needle today, you get to pick whatever you want."

"Very magnanimous of you, but I insist that you get to pick."

"Why?"

"Why what?" I ask.

She turns to face me. "Why do I have to pick?"

"Because I want to make you happy."

The answer comes so easily, so honestly, that it rocks me back a little. "That was sweet."

"I'm a sweet guy," I say, covering my emotions with humor. "Plus, I'm delirious from the drugs."

The smile she gives me makes that admission worth it. "Please, you don't have any good drugs and if I remember correctly, you told me you weren't a sweet guy when we saw each other at the play."

"I was wooing you then."

Her brows shoot up and she laughs. "You were? For our inevitable . . . agreement we're currently doing?"

"Obviously. Did you think this was all coincidence? No."

Addison pulls her lips between her teeth in an obvious attempt to keep herself from bursting out laughing. A few seconds pass and then she nods once. "I see. You were the mastermind behind all of this?"

I lean in. "It worked too."

She shakes her head and then loops her arm in mine. "All right, since you've clearly manipulated all of this, what do I pick for us to eat then?"

I've seen her eye the Greek truck three times. I'm not the biggest fan of gyros, and she knows this since we had lunch at the diner where she orders that each time. I know it's her favorite thing, and I also know she's not picking it because she is aware of my thoughts on it.

But I want to see her smile.

I want the town to see her happy and I meant what I said about giving her a measuring stick of some sort to compare anyone she dates in the future. So, I lead her over there. "I'm in the mood for a gyro."

Addison looks at me, her eyes wide. "You . . ."

I don't let her finish. "We'll eat here. This is what I want."

The thing is, when I'm staring in her eyes, I'm not just talking about the food.

fifteen
ADDISON

"I never needed anyone . . ." I sing along to the woman who speaks of broken hearts like no one else. It's ten o'clock at night, Elodie is sleeping over at her friend's house for a birthday party, and I'm alone—drunk and singing.

Because that's what a girl does.

She sings drunk in the bathtub with wine.

Speaking of wine.

I move the many layers of my dress, trying to find the bottle I put down, and then giggle when I see it on the ledge above my head.

"Oopsies. Silly, Addy," I chide myself.

Today is my wedding anniversary. Or it would've been. Three years of anniversaries have passed, all alone. However, this one is especially strange.

Celine belts out another round of heartbreaking lyrics and I drain the bottle with a hiccup. "I thought I would be happy!" I yell out to no one. "I was supposed to be happy again. You were supposed to send me a new man so I wouldn't be all by myseeeeeelf."

Then I belch.

Oh, that burns.

157

My phone rings and I find it tucked in my boob. Convenient that. "Hello?" I answer as the music blares behind me. "Can you turn that down? I can't hear myself talk."

Some people are so rude. Calling me with their music blasting.

"Addison? Are you okay?" the deep, smooth voice of my fake boyfriend comes through.

"Of course I'm okay," I say, taking another drink. "Who isn't okay? Everyone is okay."

"That's good," he chuckles.

"My life is perfect and I'm all by myself, at least that's what Celine and I are commiserating about." I sing another line of the song as I move my head back and forth. It's nice to have a friend in the bathtub with me. "She's my bestie."

"Uhh. Where are you?"

"I'm in the tub. Where are you? It's loud there. I didn't think you liked Celine. Good song. I was listening to it too. Oh! Is it on the radio? That would be just like today. Kismetic. Is that a word? Maybe it's Kismetetic? Kismosis? Kiiiiiismet."

Grady chuckles and I grin. I like his laugh. I like his lips too. Which I shouldn't.

"I like your laugh as well."

"Can you read minds?" I ask, sitting up a little but my legs don't let me go far. "I said that in my head."

"No, you said that out loud. Are you drunk?"

I shrug, not caring what I said because . . . what does it matter anyway? I'm going to be all by myself forever. "I'm drunk. I like drunk. Drunk is good. Drunk takes away all the feelings and feelings are stupid. Do you know why feelings are stupid?"

"I can assume."

"You shouldn't do that. Assume. It makes an ass out of you and me. Get it?" I snort, laughing at the stupid saying that my mother said all the time.

Damn. I'm becoming my mother.

"Where's Elodie?"

"At a friend's house."

"So you got drunk alone?" There is a lot of worry in that voice. I don't like it.

"Well, Grady, I can't get drunk with my kid. That would be irresponsible and illegal." I would think he'd know that, but . . . alas, I have informed him.

I kick my feet, which are now hanging over the edge, the crinoline in my dress rumpling.

"Maybe you should go to bed," he suggests.

I shake my head, not even entertaining that. "It's early, Grady. Besides, I'm comfy with all this fabric."

"It's past ten and you're clearly drunk."

Huh. Time is passing. Well, that means this day is almost over. Good. I hate today I hate anniversaries and reminders that my love life is a big fat zero, and I have the dress to prove it.

"I'll sleep here," I hiccup and giggle.

"In the tub?"

"Duh!"

"Addy, where's your key?"

"The key to my heart? It's broken," I reply. "I'm throwing it out."

"The key to your door, sweetheart. Where is it? Do you have a hide-a-key?"

I raise my brows. "I do! I have two, but I won't tell you that it's in the second rock in the garden. Nope. Then you could break in."

"Good, you should never tell anyone that," he says, and I beam at his praise.

I hear what sounds like a door opening and closing and I drain the remaining wine from the bottle, wondering if I have more. I brought many bottles with me when I came in, opened them all and put them . . . oh! Over here. I reach for the next open bottle, noting I only have one left.

That sucks. I can't feel my legs, so I doubt trying to get more is a good idea.

"Addy, are you dressed in the bathroom?" Grady asks, his voice causing me to gasp.

"When did you call me? Grady? You're on my phone but echoing in my head. Trippy."

"Oh Lord. Are you naked?"

"Nope, I'm in my dress, shoes, and veil." I look at my wedding shoes, remembering how much they hurt my feet, they don't hurt now. I should've just drank wine and they would've been great.

"Veil?"

I nod and smile. "Yup. I have it all on. I look like a princess. I wanted a tiara but my mother said I would look like a snob. Who says that?"

"I'm coming in."

"Coming in where?"

My bathroom door slowly opens, and I scream, dropping the phone, but not the wine. I hold tight to that.

"You're all right, it's just me. I'm here," Grady says softly as he opens the door.

And he is here. My boyfriend. Kind of. The man who kissed me like every girl wants to be kissed—and I don't even get to keep him.

He looks at me, sitting in the tub with a bottle of wine, wearing my wedding attire, and his eyes go soft. As though I'm an injured animal, he approaches slowly. "Why are you in the tub in your wedding dress?"

"Because it's my anniversary and the box hit me in the head."

Grady squats next to the tub and rests a hand on the edge as he reaches for my wine bottle, pulling it from my grasp. "The box hit you?"

"Yup. Like a sign. From above. Literally. I opened my closet and *bam*!" I slap my hands together. "Wedding dress box to the face. A sign from the Lord."

"A sign to put it on and climb in the bathtub with some wine?"

That's right, I love wine. I grab the bottle back and chug straight from the bottle because who has time for a glass? This is faster. "I mean, what else can it mean? The box fell right on my head! Not yesterday. But today, of all days. A sign it was, and I listen when God speaks. So I put my dress on, gathered my friends Zinfandel, Pinot, and Rosé, and we came to where dreams go down the drain." I lift my bottle, cheering to the sky.

Grady huffs with a sad smile and then stands, climbing in next to me. "Hand me that," he says, reaching for the wine, but I pull it to my chest. "I'll give it back."

I glare at him. "What makes you think you should come to my pity party?"

He raises one adorable brow. "You think you're the only one who had their dreams go down the drain?"

I purse my lips. He has a point there. "You don't even like wine."

"No, but no one should drink alone in the bathtub on their anniversary."

I'm sure that's a rule. "Is that a law? Asher would know."

"Not a law, but definitely a rule a friend ensures is followed."

"We're friends."

He nods. "We are."

"Who kissed."

Just the edge of his lip tips up. So cute. "We did. Is that why you're drinking?"

"Nope. I liked the kiss."

"I did too."

That's good. Since we're friends, he's at my party, and it's rude to not share, I hand him the bottle. "Here, friend, drink up."

He settles in next to me, his long legs hanging over the side like mine, and he takes a swig. "Seriously, this stuff is nasty."

"It tastes better after the second bottle," I tell him, and he takes another swig then hands it back to me. "In fact, you lose all taste."

"So, it's your anniversary?"

"It was. It's not anymore. Now it's just a day. A day where nothing happens because the past is done."

God, saying that aloud makes me hate this day even more.

"A fall wedding must've been nice."

I look up at him, my eyes swimming with unshed tears. It was the most beautiful day. "The leaves hadn't fallen yet so the trees were so pretty," I tell him. "It was not too hot or cold, the sun was out, and we were on the cliff by the ocean. It was perfect."

He takes the bottle again, drinking from it. "I got married in the winter in Oklahoma. It snowed the day before and Lisa was afraid of the ice. I remember going out to the church with the guys, salt, and shovels."

I lie my head back against the wall, slinking down more in the tub. "I bet she was the perfect winter bride. How did you meet?" I turn my head to face him and watch the smile on his lips.

"I was at a bar in California. I was flying with a squadron then and had just gotten home from my first deployment and thought I was hot shit. We were trying to be like Top Gun, singing and hitting on girls. Lisa was there with her friends, she thought I was an idiot —which in hindsight I was. After she put me in my place, we spent the night talking, and for the next six days she was there, we spent every minute we could together. Four months later, I got transferred and she moved with me, then we got engaged."

"How long were you married?"

"Two and a half years. I've been a widower longer than I was a husband. It was strange when that happened."

"Oh, that's so unfair," I say, and that makes me sad. I had Isaac almost my whole life. We weren't married that entire time, but he was mine and I was his.

Two and a half years seems so short and to lose that person suddenly is worse. I got the moments. So many of them. The drunken, late-night calls, the fights about nothing and the making up after, the family time and friend time, all of those memories I have called up when I needed to.

Tonight, when I got dressed in this gown, I was missing Isaac, but more missing the future I was promised.

Which then made me feel incredibly guilty.

Also, the box fell on my head, so really, I felt compelled in every way to wear it.

"It was a good few years. How long were you with your husband?"

I snort. "My whole damn life."

"How did you meet?"

"He defended me on the playground in fourth grade. And that was that. I was his and he was mine."

"Wow," Grady says, his head jerking back. "That's crazy."

It really was. "I've only been with one man, how is that for depressing?" I lift the bottle in the air and then drink again, feeling that familiar pang in my chest. But then I think about the sad part of it. The part my friends and I always joked about. I whisper, imparting my great secret to my bathtub buddy. "I don't even know what another penis looks like. Only his."

Grady nearly chokes on the wine he was drinking. "Well, that's . . . something."

"Isn't it? I mean, I've seen porn so . . . I guess that counts? Are they all the same? Probably not, right? That would be stupid. I know they vary because they have to."

He bursts out laughing. "Addison, you're going to regret this tomorrow. And no, they aren't the same."

"I knew that. I was just testing you."

"If it makes you feel better, I would've given up every girl before Lisa just to have her. It's quality not quantity. You had one great guy who loved you. One man who literally died for another because he was defending her. I don't think that's depressing."

"Maybe you're right."

"I'm always right."

I eye him skeptically. "You're a man, that's not possible."

He laughs. "You're drunk, you have no idea what is possible. Now, hand me the wine."

"And why, pray tell, do you think you should get more?"

"Because I'm in a bathtub on a Friday night with my girlfriend who is two sheets to the wind."

"Fake," I remind him.

"What's fake?"

I purse my lips and give him the look. "You know what's fake, Grady Whitlock, and it ain't the wine or my boobs."

Immediately his eyes go there. I probably shouldn't have said that.

"Not if you didn't want me to look at them."

"I should stop drinking," I muse.

"Nah, you're cute drunk. Now, tell me what's fake."

Grady takes the bottle from me, drinks some, and then hands it back. Stupid boy took my wine.

"*We* are fake," I answer and then drink myself. If I drain the bottle he won't be able to have more. As appealing as that is, the copious amount of wine swirling in my stomach tells me that would be a big mistake.

No one wants to see me heaving.

"I'm pretty sure we're real. Fake people can't drink wine in a wedding dress."

I roll my eyes. "I meant being your girlfriend."

"Now I'm wounded and deserve the rest of the crap in the bottle."

"Oh? Why are you wounded?"

Grady grins. "Because our dating may be fake but I'm your real friend. I care about you, Addy. I'm here, and I want the damn wine."

"Not good enough," I tell him.

"I have to earn the right to drink?"

"This is good wine."

Grady tilts his head and raises an eyebrow. "Good isn't the word I'd use."

"Even more of a reason not to share."

Wine is my friend and if he's going to insult it, he doesn't get the fruit of the gods.

"Fruit of the gods?" he asks on a low chuckle.

I keep saying things out loud. Maybe I should stop drinking. I sigh, letting my head fall back and handing him the wine. "Drink up. You definitely get to party with me."

He laughs once and then chugs. After he finishes, he places it where the other bottles are and then puts his arm around me. "Come here."

I lean in, my head resting on his shoulder as he holds me to him. I relax into his embrace, feeling alone and yet found. My eyes close and I nestle deeper into his body. "Thank you for coming."

"I'll always be here for you, Addison. You never have to be sad alone."

I smile, liking the sound of that. "Good, I don't want to be alone when I'm sad."

"Then just close your eyes and feel me here with you."

And then I drift to sleep, wearing my wedding dress in a bathtub while tucked against Grady.

sixteen

GRADY

She was completely passed out and snoring on my chest roughly four seconds after she closed her eyes. Although, three bottles of wine would probably do it.

I adjust because there's no way in hell we're sleeping in here. Then I shift her head so it's resting against the back of the tub, and I have a bit of room to maneuver my way to standing.

My plan was definitely not for her to fall asleep, I just needed to hold her, to clear the ache in her voice and comfort her. I called Brynn, told her I needed to come here, and she squealed and told me not to rush back.

Now, I need to put Addison to bed so she doesn't wake with more regrets.

Only, I'm not quite sure what the best way to move her is. Since I have to start somewhere, I remove her veil and place it on the floor, sigh, and then squat to scoop her up.

Her head flops back, arms hanging like a ragdoll.

"Great," I say with a heavy sigh.

I hoist her up high, hoping she wakes a little so I can get some help, but she just snores loudly.

I carry her into her room and place her on her bed.

She's so beautiful.

CORINNE MICHAELS

Even like this.

When I brush my fingers against her cheek, her eyelids flutter open. "We're not in the tub?"

"No." I chuckle.

"My ass hurt anyway."

At least she's a funny drunk. "Get some sleep. I'll come over in the morning to check on you."

Her fingers wrap around my wrist. "Don't leave. Stay with me."

"What?" I ask, unsure if she's even aware of what she's saying.

"I don't want you to leave me. You make everything better. Stay the night."

There's a rasp, a desperation in her voice that rips at my heart. "Addy, I don't know if that's a good idea."

However, she shifts, arm extended to me. "Please, Grady, just lie next to me. Don't . . . don't let me be alone."

I don't know that I can deny her anything, but especially not with how she's looking at me, like I'm the only person who can make this okay for her. I nod once and move to the other side of the bed before climbing in next to her. I settle on my side so I'm facing her, and she does the same. Her big dress makes a crinkling noise as she adjusts her legs.

"I thought you were asleep," I say quietly, just in case she is.

"I was." She snuggles closer so her cheek is resting on my chest, and I wrap her close to me, pressing my lips to the top of her head. "But I didn't want you to leave, which is stupid." She yawns.

"Why is it stupid?"

The truth is, I didn't want to leave her. I want to hold her while she's hurting and feeling alone.

"Because you aren't real."

"I think I'm real."

She sighs, tightening her arms. "You are."

I kiss the top of her head, pulling her to my chest and whisper as she relaxes against me. "Sleep, dove, I'll take care of you and chase your dreams away."

168

I feel a hand snaking up my chest and I grin, shifting to my side. God, that feels good. Her hands move higher, up my neck, and I find myself moving closer to the touch.

There is a soft floral and fruit scent around me and I inhale deeply, letting it flood my senses. Before I can place it, a warm body is against mine, lips on my neck, and then I hear a moan.

So fucking sexy.

But that perfume, I know it. It's not too powerful and has a musky undertone that's sexy and warm.

Like she is.

And then I know why I know it. I know who it belongs to.

Addison.

That scent is ...

Before I can breathe, she goes stiff in my arms and pulls back. Her eyes are wide, as are mine, and she gasps.

"Grady!"

I clear my throat as she sits up, her hand going to her head immediately, and she winces.

"Easy," I say quietly, sure she's got a raging headache.

She inhales a few times, looks at herself and then at me. "I'm in my wedding dress, I'm pretty sure I have never been this hungover before, and you're in my bed."

That's a pretty good assessment. "All of this is true."

"What the? How did I get? Oh God. Did we? Did I? Oh, God."

"You don't remember what we did?" I ask, feeling the urge to mess with her.

Her fingers move to her mouth. "What we did?"

I sit up so my back is against the headboard and nod.

"What did we do? Did we have sex?"

"With a dress on?"

"Skirts lift, Grady!"

Very true. "What do you remember?" I ask.

I sure as fuck would hope she'd remember if we did that.

169

Addison pulls her lower lip between her teeth. "I remember the box falling on my head in the closet. I'd already had a few glasses of wine and was trying to find my dress for our party in two days. When the box opened, I just thought . . . why the fuck not? So I put it on, grabbed some more wine, and then went to the bathroom."

I lean in. "And what about us?"

She stares off. "You came when I was in the tub!"

"I did."

"Why the hell was I in the tub?"

"Well, to quote you, it's where dreams go down the drain," I say with a laugh.

Addison rubs her head. "Ugh. I hate myself. Okay, what about the bed? I don't remember coming to the bed."

"No?"

She covers her face with her hands. "Did we . . .?"

As fun as this is, I can see it's worrying her. "No, sweetheart. We didn't do anything. You passed out in the tub, I carried you in here, and then you asked me to stay so you weren't alone, and I wasn't leaving with you plastered anyway."

"Oh." She lets out a heavy sigh. "Good. I mean, if we're going to . . . do it. I would like to be conscious."

Well, she opened the door, so it would be rude not to walk through it. "You think of us . . . doing it?" I wiggle my brows, which earns me a playful slap on my arm.

"Shut up."

"I think you can answer that one. I did listen to you sing and climb in a tub with you. Give me that much. You think about it?"

Addison's cheeks turn scarlet even with her hangover that has her a tinge of green. She does think about it. After that kiss, God knows I think about it. Not that I didn't before it because —she's hot.

Still, good to know she does.

"I might have thought about it once," she admits.

"Once a day?"

"Once as in once."

Liar, but I'll let her have it. "Was it good?"

"Ugh!" She moans and then stands. "I'll be right back. I'm going in the bathroom to change and brush my teeth."

"Don't climb in the tub," I say as she walks off, which earns me a raised middle finger.

I grab my phone, sending a text to Brynn.

> I'm at Addison's still. She just woke up and I'm leaving soon.

BRYNLEE

> Don't rush. We went to feed the animals and I got a new chicken! It's so cute. Also, I might have a baby deer, but I think it's just here to eat the food and not in need of my love and affection.

Jesus, there is no hope for that girl.

> I'm not touching any of that other than do not let my son near the deer.

BRYNLEE

> Don't tell me what to do, ass.

> Are you twelve?

BRYNLEE

> Are you going to tell me about your wild night with Addison?

> No.

BRYNLEE

> Then be nice to me or I won't watch him for you when you go away and tell Rowan he has to do it.

I pinch the bridge of my nose and put the phone away. It's best not to piss off the babysitter since I need her. It's one of the perks of being in Sugarloaf. My siblings, and the fact that we all live within a few miles of each other. Jett has had a lot of fun being around them and so have I. Plus, me dating Addison has made Brynn happy and willing to keep Jett more than she may have been before.

Addison comes out, wearing a pair of shorts and tank top that hugs every perfect curve. "I took some medicine because this headache is not my friend."

"Alcohol is never our friend the next day. When we're consuming it, it's the best thing in the world." She climbs in beside me. "Also, Celine doesn't sing much about drinking, does she?"

Addison's confused gaze finds mine. "Celine? What? Oh no! No, I didn't. I was singing. Oh . . . seriously, I want the bed to swallow me."

"Come here." Addison hesitates but then scoots toward me, I pull her to my chest and wait for her to relax. "Are you okay?"

She lifts her head to look at me, her chest falling a little, and then she speaks. "I wasn't even that sad about Isaac. Which is why I started drinking." I wait, my heart rate accelerating as I work to keep it steady. I had no idea why she was drinking other than it was her anniversary and she was upset. "I kept thinking, why aren't I distraught today? I woke up, took Elodie to school, smiled at everyone, thought about you and our kiss, got her to her friend's, and didn't even think about what yesterday was. I felt so guilty that I let the day pass and didn't once remember any of it."

A tear falls down her cheek and I brush it away with my thumb. "Addy, he would never want your life to stop."

I know this because if the roles were reversed, I would want Lisa to move on, to find a life and love and happiness.

"I know, but I forgot. So I went to find a green dress he bought me, the one I stared at for weeks in the store but wouldn't spend the money on. When I opened the door, the box fell on my head. My wedding dress spilled out and I sat on the floor, looking at it, remembering how much I loved it when I found it. How I felt when I put it on, how I looked that day. I got back in it, and by this point I was a bottle down." She laughs softly. "I was sad because I wasn't sad all day. Does that make me a horrible person?"

"No," I say with so much conviction it aches in my own chest. My hand cups her cheek and she leans into it. "You're alive, that's what it makes you. I've wondered the same on days when Lisa doesn't enter my thoughts. When I drove over here after the meeting with Cole Securities, I wanted to see you, tell you, kiss you." My fingers move back toward her neck. "When I want to kiss you again. When I lie in bed, wishing I could kiss you again and again, but you're alive, you're real. You're not a horrible person, so fucking far from it."

There is a slight hitch in her breath before she says, "You're not supposed to want to kiss me."

I smile. "No, but that doesn't seem to make it stop."

"I wanted to kiss you last night."

Our heads inch closer. "What about now?"

"I didn't say it ever stopped."

Every time I'm around her, it grows stronger. I want her so much I fucking ache for it. Almost every night I take my cock in my hand, thinking of her. The way she tastes, how her eyes light up when she sees me, her beautiful smile, the sound of her laugh, and how she feels in my arms. Each day, it becomes harder to remember that I really don't want any complications in my life.

"Sometimes I wish this wasn't fake. That all of this was real."

"There is nothing fake about desire."

"No?"

"Want me to show you?"

When her fingers brush my cheek, my hand moves to the back of her neck and the only thought I have is of showing her just how much my desire is real.

seventeen

ADDISON

T his man can kiss.

His tongue thrusts deep and my body craves more. His hand is tight in my hair, keeping me where he wants me, and I wouldn't move if the house was on fire.

Okay, maybe then I would, but only for that.

Grady moans, and then I'm on my back with him on top of me. The weight of him feels so good, I want to weep. Why do my body and heart want this? Why does he have to be so damn good?

If he kissed like shit, maybe I could tell myself that whatever feelings are growing didn't matter. If right now I wasn't imagining that hand moving down my body, touching me where I need it most, but I am.

He kisses me harder and my back arches, seeking as much contact as he can give me. His hand moves down my side, gripping my thigh and pulling it up. I let out the most obnoxious sound when I feel his hard cock through both our clothes.

If that's a prelude, I'm ready for the main event.

When he breaks away, the two of us panting, he stares into my eyes. "I want you so fucking much." I do too. "I think of how good we would be like this. How you'd look when I sank into you. I dream of it, Addison. None of that is fake."

"No, definitely not."

He moves, grinding harder, and I whimper. It feels so good. It's been so long and while my toys and my hand have worked for the last three years, they pale in comparison to this. To him.

"Grady," I moan his name, my eyes closing as he shifts again, rubbing his cock against my clit while we're fully dressed.

"Say it again," he commands and rocks again. "Tell me who you want, Addison."

Fire courses through my veins. He's not even touching me. All he's done is kiss me and yet I feel my climax building.

My fingers dig into his shoulders, wanting so badly for him to strip me down, right now, and let me feel all of him. "You. God, you, Grady."

"That's right." His cocky grin sends shivers up my spine. "Can you be a good girl and lie still for me?"

I'll do just about anything if it means this doesn't stop. I nod, not trusting my voice.

His hand drifts down my side and then hooks under my shirt, I feel the fabric shift, the pads of his fingers rough against my stomach as he watches my face.

"Don't stop," I plead and he drifts higher.

"I was hoping you'd say that."

His fingertips graze the underside of my breast before his thumb brushes over my nipple. I swear, I might come just like this.

Call it crazy, call it ridiculous. I do not care, I'm so turned on right now anything could set me on fire at this point.

Three fucking years. Three long ass years of craving to be touched and it's finally happening.

"Does that feel good?" he asks.

"Yes."

The word is breathy, but he hears it. He pushes my shirt up higher, exposing my bare breasts to the cool air. Now I'm very glad I skipped the bra when I changed in the bathroom.

"Addison, look at me." I force my eyes to open. His green eyes are blazing with intensity. Slowly, he lowers his mouth to my breast, he doesn't suck on it, though. Instead, his tongue circles my nipple, lazily as though he has nothing else to do but this for as long as he wants.

"Grady..." I'm half desperate for more.

He stills, and I can sense he wants to say something, but before he can, my doorbell rings.

Like cold water poured on our heads, we both stop.

Shit.

The two of us turn toward the door and then the bell rings again.

"Are you expecting someone?" he asks.

I shake my head quickly.

He moves off of me, and I scramble out of the bed. Shit. What the hell am I doing? I'm reckless and was literally saved by the bell because I would not have stopped that.

I would've let him take me right then and not given a shit about anything else.

Which is stupid.

Because I have to remember my very open heart wants something he doesn't.

The bell rings again. "Addison!"

Shit.

"Devney is here," I say, straightening my shirt. "Hide."

"Hide? Why would I hide?"

Now there's a bang on the door. "Addison! I know you're in there! Open up!"

I run my fingers through my hair and sigh. "Because she can't know you spent the night here, you need to hide or sneak out the back or climb down the trellis."

"Do you have a trellis?" he asks with a smirk.

"I think so! I don't know, but she can't see you here, waking up in my house." Seriously, that is like the worst thing that can happen. I shove him toward the door as he chuckles. "Let's go, out the window."

We're on the second floor and I have no earthly idea if he can escape, but whatever he has to do, must be done. Devney will ask a million questions I don't have the answers to, and the longer this takes the worse it'll be.

"Isn't the point of our arrangement to have people see us?"

"Not like this!" I screech and regret it. My head is pounding. "Okay, fine, no window jumping, but you can't tell her you spent the night."

Seriously, she's going to break the door down if I don't hurry. He doesn't say anything, just follows me down the stairs.

I stand in front of the door, huff, straighten my shoulders, and open it a smidge with a smile. "Dev, hey! Whatcha doing here? I thought you were in Florida? Maybe I'm off on my weeks. Anyway, surprised to see you."

She runs her tongue along her top teeth and then makes a pop noise. "Really? The question you want to ask is what am I doing here? I think, my friend, what everyone wants to know is what is Grady's truck doing here this early in the morning?"

Of course. I didn't think about the fact his truck has been here. I sigh, opening the door, where she can see Grady leaning against the arm of the couch. "Hello, Mrs. Arrowood."

She laughs. "Hello, Mr. Whitlock." Devney enters the house, giving me a wink as she passes. "I see you got the text messages as well?"

"What text messages?" I ask.

"The ones that came through this morning."

"I didn't send anything."

Devney hands me her phone and my jaw falls slack. There I am, in the bathtub, wine bottle in one hand as I'm staring at the phone.

I took freaking selfies.

"Please tell me you didn't show anyone," I say as I sink into the chair.

"Only Sean, and I might have sent it to Blakely, but only because this morning she sent me the video of you singing."

Please God tell me she's joking. "Video?"

She grins. "Scroll to her message."

I do, and there it is, a video of me in the tub, but there's not a chance in fucking hell I'm playing it with Grady sitting there. "Great."

I don't remember any of that, but . . . well, the evidence speaks for itself.

"Delete these."

"Not a chance." Her reply is instant before she turns to Grady. "So, you spent the night? Did she send you texts as well?"

He answers immediately. "I got the live version. I called, she sounded like she needed me, and I stayed with her after she passed out because I wanted to take care of her."

"That's sweet, but the whole town is talking about how his truck has been in your driveway all night."

"The town can kiss my ass." I'm not playing this game. Who I have sleep at my house or not is none of their business.

Devney lifts both hands. "I'm just telling you that people are talking. I was on my way when you didn't answer my text this morning after I saw yours. Then I got a text from Mrs. Symonds that Albert notified her you might have an issue with your pipes that Grady is taking care of. Good play on words, huh? However, the key wasn't where it normally is, so I had to knock."

I groan and slap my palm to my forehead. "I'm planting trees, so many trees tomorrow."

She chuckles. "I'll handle him." Devney's hand squeezes my shoulder. "I'm glad you're okay. I have to finish packing since Sean and I are heading to Tampa for a few weeks. I'll see you soon?"

I nod. "Thank you for coming to check on me."

"Of course. I'm sorry I didn't see them until this morning. It sounds like I missed a good party." She turns to Grady. "Thank you for being a good man and taking care of her. Addy means the world to me and I'm so happy she found a man like you. Even if you didn't clean her pipes out."

"Oh Jesus," I mutter.

They laugh and then she kisses my forehead and leaves.

I turn and look at Grady who is grinning. "What are you smiling at?"

"Just that I'm going to really be a legend now."

I roll my eyes. Typical man. "Yeah, I'm sure once I tell everyone you sat in a bathtub and sang Celine Dion, everyone will fall at your feet."

"You sang, not me."

"That's not the story they'll hear."

He gets to his feet, coming in front of me, his hands rest on my hips. "What else will you tell them? That I held you all night? That I kissed you in the morning? That I wanted to do so much more and hope we will soon?"

My heart beats faster and there's no hiding the fact that his words excite me. "None of that. I'll tell them you were a perfect gentleman."

His lips move lower, just brushing against mine in the most delicious way. "You do that and I'll have to prove otherwise —publicly."

"Hmm, I'd like to see you try it."

Yes, Addison, real smart. Tell the man to defile you in some way publicly.

"Don't challenge me, Addy. I always rise to challenges." I clear my throat and try to step back, but he pulls me tight. "And I win."

I don't doubt that. However, I have to regain control of this before I end up naked on my floor. Judging by the way he's staring at me, he might be wanting the same thing. I put my hands on his chest. "I'm sure you do, but that wasn't a challenge. It was, however, a belated thank you for coming last night and staying."

"It was nothing."

His arms loosen and I step back, letting out a heavy breath through my nose. "It wasn't nothing to me. It means a lot."

He shrugs. "Anything for you." His phone pings and he looks at his watch. "I have to go, will you be okay?"

I nod. "Yes, I'm going to shower and pick up Elodie in an hour."

"Okay. I'll see you tomorrow at drop-off?"

"I'll be there."

He takes my face in his hands and brings his lips to mine. "I think this is my favorite part of our arrangement."

"What?"

"Kissing you."

And then he leaves, I stand here, staring at the door wondering what the hell I'm going to do now.

eighteen

GRADY

"Why the fuck is everyone looking at me?" I ask Rowan and Asher as we're sitting in Sugarlips.

"Oh, I don't know, because you slept at Addison's house," Asher tosses back.

I put my fork down and lean back. "Seriously?"

Rowan laughs. "Dude, she's like the town's princess. She does charity work, is a good mom, is practically a part of the Arrowood family. You're the first guy she's ever had sleep at her house, what did you think?"

"That maybe they'd be happy for us."

Although, all of this leaves me wondering what the hell is going to happen when we break off this agreement.

Asher snorts. "Not a chance."

"Also, you better hope to God she dumps you and says it was her fault if this goes bad."

I guess that answers that one. "Why?" I ask stupidly.

"Because of the aforementioned reasons as to why they're staring. They love her. I wouldn't put it past them to hold some kind of town hall meeting to discuss why you broke up and who is choosing what side." Rowan looks to me. "I would probably go with her. You're a dick and she can do so much better."

I glare at him. "Yeah, you're a total winner."

"Never said I was, big brother. Never said I was. However, Addison is a delight."

I sigh heavily and look to the one brother I don't want to choke. "Did you have this with Phoebe?"

He pushes his plate back and lifts one shoulder. "Yes and no. Phoebe is loved, but I'm also well liked. We had the whispers because—"

"He's old as fuck and knocked her up," Rowan unhelpfully adds.

"Of the age difference and the fact that I work for her dad," Asher finishes as though he wasn't cut off. "Now, no one bats an eye. If anything, they see how much I love her, how I would literally die for her. It helped when people found out I drove twelve hours to punch someone in the face who hurt her."

I grit my teeth, not wanting to think about why else Asher went to punch that piece of fucking shit.

"I'm going to a wedding across the country," I remind him.

"Wow, what a selfless guy you are," Rowan says with mock approval. "You're like, fucking amazing."

"Can we get rid of him?" I ask.

Asher sighs heavily. "Unfortunately not. One of us would have to care for the cows and the new land the idiot bought."

"Hey, I'm going to increase our profits and I beat out the She-witch."

"Her name is Charlotte," Asher corrects.

"Is it? I'm not sure, she's got a green tinge to her that would lead me to believe she's a witch."

One day he's going to grow up and I can't wait for it.

"Anyway," I shift the conversation away from this rabbit hole. "I'm just saying I'm a good guy."

Asher shrugs. "You might think so, but they want to see it."

"I didn't realize I have to woo the town."

Rowan snorts. "Mistake number one. The town is your wife, and your girlfriend is your mistress."

Both Asher and I give him a look that clearly says he's a fucking dumbass.

"Do us all a favor and stop talking, Rowan," Asher urges and then turns his attention to me. "As dumb as he is, his thought process is correct. This town is a family and while you're a Whitlock and have family ties, you're not from here. I wasn't and neither was Rowan, but we've been here long enough now. We both do a lot for the community. While Addison is newer, she's got three years ahead of you and she's . . . loved. The chili cookoff was a good start, but you need to win over four people and this town will be putty in your hands."

"What four people?"

"The Arrowood women."

I sit back and lift one shoulder. "Well, I think I have one down."

"Which?"

"Devney. I saw her this morning."

Rowan nods approvingly. "Ellie will like you just because she is incapable of being mean to anyone. Brenna is a therapist and always gives people the benefit of the doubt, so she'll follow. It's Sydney who is the tough nut to crack. She loves me, though."

"Sure she does," Asher laughs. "Rowan is right, though. She's tough."

Rowan raises his hand like we're in grade school. "I'd just like to point out that it's twice now I've been right, and you assholes keep acting like I'm incompetent."

"You are," I cut him off, then say, "So, win over Sydney Arrowood and the town will stop glaring at me?"

Asher pops a fry in his mouth. "It'll get you closer than you are now."

***

"You're sure about this?" Addison asks as we're waiting for Sydney and Declan to arrive for dinner at Addy's.

"Absolutely."

After my talk with my brothers, I thought about the best way to do this. I thought about making up some bogus legal thing, but then I figured she'd see right through it. So, in the morning, when Addy and I were dropping the kids off, I asked if she thought we should do dinner with the kids.

She thought it couldn't hurt and might go a long way once we parted to have Sydney and Declan on our side.

Two days later, here we are. Jett pulls on my arm. "Daddy, we go horses?"

"No horses, buddy."

Elodie twists her body side to side. "Mommy said no pony."

I squat down in front of her, taking both her hands in mine. "Want to come ride the pony at my house?"

She nods, her big blue eyes getting even wider. "Please! Now! We go ride the pony?"

"Tomorrow, you come over and I'll take you."

Elodie rushes to Addison, her smile so wide it looks like it could break her cheeks. "I get to ride the pony, Mommy!"

"What do you say to Mr. Grady?"

"Tank you!"

She runs over, her arms wrapping around my neck, and I squeeze her tight. "Of course, sweet girl."

The two kids run out back to the play area, which I can only imagine the damage they've done. Those two are like hurricanes when it comes to that room.

I walk over to Addy and pull her close. "I love that they get along."

She grins at me. "Me too. She really adores him—and you."

"Feeling is mutual from both of us."

Jett loves Elodie. He tells everyone that she's his best friend. It really is great to see him so happy when he's around her. He also loves Addison. She bakes him cookies and always gives him big hugs.

When the sounds of their laughter fill the room, Addison's blue eyes get misty and she stares at me. "When this ends, when we walk away from this arrangement, I don't want the kids to suffer. Promise me, Grady. Promise that Elodie and Jett won't suffer another loss."

I'm stunned for a moment. I never would allow the kids to be hurt by this. "Addison, we're still going to be friends. I don't plan to lose you or Elodie when our arrangement ends. Look, I know this is our way to get what we want, but I hope that you know I would never let the kids be affected by this. They're friends, hell, we're friends and that isn't going to change."

She steps back, her hand resting on her chest. "Good."

I can tell that is absolutely not what she wanted to say, but Sydney and Declan should be here any minute and now is not exactly the best time to get into a discussion like this. So I nod once. "Okay. Now, will you let me kiss you before they get here?"

Her lips quirk up. "I guess so."

I take two steps, cradling her face, and slowly bring my lips to hers. "Thank you."

She sighs heavily. "Keep that charm going, babe, you're going to need it with Syd."

"And what exactly are your intentions, Mr. Whitlock?"

"Syd," Declan says as a warning.

"What? I'm asking a question. Besides, I don't get to make the Whitlock brothers sweat often, this is fun." Her smile is friendly, but it's clear she's enjoying herself.

All night I've done my best to answer her questions and not look like a total asshole. Which normally would be no problem, but this woman is fucking devious and I love it.

Each word is carefully measured and if I let my guard down even a touch, she pounces.

Declan shakes his head and drains his beer. "Come on, Grady. We can go out back and leave Addison to chastise my wife for her interrogation habits."

"I can handle it."

He quirks a brow. "But do you want to?"

Sydney crosses her arms over her chest and grins. This is a test, but while Sydney is important to win over, Addison said that Declan is actually just as influential and has a lot of contacts I might need for my business.

I get to my feet, take the beer he is extending, and smile at her. "After a beer or two, I'll be back in here and I'll answer all your questions."

She makes a humming sound and tilts her head. "You think you're getting out easy by going with Declan, but he's ruthless. Watch him."

As much as these two are a pain in the ass, I really like them both. It's clear they care about their friend and their family. Declan seems like a pretty laid-back guy, but I can see there is a lot more to him. He's protective, almost as though he's on alert when it comes to his wife, which I respect.

We get outside, sitting on the chairs out on the porch.

"You know I almost lost my wife?" he says as sort of a statement and a question.

"I didn't know that."

He nods slowly. "She was pregnant with our son, she had a tumor in utero and needed to have it operated on immediately. The surgery went well, but she didn't wake up from the anesthesia for six fucking long days. I pleaded with God to take me instead."

"I understand that," I say, because I do. I remember when I woke and found Lisa on the couch, unmoving, for hours, she was gone, but God, I tried.

I screamed, prayed, negotiated for her to wake, but it didn't work. She had died, alone, while I slept and Jett was in his bassinet beside her.

"That fear never leaves you, does it?"

"No, it doesn't."

He exhales. "You and Addison share that type of experience, and while Syd recovered, it is something that haunts me still, all these

188

years later. It's like a part of you is irrevocably changed from loss or even fear of loss like that. Addy has worked hard to come out on the other side, and I'm really glad she found someone who understands it. She means a lot to my family, she's like a little sister to me and my brothers. We hoped she'd find a guy we wouldn't want to beat the fuck out of and the fact that the first guy she's opening herself up to is you makes me not want to kill you."

I chuckle. "That's something."

"Yeah, it is."

Those fears Addison had about her friends finding out? I get it now. While I don't know Declan Arrowood for shit, I will really hate it if he ever learns that the things he's happy about aren't real.

Addison hasn't found someone, because we aren't that. We're just pretending for money and so she's not alone at that wedding. Sure, we're friends and our kids get along great, but it's not a relationship that goes past a certain timespan.

We're friends.

Friends who are seriously attracted to each other, and the whole point of tonight was to smooth any possibilities of being run out of town.

Now he's talking to me like a father talks to a guy coming to date his daughter and I'm not really sure what the hell to say.

"Well, I care about Addison. We're taking things slow."

"Slow?" he asks with a laugh. "Good luck. Those are every man's famous last words. Just like . . . we're just friends. That's the kiss of death."

Great. And I've said both of those things.

The back porch door opens and Addison pokes her head out, saving me from the rest of this conversation. "Come in for dessert."

We stand, but Declan puts his hand on my arm. "Be good to her, Grady. Not because anyone is going to threaten you or whatever, but because women like her don't come around often, and the guys who let them go never forgive themselves. Trust me, I know all too well, and I just was lucky another man didn't steal my wife before I could smarten up to win her back."

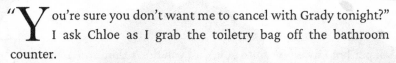

nineteen

ADDISON

"You're sure you don't want me to cancel with Grady tonight?" I ask Chloe as I grab the toiletry bag off the bathroom counter.

She is sitting in the middle of my bed with Elodie on her lap while I frantically pack for an overnight date with Grady.

And when I say date, I mean where I'm arm candy. It's not a date. It's a business meeting with two investors at a party he was invited to once the rumors of our relationship reached outside of town.

Apparently, my kissing him in front of everyone did the trick. Then the sleepover really spread like wildfire and Declan said something to someone about how much he likes him and now everyone is on board, whatever that means.

Not that it was my plan to be town gossip, but it's working for the goals that Grady has, so there's that.

"Oh my God, you're ridiculous. I'm more than capable of hanging out with Elodie for a night. We're going to have so much fun," she says as she kisses her cheek. "Right, Els?"

Elodie giggles and reaches for my bag. "I go too?"

"No, baby, Mommy is going away, but you'll be with Aunt Chloe and I'll be home in one sleep."

I swear, my friends are so intent on this working, they're lining up to watch Elodie any time Grady mentions a date.

Hopefully, Grady can secure his funding tonight because we leave for Oregon in a week, which means I can put an end to this fake dating shit quickly because my fake feelings are becoming much too realistic.

"Okay," Elodie says, clearly not caring that I'm leaving.

"Do you have everything?" Chloe asks as she looks at the clothes laid out.

"I think so. Makeup, hair stuff, fancy dress, shoes, stockings, jewelry, and change of clothes . . ."

She lifts one brow. "Errrm . . . you know . . . protection?"

"I don't own a gun, Chloe."

Her laugh is instant. "Not that kind!"

"Oh! Oh my God! We don't need that."

"No? You're going away to a fancy party, overnight . . . with a super hot guy who is into you, and you don't think you need to be" —she covers Elodie's ears—"prepared?"

I stare at her, wishing I could tell her the truth about this, but that would be stupid and defeat the purpose of the last few weeks. "No, we don't need to worry about things because those things aren't things to worry about."

"Okay . . ."

I huff, feeling better having said it, but also not really because what if? What if I . . . we . . . well, what if? There's no reason I can't. There's no reason to really say no other than I have only ever been with one man, and I married him. Though, the other morning that fact hadn't seemed to bother me all that much.

I turn to Chloe, that calm now completely gone. "Oh, Lord. I can't . . . I don't know. Do I need *it*?"

She smiles softly. "Not if you're not ready."

"Am I ready?" I ask, because maybe she knows.

"Addy, you don't have to. I didn't mean to freak you out." She places Elodie down. "Can you go set up your doll house for us and I'll come there in a few minutes?"

"Dolls!" Elodie yells and rushes out of my room.

I shake my head, trying to dispel the panic in my chest. "I didn't even think about it. I mean, we've kissed and done a little petting. Do they call it that still? It's so weird. Anyway, since the other night when he took care of my drunk ass, he hasn't tried. He wouldn't be expecting it, would he?"

Chloe comes to me, taking my hands in hers. "No, babe. No one calls it petting. It's messing around, but . . . not the point. Considering that Grady understands and is in the exact place you are, I don't think he would expect anything. I shouldn't have said anything and I'm sure that he will never push you. It's clear how much he cares about you and Elodie. You guys said you're taking it slow, and maybe he got you your own room and this is a moot point . . ."

He's never even alluded to it, especially since, while others are buying this budding love, we both know it's not true. Also, I didn't even think to ask about the room and she's probably right.

There's no reason not to have sex, but then there's no reason why we would. Other than I really, really want to.

I nod once, putting my fears aside, and release her hands. "You're right. Okay. Pack for sleeping though."

"What time will he be here?" she asks, looking at the clock.

"He has to read to Jett around seven and then he was coming right here."

So, about five minutes. Great.

She helps me fold everything and put it in my overnight bag. The party is at nine and the flight should take about forty minutes. It would be a six-hour drive otherwise, so this was definitely the better way to go. Plus, the whole point of Grady's business is to show the convenience of having a plane and pilot for just this reason.

However, the idea of flying with him has me a little freaking terrified. I don't like flying in general, let alone in a small plane.

"I think you have everything," Chloe says, looking at the bag once more.

"Thank you for watching her."

"It's nothing. Have fun and . . . look, be honest. If you're not ready, don't convince yourself you are. Grady should understand that."

I nod, because if I open my mouth, the truth might spill, and I have another week of this charade that I need to keep up. Chloe has a big mouth and she'll tell Devney, which will lead to issues for my Rose Canyon adventure. Plus, he still doesn't have his money secured.

So, until then, lips closed.

My phone pings.

GRADY

I'll be there in two minutes.

Shit.

"He's almost here," I explain to Chloe.

We grab the bags and I head to Elodie's room. I brush her blond hair back as she moves her dolls around. "You be a good girl, okay?"

"I will," she answers in her sweet little voice.

"I'll be home tomorrow morning."

"Okay, Mommy."

My heart aches at the idea of being away from her for the night, but I need to go. "I love you, Els."

She wraps her little arms around me. "I wub you, Mommy."

I squeeze her tight, kiss her temple, and stop in front of Chloe. "No candy, cookies, or any other crap she asks for."

"I know, trust me, I'm not giving that kid an ounce of sugar. It's not like when you're coming back and have to deal with her."

I roll my eyes. "I'll see you in the morning."

"See you tomorrow. Have fun!"

I'm going to try.

I get downstairs right as Grady is pulling in and head to the car. He gets out, kisses my cheek, and then takes the bags from my hand. "I got this."

"Thanks."

I get in the car, and as he puts the bags in the trunk, my nerves start to build again. I don't think I'm ready.

I mean, I could be.

I want to be.

It's been a really fucking long time of no sex. I liked sex. I was pretty good at it too, I think. I mean, Isaac never complained. Not that he was vastly experienced either, since we were both virgins when we met.

Being that we were eight.

Oh God. What if I'm bad at it? What if I really suck, and not the good suck, like the sucking that's not wanted? That's a possibility. Maybe I never heard complaints because there was nothing to compare it to.

Grady can compare.

He climbs in and lets out a sigh. "Are you ready?"

"I don't think we should have sex because I might be bad at it," I blurt out because my anxiety is at a ten and I can't help it.

He doesn't say a word. He just looks at me with wide eyes as his jaw drops, closes, and then drops again.

Great. I broke him. See, I'm bad at this too.

"I ... I ... ummm," he says and then shakes his head, blinking, and returns to me. "Okay, first, I doubt you're bad. No one kisses like you do and is bad at the rest. So, that's point one. Point two is that I have no idea where the hell the first part came from. Did I insinuate that you had to have sex with me?"

"No!" I say quickly, feeling like an idiot in a hundred ways. "Chloe asked if I packed protection, which caused me to spiral into wondering if we were going to have sex or if we wanted people to think we did and then ... well, I panicked."

He takes my hands in his and brings them to his lips, dropping kisses against my knuckles. "You don't have to panic. The only expectation I have for tonight is that you dance with me, and I hope you let me kiss you because I really want to kiss you, Addison, but that's it."

"Okay," I say, my blood pressure starting to come down from

panic but rising for another reason. Because he wants to kiss me. Because he's looking at me like he really wants to kiss me right now. We need to not kiss right now though, because we have to go, and I need to think. So I pull my hands back and let out a deep sigh. "Okay, we better go then."

He gives me a tight-lipped smile and heads down my driveway. I feel stupid. So freaking stupid.

With each minute that passes, I try to put that blunder behind me and go forward because what other option do I have?

However, the farther we get and the closer to the airport, I find that my internal bravado is all bullshit.

We're nearing the airport, which now means it's been almost ten minutes of silence. It's now or never.

I shift a little and smile. "So, how was your day?"

Grady bursts out laughing and then gains control of himself. "It was good."

I ignore his reaction and soldier forward. "How so?"

He arranges his features as to attempt to hide his amusement. "I was able to get the horse to cooperate, but the setback isn't his fault since I haven't been riding him as much as I need to, I got Jett into school without you and without bribery, and now I'm with you."

"I'm going to pretend the last part is the best."

"It is," Grady says without pause. "Even though we're not having sex."

I groan. "You had to say it."

"You said it first, I was just assuring you that I hear you loud and clear." He shrugs, shows his badge to the gate guard and then the bar lifts.

As soon as we're away from there, I clarify my earlier statement. "I didn't say we *weren't* having sex. I was just saying that we *shouldn't*."

Grady parks the car outside a big building and then turns to me with a smirk. "There's a distinction in there somewhere. Do you want to have sex with me?"

I want to fall through the floorboards and die, that's what I want.

"Let's talk about the Jett thing, that sounds like there's a story there."

"He went inside without a tantrum. Now, back to what we were talking about."

Seriously, sometimes I hate myself and my big mouth. "What about Jett and his story time, how did that go?"

I bring it up because it's the one thing that Grady will not give up. He either does it over the phone or video call if he's working or he'll rearrange his schedule to ensure that every night, he reads to Jett.

He chuckles again. "It went like it always does."

Of course it did. Even if it hadn't, I'd bet my ass he won't tell me anything different.

I'm a grown woman and I can handle this discussion. So I turn my body to face him as much as I can in the car and tackle this head on. "Fine, we'll have this conversation. I don't know if I want to have sex with you. I know that I like you, I'm very much attracted to you. I know that I like how you kiss me, make me feel when I'm around you, but I also don't know how much is pretend and real."

He leans forward, his hand cupping my cheek. "I like you too, Addy. I don't have to fake much with you. You know how I feel and why I won't make the relationship part real. I can't do it. I just . . . it wouldn't be fair to you. However, the attraction, the friendship, the way I care about you isn't fake."

A warm feeling moves through my veins and I hate that right now, I want the lie to be real.

"So you want to have sex with me?"

He chuckles low and runs his thumb against my cheek. "I don't know a man alive who wouldn't want that, but I have no expectations and I would never ask that of you."

I really should learn to keep my trap shut, but I haven't so far. "Why?"

"Why what?"

CORINNE MICHAELS

"Why would you never ask that?"

Why am I so dumb and why do I keep talking?

"Because I think you're a woman who only gives herself to a man she loves and who loves her back. I think you're the kind of woman who men dream of finding because you're honest and giving. You give your heart and that's a gift I wouldn't take from you, but I wish to fucking God that I was deserving of it, Addy."

His thumb strokes my cheek again, then drops and I feel the loss everywhere because I wish it too, and I wonder if I am that woman or I can be a new version, one who can take what she wants and walk away unscathed.

twenty

GRADY

"Only one bed?" Addison says with a laugh as we walk into the hotel room. "It's like we're in a novel where this is the exact thing that would happen."

"Well, it is the exact thing that happened and I promise, we're not in a novel."

She turns to me. "Yes, funny that."

As luck would have it, the room I booked was given away accidentally, leaving us with one option and this is it.

"I swear, I didn't plan this," I say.

"Sure you didn't."

I take a step to her. "We can fly home after the party if you want. I don't want you to be uncomfortable." I also don't want her to think I'm responsible for this or that I expect anything.

Tonight may have started rocky or at least strange, but we found our way back to the carefree friendship we have. She was definitely not excited when we got in the plane, but as soon as we were airborne, it was different. We flew into the small airport in upstate New York. There were stars in her eyes the entire flight, watching the lights below and talking to me on her headset.

Gone were the conversations in the car and here was a free and happy Addison.

201

One I was enjoying immensely.

And one I don't want to lose.

"It's fine, Grady. I know you didn't really plan this, I was there when the front desk stated what happened. We're adults and we'll be fine."

"Right." I'll just have to jerk off in the shower when we get back to the room and fight every urge I have to touch her—at all. No touching or I'm going to end up between her legs.

She smiles and lifts her bag. "Now, we're late and I have to get ready to be the arm candy you need."

I don't need arm candy, I need her. Just her. The way she is because it's impossible not to fall into her charm once she speaks. I want to tell her that, but I worry she'll think it means more and there can't be more when it comes to us. Jett is already too attached. He needs me to protect him from it getting deeper. "Addy . . ."

She taps my nose. "Let me get ready without another weird conversation happening. Okay?"

"Okay," I acquiesce.

I hear the bag hit the floor and a lot of things opening, moving, thumping as she starts to get ready. I flip the television on and lie back on the bed, letting her do her thing. It'll take me a total of eight minutes to get ready, so I lounge and wait for Addison to emerge, hopefully soon, since we're running late as it is.

"I'm almost done!" she calls from the bathroom about thirty minutes later and I take that as my cue to get ready.

I pull out my tux from the closet, since this is a black-tie event, and get dressed. I had to dress up for balls and events when I was on active duty, but I was in uniform, which felt like armor in some ways. There's a nervousness that I can't explain.

Maybe it's because this is really one of my last shots to secure the funding.

Maybe it's because the last time I wore a tux was for prom, since Lisa and I got married in a traditional military style wedding.

Or maybe it's because I'm here—with Addison.

A woman I'm coming to like more than I thought I would. More than I want to. More than what our arrangement was supposed to be.

All of that could be it, but I don't have the time to pinpoint it because about ten seconds later, the door opens and she walks out.

Stunning.

Fucking stunning.

She smiles, glances down at her dress and up to me. I should speak. I should have words coming out of my mouth, but I can't.

She's fucking fantastic.

Her long blond hair is swept up with hanging curls, her makeup is darker than I've ever seen, but it's perfectly subtle at the same time. Except her ruby red lips, there is nothing subtle about those. Her beauty is beyond words, but the showstopper is her dress. Red silk falls against her body as though it was fashioned exactly for her. The front dips down low, just the traces of her breasts visible.

"Do you like it?" she asks when I still haven't said anything. "I saw the dress in the store and really thought it was pretty. Chloe and Devney demanded I buy it after I tried it on, but if you think it's too—"

"Exquisite," I finish. "You. The dress. You're . . . perfect."

The fear in her eyes vanishes and she smiles softly. "I wouldn't say perfect, but . . ."

"I would. I do. You're perfect and you left me speechless."

Her cheeks redden and it takes everything inside of me not to lift her in my arms, toss her on the bed, and see what that red lipstick looks like on my cock, but that's not going to happen for several reasons.

"Well, thank you."

I extend my hand. "Ready?"

She nods, and I focus on heading to the door and not the bed.

203

"Addison, my dear, you look absolutely stunning," Mateo says as he approaches us.

"Mateo, you look very handsome yourself."

He chuckles and then his wife appears next to him. "It was a lot of hard work getting him to look this good."

Addy laughs and kisses Lily's cheek. "You've done an exceptional job."

"Thank you." Lily beams and slaps her husband's chest. "See."

He rolls his eyes and looks to me. "See what I put up with? Once you put a ring on their finger, it's over."

We shake hands and then I wrap my arm around Addison's back, hand resting on her hip. "Thankfully, Addy hasn't had to do much work with me yet."

"Yet," Addy echoes.

Mateo grins. "It'll come, trust me."

"Well, hopefully I don't have too much to do. He's a pretty great guy as it is."

Lily's eyes glimmer. "So things are good with you both?"

Addison looks to me, a smile on her perfect red lips. "Definitely."

"That's great to hear. You can't do better than Addison, other than my Lily. But Addy is truly a wonderful person."

"I agree," I say quickly. "She makes me want to be the man she deserves, that's for sure."

He nods. "Is that one of the reasons why you've been working so hard to secure the investment you need?"

"It is." Her back stiffens just a little and if I wasn't holding onto her, I probably wouldn't have noticed it. I squeeze her hip just a little and she relaxes again. "When I moved Jett up here after his mother died, I promised him that I would do anything to give him a good life. That includes being able to provide for him—and any woman I'm building a life with."

"Has Grady told you about the new investor he met?" she smoothly asks.

"A new one?"

"Well, he's not an investor as much as it's a security company that sees the value in the private standby service. They have parties, much like this, and clients they need to fly often. It's just an idea we're tossing around."

Mateo nods, taking a sip of his whiskey, and I do the same. "I see. If you could keep things as your original plan, then what?"

"Then that would be my first choice."

I feel a jolt of excitement because this is exactly what I want.

"Maybe when we return to Sugarloaf in two days, we can have a drink, talk a bit more about it? I talked to a few friends here and after the two hours of traffic they sat in yesterday, I think the idea is very appealing to them now."

"That sounds great," I say, keeping my voice even. "I'll reach out on Monday."

He inclines his head, then turns to Addison. "And I look forward to our meeting about the grant paperwork."

"I can't wait."

Lily reaches her hand out to Addison and squeezes it, then the two of them walk away.

As soon as they're out of earshot Addison turns to me, her smile wide and eyes alight with joy. "Oh my God! You're totally going to get the money."

"It's not for sure yet."

"Well, it's closer than it was."

I let out a heavy sigh, draining the rest of my drink. "Closer is better."

"Why don't you seem happy?"

"I am happy. I'm just reserved. I don't want to get my hopes up."

Addison rests her hand on my chest, right over my heart. "Hope is what keeps us going forward. Don't ever lose it, Grady."

"And what do you hope for?"

She pulls her lower lip between her teeth for a second. "Love. I hope for love."

I wish I could be the one to give it to her. However, I can give her a good time tonight. So instead of saying anything about her hopes, I step back. "Dance with me?"

The flash of disappointment fills her eyes, but she masks it quickly. "I would love to."

We walk out to the dance floor, and I swear every man turns to look at her. How anyone could stop themselves is beyond me. She's the bright light in the dark skies, the light in the lighthouse that cuts through the fog and guides the ships home.

It doesn't matter how bleak or dark it is, she's there, bright and ever shining.

Her hand rests on my shoulder, the other one against my chest, and we move to the soft music.

"Everyone is looking at us."

"No, dove, they're looking at you."

She blinks and then shakes her head. "I assure you, the women here are feral to be the one in your arms, sir."

"It's the men who are staring, hating me, and I don't blame them. If I weren't the one you were dancing with, I'd be jealous too."

Addison rolls her eyes. "You're ridiculous."

I am. I am because I should be worried about keeping up this ruse and not asking her to dance because I just wanted to hold her. This isn't for show, this is for me, and that's the mistake I keep making.

"You have no idea."

"Well, if you wanted people to believe our dating is real, you're selling it," Addison says, her eyes not leaving mine.

"It's not hard to sell."

I need to shut the fuck up and take a cold shower and remember that Addison is selling it as well.

"Grady?" Addison's voice is hesitant.

"Yes?"

"Do you think we'll ever find love again? Do you think one day I'll find a man who wants to dance with me every night?"

The anger that rushes through my veins is unexplainable. I shouldn't hate this man that doesn't exist, but I do.

I fucking hate the idea of him. That anyone is deserving enough to touch her, kiss her, know how it feels to hold her is impossible.

I swallow down the knot in my throat and force a smile. "You'll find it," I promise.

My chest grows tight as again, I picture her with another man, laughing, smiling, and dancing in the kitchen of her home.

And then, as though the red in her dress is fire, I step back, feeling the burn from touching her.

"What's wrong?"

"I need to . . . I have to . . . go get a drink and I'll meet you over there. I need to talk to someone and call home to check on Jett."

Jett. He's who I have to think about. I can't be angry about some guy who doesn't exist because I didn't exist for my son for far too long. This fake dating already takes me away far too much. He needs stability and his father, not half of my time because I'm giving it to someone else.

I walk her over to the bar, kiss her cheek, and then head down the hall. Once there, I grab my phone and shoot a text to my sister.

> How is Jett?

BRYNLEE

> He's fine. Stop worrying. He doesn't even miss you.

I let out a sigh and despise myself for being a pansy and rushing out. However, I'm not ready to face her right now.

Thankfully, there are three guys standing around shooting the shit at the bar, so I grab a drink and insert myself when they start talking about the military.

"I think the government should cut the spending. Why the hell do we need a six-thousand-dollar screwdriver? We're wasting money building an already strong military. We need to work on limiting their budget, not increasing it," the one guy with a really bad unibrow says. b

The one to the left, we'll call him Stringbean, agrees. "There's no need for it."

The only one with a brain laughs. "You're all idiots. While I don't disagree there is mismanagement of funds, you have no idea what that screwdriver does. I doubt it's what you think and unless you've served, you don't get to make that call."

I instantly like this guy. "I don't mean to intrude, but having served eight years and as a pilot, I can attest that while it seems frivolous, and agreeing with your friend, there's plenty of waste, that screwdriver could be the one that tightens the bomb attached to my plane."

Stringbean and Unibrow jerk their heads back a little. "I'm sorry, I didn't mean to offend."

"No offense taken, I just overheard you and wanted to explain my position. Now, if we're talking about the vast amount of paper-work they distribute, that's where we can afford to cut back." I smile, not wanting to piss any of them off. Who knows if they're possible investors.

All three chuckle. The smart one extends his hand. "I'm Javier Santiago."

"Grady Whitlock, nice to meet you." I turn to Stringbean and introduce myself, his name is Killian, and then the same to Unibrow who is Ethan.

"So, you said eight years?" Javier asks.

"Yes, in the navy. I would've stayed longer, but life happens and we do what's best for our family."

He chuckles. "I understand that more than most. I moved to New York to better my life when I was fifteen. My uncle taught me everything he knew about his business, and when he passed, I took over and have been able to give my wife and kids a life we dreamed of."

Admirable. He seems like my kind of people. "I'm sure your uncle would be incredibly proud."

"I'd like to think so," he says and then slaps Killian's shoulder.

"Killian here is the same, he owns a trucking company that he started from the ground up."

I nod to him. "Congratulations on your success."

Killian bows his head. "And what do you do now that you're out of the service?"

I start to tell him a bit about my company, how my goal is to do more private services and have a fleet by the end of year three. All three men seem impressed with my business plan.

"I can see a need for it, at least amongst this crowd," Javier says. "I wish you luck, my friend."

"Thank you. If any of you three would like to invest, I won't turn it away," I say, half joking, but really serious.

All three men laugh and Ethan starts telling me about his new business venture. He's opening a resort and brewery.

"It'll be great. We're going to have so many options for food and I think guests will enjoy coming to one place for a bit of everything," the one dude says.

I nod. "I can see the appeal."

"It'll be great if you can get your business off the ground, no pun intended," he jokes and the group laughs. "You could fly guests out and make some money."

I take a long pull from my gin and smile. "That's the hope."

The three men start talking about the resort and my eyes scan the crowd, looking for Addison. I left her suddenly and guilt fills me as I didn't intend to stay away this long. As I turn a little more to the left I see her, only she's not smiling, she looks uncomfortable.

He leans in, whispering something, his hand trying to move against her back.

"Excuse me," I say as they're talking and I'm moving toward her.

There's a man standing there and he slides his hand around her hip, and she tries to pull it back but can't.

I'm there in three seconds and my voice is like ice. "If you want to keep that hand, I suggest you release her immediately."

His eyes lift and I see the surprise for a moment. "I'm sorry, what?"

"I said if you don't let go of my girlfriend, I'll break your fucking hand."

He tilts his head and then lets go of her. I step between them, putting Addison behind me.

He looks like he wants to laugh, but something stops him. "Relax, we were just talking."

"And now you're done."

I feel Addison's hand on my back. "Grady, it's fine."

No, it's not. I could see the panic in her eyes. Whatever he whispered to her made her back stiffen.

I stare at him, he shakes his head and walks away.

Forcing myself to control my anger, I turn to her. "Are you okay?"

"I'm fine. Perfectly fine."

"I shouldn't have left you."

Addison lifts her hand to my cheek. "You came back at the perfect time, just like I knew you would."

I close my eyes for a heartbeat and try to fight off the emotions her words are stirring.

***

I put the card in the lock, removing it as the light turns green.

I open the door, holding it so Addison can walk in first. She has her heels in her hand, having taken them off the minute we got out of the elevator.

She stands there in the middle of the room, looking at the bed, her back to me.

I have thought about this all night, wondering what the right thing is and I'm still not sure. I want her. There's no doubt about that, and tonight only solidified that desire. It's more than just her beauty, it's her grace, kindness, and I like being around her.

Addison is different than Lisa in a lot of ways. My wife was commanding and argumentative at times. She always had to have the last word and challenged me at every turn. Addison doesn't seem to have claws that are ready to slash out at the first person who pisses her off.

I move behind her, not touching, but knowing she feels me there because she tenses and then turns.

My heart is pounding as we both stand here, arms at our sides, waiting for whatever from each other.

Her blue eyes are filled with a million emotions, each moving so fast I can't begin to read them, and then her lips part and her voice is soft as she speaks. "I know that I said I didn't think we should ... be intimate, but ..."

I wait, praying she says she changed her mind. Hoping at the same time she hasn't because, if I have her, if I have a taste of her, I don't think I'm going to want just a little. I'm going to want to consume every drop of her.

"But?" I urge her to continue.

"I trust you. I like you." Her hand lifts barely a whisper on my chest. "We're both very attracted to each other and ..." Addison's eyes find mine again and I swear I can't fucking breathe. "I take it back."

"You take what back, dove?"

Her lashes lower and then lift slowly. "I want you. I want us. I thought of nothing else but what we'd do when we got back here alone."

In that exact second, any resistance I had disappears. I cup her face in my hands, rubbing my thumb against those red lips that I thought about all night. "Whatever you want, Addison, I'll give you."

"Give me tonight. Kiss me."

I lean in, using all the restraint I have to go slow. I want this night to last. Every second, every breath is going to matter.

Our lips are almost touching, the scent of her perfume, a mix of flowers and pears, grows stronger. All night I've wanted to run my nose down the column of her neck, memorize the way it hits my senses. I tip her head back bringing my mouth to the corner of hers, along her cheek, and then I do what I wanted. I inhale deeply as I move down her neck and then back up.

I can feel her heart pounding beneath my fingers, and I grin against the shell of her ear. "I'll kiss you all night, but you have to tell me where."

twenty-one
ADDISON

Oh my God! I think I might perish right here.

A shiver runs through me as Grady's lips run along my ear and then he nips it. "Where do you want me to kiss you, Addison? You have to ask for what you want, dove."

The endearment does me in.

The way he says it, so sweet and careful, like I'm precious. I want him even more. The rasp in his voice is so damn sexy, I feel it all the way to my toes and definitely somewhere else.

I have never been vocal in bed. I tried, but it felt so uncomfortable for me. Telling a man what to do, where to go, just was . . . hard for me. Now, it's even worse. I don't know that I'm going to be good at this and now I'm terrified I really won't be.

"I can't," I admit.

Grady's deep green eyes find mine. "I don't want to take from you, Addy. I want to give you whatever you want."

"I just . . . I might not be good at this," I let it out because at this point, it is what it is.

He smiles at me and then his hands slide back up to cradle my head. "You're too good at this. You have no idea how beautiful, sweet, wonderful, and alluring you are. There's no way you're not good at this and we'll find a way together to be even better, but I need to know what you like, what makes you feel good, what you need, to make sure that I give it to you."

That was incredibly sweet and also melts away a very small amount of my trepidation. I bring my hand to his chest, playing with the buttons of his dress shirt. "I've only been with one man and we weren't exactly . . . adventurous." I don't want to say his name. I don't want to admit that Isaac, while very tender and sweet, was never really . . . rough. He treated me with kid gloves. I was precious to him, and I loved it, but he was always so worried that he'd upset me.

"Do you want to be adventurous?" he asks.

Please Lord, just let me expire now. I don't want to answer that, but Grady tilts my head back and waits until my eyes meet his. "I don't know what I want. Are you, I mean, tell me what you want."

He doesn't hesitate as he looks in my eyes with so much heat I could melt. "Right now, I want to kiss you, Addison. I want to watch this dress fall to the floor and see if you really aren't wearing anything underneath. I want to run my hands along every inch of your skin and then follow that with my mouth. Then, I want to lay you down on that bed, spread your legs, and make you come on my tongue. If after that, you want more, I'll fuck you until we both can't walk."

Safe to say he knows what he wants and every single desire he just named, I want as well.

Instead of looking more ridiculous and inept, I lift up on my toes and bring our lips close. "I'm not wearing anything underneath."

He practically growls and then crushes his lips to mine. My arms go around his neck, as his are on my ass, definitely not feeling panty lines. There really weren't any options in this dress so I used tape to keep my breasts covered and went commando.

Grady pulls the fabric up and then dips down, lifting me so my legs wrap around his waist. He moves us to the bed, stopping before it and standing me up. "Turn around, dove."

I move, my back to his front, and I feel the loss of heat as he steps back. His hands are at my neck, massaging slowly, and then they move lower. Then I feel him tug at my dress and the sound of the zipper sliding is the only thing I hear.

This is happening.

His lips are right where my shoulder meets my neck and I close my eyes when I feel the heat of his tongue.

"Grady," I sigh his name.

"Where do you want me to kiss you, Addison?"

I grit my teeth and force myself to be brave. "My neck."

"Good choice," he murmurs and then kisses there. "Where else?"

"My mouth," I say, wanting to kiss him so badly.

He turns my head, keeping my back to him, and kisses me hard. His tongue thrusts in my mouth, pushing against mine in the hottest kiss I've ever had. The heat rises in me as his hands cup my breasts, pinching my nipples gently.

I want his mouth there. I want his mouth everywhere.

I break away, needing to catch my breath, and then his fingers are at the straps of my dress. "I'm going to take this off you, watch the red silk pool at the floor, and then I'm going to lay you down and wait for you to tell me where to kiss you next."

So I have a few seconds to come up with the ability to form words. Good.

Sure enough, the straps fall to my elbows, then my wrists as the fabric falls away and to the floor. I'm naked and vulnerable, but at the same time, I feel safe.

Grady didn't ask for this, I did, and he's giving me the power in so many ways.

Instead of waiting for him to tell me what to do, I turn to face him, allowing him to drink me in.

"I thought you were exquisite before, but I didn't know the meaning of the word until now."

I can't stop the smile that forms and I lift my hand, hating that I'm naked and I can't see any of him.

"You asked me what I want?"

"Yes."

"I want to see you—all of you."

He shucks his jacket off, tossing it to the chair, and then starts to unbutton his shirt, but I stop him. My fingers move to the buttons and start to do it myself. However, he doesn't just stand there and let me do it, instead, his hand lifts to my chest, trailing his knuckles from my belly up to my breast. I miss a button, my body trembling as he touches me.

There is a devilish gleam in his eyes, and I let out a sigh, frustrated and desperate, and grab the two hems and rip it open.

"Fuck," he groans and then his hands are in my hair, tipping my head up to meet his lips. He kisses me hard, as though I tore more than just his shirt. The restraint from the first kiss is gone. This one is rough, primal, and I never want it to stop.

Grady doesn't treat me like glass, he's willing to risk breaking a piece and cutting himself as he takes and also gives.

I manage to tear my lips away, breathing heavy and loving the red stain on his mouth from mine.

"I want to touch you."

He pulls the shirt off and the undershirt over his head by doing that manly one-arm thing. His chest is bare and I gasp. I thought I knew he worked out, but this is beyond what I imagined. There are ridges, valleys, and peaks of muscle everywhere. He looks like he's chiseled from stone. His hand moves to his pants, unbuttoning and then lowering the zipper. They hang there waiting to fall free.

"If you want to touch, then touch, Addison."

His raspy voice travels straight to my core and I clench my muscles.

I want to touch. I said as much, so I do. I move my hands to his waist and push the material down. He's in nothing but his boxers and if this is what his erection looks like now, I'm almost afraid just how big it will be when it's not restrained.

Without thinking on that too hard, I hook my fingers there, pulling down.

And yeah, I was totally right about the size. He's huge. He's huge and it's been three years since I've had sex, so this is going to be . . . interesting.

"You're incredible," I say to him.

Grady waits for my eyes to meet his. "No, dove, you are. Climb on the bed," he commands. I slide up onto the bed, and he follows, we face each other and his hand glides across my cheek. "I have never wanted anything the way I want you right now."

"I'm right here."

"You are," he says it as though he can't believe it's true. "I'm going to make good on my promises now. Lie there, and let me kiss every beautiful inch of you."

Grady shifts up and starts at my hand. He kisses each finger, palm, my wrist, and up my arm. Without releasing my gaze, he moves across my chest to the other arm, going backwards this time. Then he kisses my lips, eyes, nose, cheeks, before grazing my neck again. The low rumble in his chest vibrates through me before he's at the valley between my breasts.

I watch as he runs his tongue around the left side, flicking my nipple before taking it deep in his mouth. My hands move to his hair, groaning as he sucks harder. "Oh, God," I pant. And then he does it to the other side, the same exact thing, and this time I squirm.

"After I make you come on my tongue, I'm going to suck these while you ride me."

"Is that what you want?"

"To see your beautiful tits bounce as you're on my cock? Yeah, baby, I definitely want that."

Okay, this dirty talk thing is really hot. I wish I was better at it, because he's pretty damn fabulous.

I moan because instead of saying more, his mouth is back on my skin, trailing down my stomach. He pauses, his breath hitting where I'm desperate for him. I feel just the barest touch, heat washes through me and I curl my legs up and lift my head.

He looks at me, his eyes wild. "Do you want this, Addy?"

I'm practically vibrating with need. It's not a want at this point, but I know what he's asking, why he's asking. I know that for the two of us, this is different.

I push up on my elbow, resting my one hand on his cheek. "I want this with you."

"Thank God," he says, releasing a breath, and then pushes my legs apart. I fall back as the first swipe comes.

He moans and I melt into the bed. His tongue moves over and over, flicking and swirling around my clit. My fingers tangle in his hair, the dark blond locks like silk as his rough tongue keeps up its friction.

I feel my back start to lift off the bed while he pushes me higher to climax. "Grady!" I pant, feeling the fire burn through my veins. "Oh, oh, God."

There's no relenting. It just keeps going as my fingers now grip the comforter. My orgasm is fast approaching. I wish I had the strength to hold it back because this is incredible. I never want this part to end.

He flicks his tongue faster and my breathing is so erratic as my climax is barreling forward. He fingers me, thrusting inside of me so hard, and I can't control myself. I fall, letting out a moan as waves of pleasure crash into me, dragging me down before pushing me back up for air.

Grady crawls up my body slowly, kissing back up the way he came. "You know, each time I think you're perfect, you show me another side and I think I'm wrong."

I smile, turning my head to face him, blissed out and panting. "You think I'm perfect now?" I ask, with a raised brow.

He nods, brushing his nose against mine. "I do. I think I'd like to see if you're perfect when you come on my dick."

"I'm pretty sure I'll think you're perfect then."

"How about we find out?"

I run my finger from his lips down his chest, finding the courage to ask him for what I really want. "How about we see if I'm perfect with my lips around your dick first?"

twenty-two

GRADY

Addison pushes me so I'm on my back and I think of every fucking thing I can to keep from losing it here.

Her red lipstick is still on, and I'm going to get my wish.

She moves down, pushing her hair to one side, and I love the feel of it against my thighs. I open my mouth to say something, but her blue eyes lock on mine and she takes me deep in one move.

"Fuck!" I say loudly, fisting her hair. "Yes, baby, just like that."

The heat from her mouth is almost too much. I think about anything other than the feel of it or the way her tongue runs up the underside of my cock. I absolutely avoid thinking of how her moans vibrate as she takes me deeper.

I stop myself from thrusting up, fucking her mouth faster and harder, and focus on staying still.

Addison does something with her throat and that restraint I was working on frays a bit more. "Addison, don't do that unless . . ." I try to warn her, but she does it again. "Fuck! You're going to . . . you can't!" I try to make sense, but Jesus Christ, I can't take it.

Her hand moves to my balls, and that's it. I'm going to lose it. I have to tell her to stop, I have to be inside her when I come. "Too good, dove. Too much. Not . . . Addison . . ."

She takes me deep again, and I feel the back of her throat. Nope. I'm going to come if I don't stop it right now.

I guide her head back and flip her quickly. She gasps and stares up at me. "Did I do something wrong?"

I push her hair back. "No, you did everything right. I want to come inside you. I want to feel you around me, and if you kept going, that wasn't going to happen."

"Oh." She sounds genuinely confused by that.

I stroke myself, watching her eyes as I tell her the truth. "That was the best fucking blow job I've ever had. Your mouth wrapped around my cock was the most beautiful thing, but, sweetheart, I want to be inside your pussy. I want to fuck you until neither of us can move, and then I'll take you again."

She smiles. "Good."

"Yeah, it was good, but this is going to be better," I promise.

I stop stroking long enough to slip the condom on and then shift so my arms are by her face, and I wait for her to look up at me.

I want her eyes when I take her.

I want to watch her as I slide inside of her.

When she finally does, I see her fear. "We can stop now, if you don't want to do this, I'll stop."

It might just about kill me, but I'll never pressure her.

"It's been a long time and I worry . . ."

I lean down and kiss her perfect lips. "Shhh, I promise I'll never hurt you."

And I'll do anything in my power to make sure I never do.

"I know you won't."

"Do you want to stop?" I ask again.

Addison's finger brushes my cheek. "No, I don't want that. Not even a little." Her legs part even more, wrapping around my hips. "Take me, Grady."

Her trust. Her words. The way her eyes swim with emotion does something inside me, but I shove that back.

Addison is perfect—in every way.

I open my mouth to tell her this, but she presses her heels

against my ass. "Please. I have no expectations, just that I want this. Please."

Her plea is my undoing and slowly, I push into her just an inch and watch her face. I kiss her again and slide a little deeper. Addison shows no signs of discomfort. "Are you okay?" I ask through gritted teeth.

The restraint it's taking not to go balls deep is real.

"You feel so good. God, so good."

"Your pussy is tight around me, I think you want more of my cock, don't you?"

Her eyes flash to mine. "I want all of it."

She said it's been a while and she's so goddamn tight, so I don't want to slam into her. No matter how much I need to.

Addison brings her hand to my cheek. "I want you inside me, Grady. Fuck me."

I close my eyes. rest my forehead to hers, and wonder what the hell I've ever done to deserve her like this.

I push all the way in, feeling complete for the first time in years.

We rock together, going slow and steady, feeling each other as she relaxes, allowing me even deeper.

I shift my weight and grab her right leg, hooking it up over my shoulder, giving me even more leverage. Addison moans, her finger-nails scoring down my back as I move my hand to her clit. I want her to come again and again. I want her to remember this, us, the way I make her feel.

"That's it, baby, feel how fucking deep I am," I coax as she whimpers. "Feel how full you are with my dick."

"I can't."

"You can. Tell me. Tell me how good it is."

"It's too much!"

Her head thrashes, and I slow. "It's not enough. Give me more. Give me everything. Tell me, Addy. Who is inside you?"

"You are!"

"Who is going to make you come again?"

"Oh, God, Grady, I can't."

"You're going to, dove," I tell her. And I mean it. Lifting her hips off the bed, I drive into her from a different angle. I fuck her harder, bucking my hips and feeling the burn of the muscles in my legs.

Her face contorts as her muscles contract around me, milking my dick as her release nears.

Addison's eyes find mine. "You're killing me!"

"No, dove, this is living. This is flying. Come again while I'm inside you."

I find her clit again and flick my hand faster. She's close, and I'm hanging on by a thread.

She lets out a loud moan as her eyes close, head tips back, and her back bows. While that's the most beautiful thing I've ever seen, it's nothing compared to the way it feels inside her. Her pussy contracts around me so hard I swear I'm going to see stars.

I couldn't stop myself from falling over the edge if my life depended on it.

I let go, allowing my own release to take hold, and I call out her name as I let it go.

The two of us are fighting for breath as we find our way back to the moment.

When I roll off her, I pull her to my chest. "That was fucking perfect. You're *not* bad at this, Addy. Not even a little. Not at all," I say as soon as I can speak.

She laughs softly. "Yeah, that was . . . well, I have never ever orgasmed twice."

My male ego loves that. "I'm glad I could be your first, and I promise, if we do this again, I'll strive for three," I tell her and then shift. "I need to clean up, don't move."

I head into the bathroom, doing exactly that, and stop when I see my face in the mirror. I don't look any different, and yet, something feels changed.

I climb back into bed, pulling her to me. Addison's hand is on my chest with her chin atop it. Her soulful eyes gazing at mine. "I want you to know that this was really incredible, and I have zero expectations going forward."

"Zero?" I ask dubiously. "Not even the three orgasms I just promised?"

While I know women are completely capable of having a friends-with-benefits relationship, Addy doesn't seem like one of them. She wants to get re-married and have more kids, which I absolutely do not want. At least not anytime soon.

She shakes her head minutely. "I mean, I'd like you to make good on that orgasm thing."

"That, I can promise."

"What happened between us was . . . amazing, and while sex complicates things often, it doesn't have to with us."

"So you're using me for my body? Not that I'm complaining if you are."

"More like *certain* parts of your body."

"Which ones?" I ask.

"Well, your mouth for one. You're very talented with that."

I'll take that compliment. "You share the same talent, dove. However, I'd like to know what other parts you're using me for."

Addison looks over to the left, pursing her lips. "Hmm, I think your hands were good."

"Think?" I toss back.

"Okay, fine, they worked wonderfully."

I pull her up, so her face is right at mine. "What else did you like?"

"Can't say there is anything else."

I grin, loving this playful banter, and then rub my nose against hers. "No?"

"Did you have something in mind?"

"Want me to name what I liked on you, and we'll see if it jogs your memory?"

She giggles and the sound causes that body part to stir again. Shit, I'm going to become addicted to her and that's going to be an issue.

"I remember now," Addison says with a smile.

"Do tell . . ."

"Your feet."

"My feet? Think higher, dove."

Her lips part and she sucks in a short breath, as though it just dawned on her. "Ohhhh, that part. You want me to say it?"

"I do."

I want to hear that word fall from her lips. "Your dick."

"Not the right word," I say as though I'm disappointed.

"I can't say it."

"Cock. Say it. You like my cock."

She pulls her bottom lip between her teeth and then sighs. "You really want me to say it?"

"I really fucking do."

"I like your cock."

"What did you like about it?"

"Grady!" She tries to roll off me, but my arms tighten, keeping her right there.

She seems to struggle with the talking part, and I'm going to break her of it. "I want to know, Addy. Did you like when my cock was in your mouth or inside your cunt? Did you like stroking it or maybe you like them all?"

Her cheeks redden and it's so damn adorable. "I liked everything about your cock."

"Good because my cock feels the same, dove."

I slide the tips of my fingers up and down her back, hoping to soothe her as I make her uncomfortable at the same time.

"Why do you call me dove?"

"Because doves are precious, beautiful, innocent, and calming. They symbolize grace and beauty and inner peace. When I look at you, Addy, I see only that."

She smiles. "That's sweet."

"I can be sweet."

"I guess so."

I tickle her for that comment. "Let's get some sleep while we can."

"What do you mean while we can? I'm not even tired now."

I grin and flip her on her back, growing hard again. "No?"

She shakes her head. "Nope."

"Good. Because my mouth, fingers, and cock are nowhere near done with you tonight. Let's see if we can go for three."

I walk her up the stairs to her house, our fingers entwined, both of us with ridiculous smiles on our faces.

"Will you come over later?" she asks.

"I need to do some things first and read to Jett."

"I know, I mean *later*, later."

I laugh once, gently pulling her closer and softly kissing her. "You're going to make me obsessed with you."

"If it leads to more nights and mornings like last night, well, I can't say I'll mind."

Last night was one of the best nights I've ever had. Four times we had sex, and each time was better than the last. Each one fucking with my head as I tried to negotiate some kind of relationship where we continue doing this at least because . . . that would be perfect.

Addison and I can continue to hook up and when she finds someone, then we can stop. Because really, why not?

We're both single, consenting adults who like each other and have really fucking good sex. Two people who care about each other, but there are no strings or requirements. I want to say all this, but we're both worn out and as much as I want to come over here tonight, I have things I need to do on the farm.

"While the idea of coming over here is incredibly appealing, I have to work with the horses tomorrow and I promised Jett I'd take him riding. Not to mention, you need sleep since neither of us got any of that last night."

"You're right."

"Besides, we have next weekend in Oregon where I plan to fuck you six ways till Sunday."

Addison wiggles her brows. "I like the sound of that."

"I like the sounds you make when I'm inside you."

"I like those too."

I shake my head with a chuckle. "Get in the house, dove."

She walks up the steps, stopping at the door, and turns. "Grady?"

"Yes?"

"If you change your mind about tonight, the key is back under the second stone. I wouldn't mind if you used it."

I take the stairs two at a time, standing in front of her half a heartbeat after she uttered the last word. "I want you to climb into bed tonight naked and fall asleep anxious for when I might show, so I wake you up with my tongue buried inside your sweet pussy."

She lets out a soft moan as she pulls my head to hers. "I think I like this new arrangement."

"I know I do." I kiss her, knowing our insane town is watching somewhere. "I'll see you tonight."

twenty-three

ADDISON

There is something to be said about anticipation and it's not good.

It's absolute torture.

Since he dropped me off, I have been nothing but a ball of nerves. I want to talk to someone. I need to talk to someone, which is why, once again, I find myself in the side by side with some ridiculous excuse of needing to bring Brenna her sweater.

Which is actually my sweater.

We pull up to the house and Elodie is already trying to open the door before we stop. She loves Jacob, Brenna's husband. She tells everyone how much she loves him and she wants to marry him.

When she sees him, she squeals, and he scoops her up. Since I've been here, they've become our family. They've welcomed us in and filled the loss we've felt from leaving our home in Oregon.

"Hello, my favorite Elodie," Jacob says and kisses her temple. "You look beautiful."

She blushes and Brenna rolls her eyes. "I swear, kids love him."

"Don't forget the old ladies too. They all like to watch me walk by and make comments about my butt."

I laugh. "Oh, Jacob, you used to be admired by the women my

age too, we all thought, oh that Jacob Arrowood, he's so hot. Now we're like, man, he got old."

He glares at me and his wife bursts out laughing. Jacob is still incredibly good looking, but it's so much fun to watch him get squirrely about aging.

Brenna hooks her arm in mine. "Did I tell you his agent called and wants him to take a role where he'd play an aging actor who can't get hired anymore?"

This is too good. "No? I didn't hear. So it's an autobiography?"

"If I didn't have Elodie in my arms, you'd both be in trouble."

Brenna looks back at her husband from over her shoulder. "Why do you think we're saying it?"

"We go to the treehouse, Uncle Jacob?" Elodie asks.

It's no surprise that's where she wants to go. The Arrowoods have the most incredible treehouse that Connor built for his daughter, Hadley, when she was young. It is literally the most insane thing I've ever seen, and he maintains it still, mostly for Elodie since we lived on their land until we found a place about a year ago.

"Of course. Let's go and leave the women to their cackling."

"We'll be sure to talk about your gray hairs when you're gone!" Brenna yells out as he heads toward the tree line.

When we enter the house, we head back to the open kitchen, and I sit at the counter while Brenna's assessing eyes find mine. "I normally live for our staring contests, but since I know you went to upstate New York with Grady, stayed in a hotel, and you're here the morning after he dropped you off, I'm going to break our trend and demand you spill it."

"We had sex. But it's still fake."

"Fake sex?"

I shake my head. "No, I mean . . . I don't know what I mean. I kept telling myself none of it was real. This relationship wasn't going to last so I wasn't letting my heart even consider this could be anything worth caring about."

"But the sex is?" Brenna asks.

"Yes, of course the sex is real. God, was it real. Did you know that a body can orgasm itself into a coma? Because I feel like that happened."

"Oh, I need to hear this."

Yeah, I can't believe I just said that, but it's true. "Sex with Grady was like nothing I knew possible. The orgasm after orgasm had me seeing stars at some point in the night. It was . . . the best sex I've ever imagined."

Her eyes widen and her smile grows. "Well, that's good!"

"So good. So, so good."

She nods approvingly. "Good job, Grady."

Yeah, if this was a grade, he'd be an A+ with honors. It's why I said what I said before he left, because I'm really hoping for more of that.

"Okay, so sex is real and what's the problem? Did you guys talk about what you're going to be now that you've crossed that line?"

And that's why I'm standing in her kitchen. Because we kind of did. I think we did. I mean, I said I didn't want anything from him, and I mean that.

"Sort of. I told him that I don't want anything from him, that we're adults and it changes nothing. Which I'm completely and totally fine with because I still don't think he wants a serious relationship."

She purses her lips. "You're fine with this?"

"Yes. I mean, we're two adults who are enjoying a little . . . carnal fun."

Brenna stares at me for a heartbeat. "Did you practice that speech on your way over?"

"No."

"It wasn't bad. Slightly believable, a little weak on the ending. I bet Jacob could give you lessons on selling it better."

I sigh heavily, letting my head fall to my arms, unwilling to look at her. "Don't judge me. Please."

My incredibly well-trained friend keeps quiet until I lift my eyes to find hers. There, I find what I always do with her . . . understanding. "I'm not judging at all. I'm happy for my friends or anyone really, when they're doing what they want and makes them happy. My arrangement with Jacob was far from perfect and I have a lot of friends who are completely fine with a friends-with-benefits deal. I guess I'm asking if you are or you're telling yourself you are."

It's hard to answer that because the reality of my life is that I met a boy when I was just a girl, fell in love with him as we both grew up, married him, and then he was killed. I don't really have a clue as to what I am okay with.

Which is probably why I really like that I'm doing this.

I was so ready to have this serious relationship again, to have kids, and a family, but what if this is what I really want?

Just a companion. A friend. Someone I like and who likes me, but there are no strings attached at the end of the day.

If this stops being convenient, then we walk away and no hard feelings.

"What if I don't know?" I ask her.

"That's fine too, Addy. I don't think we have to know the answers, but I remember you were worried that your feelings for Grady weren't at the same place his are."

"I know. I do like him. He's a great guy, but I also am aware of his stance regarding loving someone again."

Brenna watches me. "I need you to explain that."

"He doesn't want it. He has endured the loss of his wife and that was enough for him. Then, he had to give Jett up while he was deployed and I think he struggles with giving a part of himself to anyone else right now."

"That doesn't mean he won't change his mind."

I shrug. "I can't expect or hope for different."

And I get being afraid. I'm still scared, which is why I think this might work out.

"Okay, I'm going to give you advice you aren't prepared for," she warns. "I think you should have as much sex as you want with Grady Whitlock. I mean, bang him until you can't walk and then bang him again if it makes you feel good."

I nearly choke on my breath. "What?"

"I'm serious. You've spent your entire life being in a grown-up relationship. I admire that you want to start dating again. I was *so* not ready, and I don't know that I ever would've been if it weren't for Jacob. What you're doing now is fun and it's consensual and safe. You and Grady are in a committed relationship, no matter where it goes from there. Have fun, Addison. Have orgasms that make you run to your friend's house to tell them about it and question life."

"Like I'm doing now."

She raises her coffee cup. "Exactly. Now, tell me the fun details."

And I do, I tell her about the whole night and the possibility for tonight.

What does one do when waiting for their non-boyfriend/boyfriend to come over and fuck their brains out?

Am I supposed to watch TV? Porn? Does he really want me to be naked? So many questions and so much anxiety around it.

I look at the bed that I am supposed to be naked in when he arrives and then wonder if I can actually do it.

I'm so damn inexperienced. I imagine being someone else, someone like Blakely, who has no reservations about anything in life, and try to channel that.

"Come on, Addy, take the shirt off," I try to pep talk myself, but I can't do it.

I grab my wine glass and drain the contents. Trying not to have a repeat of the last time I drank wine, I only have a glass—not the bottle.

My phone pings and I grab it quickly.

GRADY

Do you still want me to come over tonight?

I chew on my thumbnail. This is my out. I can tell him no,

pretend I'm sleeping, go move the key, and just . . . wait for our trip in a few days.

Or I can do like Brenna said and have all the orgasms I can get.

> The key is where I said it would be.

GRADY
I'm aware. I'm holding it in my hand. Should I use the key, dove?

I squeak and drop the phone. Shit.

I'm not ready. I'm not naked in bed like he said to be.

But again, what if that was a test?

Maybe he'll spank me for not listening.

Do I want that? Gah! I'm so not sexy.

I reach for the phone that fell under the bed and see another text.

GRADY
Addy?

> Yes. I want you to use the key.

Okay, I said. I did it. I sent the text. I'm a grown adult who is committing to a sexual relationship with a man who is very good at it.

Go me.

GRADY
Are you wet?

I'm beet red, that's what I am.

> Nope. I showered earlier.

GRADY
That's not what I mean.

I really wish I was sultry and not awkward.

> You weren't very specific.

GRADY

> Fair enough. Is your pussy dripping wet, knowing right now I'm sliding the key in your door, turning the lock, and when I find you naked, legs spread, I'm going to put my mouth there and make you come in less than five minutes?

Yeah, it totally is.

However, he's not going to find that if I don't get a move on. I tear my shirt off, tossing it to the floor. I hear the front door close, and I'm filled with excitement and nerves.

I walk around the other side of the bed, grab the photo of Isaac, and smile. "Sorry, honey, not tonight." I quickly place it in the drawer, rushing back around.

Grady's footsteps grow closer, and I hear him hit the last step.

Shit.

I work my shorts and panties down, but I'm too late.

"You're not naked," his deep voice is soft, but still startles me.

I go to turn quickly, but my shorts are down around my knees and my legs tangle. I flop on the bed—ungracefully I might add— and I hear him chuckle.

"I did say I wanted you on the bed."

"I seriously suck at this sexy thing," I mutter to the sheets and start to press myself up, but his hand on my back stills me.

"Stay there," Grady's raspy voice commands, his face at my ear.

The heat from his body leaves me and I obey him, laying here, ass up, on the bed.

Something hits the floor, I'm guessing his belt by the way the metal clanks. I go to move my head, wanting to see, but he makes a noise in his throat.

"Don't move, Addison." The tip of his finger moves from my

thigh up over one ass cheek. "I wanted you naked, on the bed with your legs spread."

"You're early."

"I couldn't wait. All day long I've been imagining this. Imagining you waiting for me. Have you thought about it?"

God, have I ever. "Yes."

His palm slides over my ass and then squeezes. "But not enough to let me walk in and find you ready?"

He's toying with me, and I'm so fucking turned on by it. "Grady . . ."

"Have you ever been spanked, dove?"

I want to bury myself in the covers and die. However, I remember my entire damn plan so I don't back down. "No."

His finger rubs against my clit and then he pushes inside me. The intrusion is so sudden, I gasp and rock forward. "While I wish this was my tongue, I'm going to finger you and then slap your ass for making me wait."

"O-Okay," I say hesitantly.

He leans down, lips at my ear. "Next time I tell you to be ready for me, I won't have to do this, but by how your cunt is milking my finger, I think you want to be spanked and then fucked."

I swear, I am going to orgasm at just his words. He pushes his finger deeper, harder, and then I feel it. The slap of his hand on my ass.

Before I can draw another breath, he does it again. I let out a moan and I'm not sure if it's pain or because I really fucking like it.

Grady grunts as he pushes another finger in and then he shoves me up on the bed, my knees bent, ass up in the air, as he slides under me before I feel his tongue. He slides it against my clit as his fingers pump hard.

I want to cry out, to beg him to stop because my body is falling apart. He pulls his fingers out and I whimper at the loss. "No!"

"Shh," he coaxes and then his tongue is doing these delicious circles against my throbbing clit. I feel as though I am being pulled apart as the pleasure builds.

I start to shift, and then a loud slap on my ass comes again, but his mouth never leaves me. He keeps going, his other hand gently rubbing the spot he just swatted. Then he slides it down my ass and pushes his fingers deep again, fucking me with his hand as the pleasure becomes too much.

Between his mouth and his fingers, I can't hold back.

I bury my face in the bed, biting down as the most incredible orgasm washes over me. Each wave is stronger than the last and I swear it's going to wash me out to sea when it leaves.

Grady adjusts me so he's hovering over me now and I can look at his beautiful face.

"Hi." The cocky edge to his voice makes me smile as I pant.

"Hi yourself."

He grins, and I wonder if that wasn't his way of checking if I am okay with what just happened. Although, if my orgasm was any indication—I am incredibly okay.

"We're good?"

I nod. "Very."

His hands move to his shirt where he tugs it off from the back of his neck, leaving me to look at his glorious body. I swear, this man has muscles where I didn't even know someone could. His skin is tight against every part of him, and those arms, dear Lord, save me. I love the way they flex as he moves his body. Then he drops his pants, his thick, hard cock jutting out.

He wraps his fingers around it, stroking. "Do you know how many times I wrap my hand around my cock imagining it's your lips?"

I shake my head. "Tell me."

"Every fucking day. I get in the shower, my hand resting on the wall as I stroke myself, wishing it's your mouth that's making my cock slick. Imagining it's this pretty pussy and all your sweetness and heat coating it. Tonight, I get to have that wish again."

"Grady," I say his name softly.

"Do you want me to fill you, dove?"

"Yes," I pant.

"Do you want it hard and rough?"

"Yes."

I want it so much. I want to feel good and lost with him. It's not the same kind of loss I've had before, it's more of a euphoric freeing that's addictive.

"Thank fucking God."

Then he rams into me. He grabs my legs, hooking them over his arms as he drives into me. I'm still sore from all the sex we had last night, but it feels good.

He shoves deeper, lifting my hips and thrusting savagely. Every part of me is owned by him. The sounds of our skin slapping, his breathing, my panting, and the thick smell of sex in the room.

It's everything I've never known I could have.

Grady digs his fingers into my hips as he works to find a new angle, and then, like a train without brakes, my orgasm crashes over me. I bite my lip to keep from screaming, tears fill my vision as the force of my climax is so intense.

I score my fingers into his forearms, needing to grip something as I fall apart.

"Fuck, Addison!" he moans loudly and follows me over.

Grady slumps forward, his breathing labored as the two of us fight for air.

I swear, I have never in my life had anything that intense. I think I might be dead.

Because no way was I living before that.

He pushes up, smirking down at me. "Feel free to disobey me anytime if that's the kind of sex we have after."

I laugh once and exhale. "Feel free to break into my house every night."

And the sad part is that I mean it.

twenty-four
GRADY

It's midnight and I can't sleep. Tonight is the first night in three days that I'm not sneaking out to go to Addison's and fuck her until I can't see straight. This living with my sister thing is making that part easy.

However, we both need sleep before we leave in mere days. Only, that's not happening.

I grab my phone and text her.

> Hi.

Addison replies a second later.

ADDISON
> Hi to you too, sailor.

> You're awake?

Obviously, she's awake.

ADDISON
> Yes, but why are you?

> Thinking of you …

. . .

I type the above message, but delete before sending and then rewrite what I should say so she doesn't get any ideas that I lie in bed at night thinking of her. Because I do, but I don't. Not like that.

> Thinking of work stuff, the meeting when we get back from the wedding, being away from Jett for a few days. And then the fact that I really wish my cock was deep inside you right now.

ADDISON

> We'll take these issues one at a time. First, work stuff . . . you had a big job today so clearly the courier business is picking up. For the meeting . . . you're going to get the investment. It'll be great. Being away from Jett, that's always hard. I can't say anything because when we go and Elodie is here with my mother-in-law, I'll be the same.

That's another big thing. Addison's mother-in-law is coming in a few days to stay with Elodie while we go to Oregon. At first, Addy was bringing her, and she was going to stay in Rose Canyon with her grandma. However, once the news that Addison was dating hit her radar, she decided she wanted to come out here instead.

I have two choices, I either man up and be the guy that she needs me to be to her or I hide out and come up with some bullshit excuse.

Addison's friendship matters to me, so I'll go there, meet her mother-in-law, and hopefully pave the way for the next guy.

> You forgot the last issue I was having.

ADDISON

> You'll have to figure that one out.

I grin. This conversation I can handle.

> Are you saying you want me to come over?

The bubbles on the screen pop up. Then go away. Then pop back up, before finally the text comes through.

ADDISON
I'm saying we should be sleeping.

> That's not a no?

ADDISON
You need a hobby. You should take up flying. I hear it's a real time suck.

> I have something else that needs to be sucked.

ADDISON
That sounds like a you problem.

> It does, huh?

ADDISON
Yup.

I laugh, imagining her face turning red with embarrassment. She's so fucking cute and I wish I was a different man, a better one. I wish I could unlive the hell I've been through so that I was in a head space that would allow me to be more for her.

However, already the relationship she has with Jett terrifies me. The kid doesn't even want to go into daycare without Addison and Elodie. He asks about going to their house almost every damn day for dinner or to play.

While a lot of it is that he adores Elodie, I see how much he likes Addy too.

I have to protect him as much as I can. He is lucky that when he lost his mother, he was too young to ever feel that pain. I did. I felt it for him and for me. I grieved for the both of us and it's my job as a father to ensure he doesn't know that incredible level of sadness.

Not to mention, this has been a huge adjustment for the both of us. I'm trying to be a full-time father after he was living with her parents. I visited all the time, and they came to me, but there were months when I couldn't. Times where Jett only saw me on a phone screen. I need to build this relationship with him.

I roll over, adjusting the pillow and forcing myself to put some more distance between us. In a week or two, I might have my funding and the wedding will be over. Which means this arrangement will be too.

> It's late, dove. Get some sleep. I'll see you tomorrow.

ADDISON

> Are you okay?

> Yeah, why?

Then her face is filling my screen as the video ring plays. I swipe to answer and I swear my fucking heart stops when I see her beautiful face. Her eyes are soft, hair pulled up on the top of her head the way girls do, and there's just a soft glow from her bedside table. She's so fucking gorgeous.

"Because you went from playful to going to sleep," Addy says before I can speak.

"I'm fine, just finally got a little tired. Why couldn't you sleep?"

She rolls over so she's on her stomach and sighs. "I guess I'm nervous about my mother-in-law. I have always been really close with Judy, and it feels different having you meet her. She was Isaac's mother and I can imagine the pain she's going to feel when she sees me with another man."

"Maybe I shouldn't meet her," I suggest. "I can take a courier job and then she just doesn't have to meet me."

"I thought of that, but you know, one of the perks of us is that the hard stuff isn't so hard. Having her meet you might be the best possibility. If she hates you, then you're gone in a few weeks and all is well."

I laugh and shake my head. "I haven't met a woman who doesn't love me."

"I can think of a few."

That has me sitting in a second. "Who?"

"Mrs. Symonds doesn't think you're good enough for me."

Jesus, those women are maddening. "She's right."

Addy nods. "I know, I told her we were both aware of the fact that I am much too perfect for the likes of you."

"And yet, you still begged for my cock last night."

The blush I love so much returns to her face. "You say things just to shock me."

"I do," I admit. "I'm breaking you out of that box you put yourself in."

It's one of the things I'm enjoying the most. Watching her learn what she likes and trusting me to give it to her is something I don't take for granted. It's also been the best sex of my life and why I crave it so much.

"You're doing a good job of it."

"I wish I was doing it right now."

Her smile is soft as she rolls onto her back. She bites her lower lip for a second and I know that's her sign that she wants to say or do something, but is building the courage. I stay silent, hoping to all that's holy it's that she wants me to get up and go there. If she asks it, I won't have the strength to say no.

"Grady?" She moves the phone to the side table and her hand moves down her chest to her shorts. "How fast can you get here? I'm starting without you."

I'm already out of the bed, throwing my shorts on. "Don't touch your clit."

"But it's aching."

"I want it throbbing when I get there," I say, searching for my damn keys. "I want it pulsing knowing I'm coming to make it feel better."

"What can I do? Can I finger myself as I imagine it's you?"

Fuck the keys. I'll run.

I'm down the stairs in the fastest I think I've ever done and out the back door. It's fucking freezing, but I give zero fucks. I start to jog to her house, wishing so desperately I was there already.

"I'll be there in five minutes and, dove, you're not getting any sleep tonight." I hang up and run, eternally grateful I live with my sister.

I'm slipping back in through the back door, trying to keep quiet after spending thirty minutes trying to find the key my sister hid because my asshole-self left without my keys, which meant I couldn't get back in the house after leaving a very sated and sleeping Addison in her bed.

The light flips on as soon as I close the door, my sister sitting at the table, coffee in hand, leaning back like my mother would've done if I were seventeen.

"Late night?" she asks with a smirk.

"I went for a run."

"Did you?" Brynn pushes. "A run to where?"

"Does a run have a place when you end up at home?"

Brynn quirks a brow. "What time did you leave for said run?"

"Early."

She nods. "I see. And did you stop, maybe get some water, or engage in another type of workout?"

I let out a heavy breath. Not a chance in hell am I telling her any of this. "Let's remember you're my baby sister and not my mother."

She grins. "I am that, but I also love you and it's my job to make sure my asshat brothers don't fuck things up."

"When did you earn that responsibility?"

Brynlee shrugs. "The day I was born."

"Missed that memo."

She pushes a coffee mug to me and while I'd love to tell her to eat shit and walk upstairs, she has also been a huge help and it's

250

pretty much impossible for me to hurt her feelings and not hate myself later.

Pity I have that trait.

"Thanks." I take the coffee, knowing I'm going to need many cups if I have to get through today, and make a note to cancel any flying for the day. No way should I be operating a plane when I'm this exhausted.

Brynlee sits quietly while I take a few sips. God knows it's not going to last long so I soak it up and think of some good comebacks when the interrogation begins.

"Grady?"

"Yes, my beautiful, annoying, and intrusive sister, Brynn?"

"I hate brothers." She sighs and then her tone turns serious and concerned. "Are you okay?"

Okay, not what I thought was going to be her strategy. "Why wouldn't I be?"

"Oh, I don't know, this is the first time you've dated and slept with someone since you lost Lisa, you're starting a business, raising Jett on your own, and just moved here. Why would you possibly be a mess?"

I really don't want to talk about this with her.

"How do you know it's the first since Lisa?" I figure that's the most uncomfortable part for her and where I'm likely to have an out.

"Because you told Rowan and he told me."

"So do you all sit around and talk about me?"

I pretend to be offended.

Brynn doesn't buy it. "Like you don't talk about the rest of us? I'm serious."

"I'm fine, Brynn."

"Are you?"

I drain my coffee and grab the pot, filling it back up. "I really am."

"So your feelings for Addison don't scare you?"

No, they terrify the fuck out of me. In fact, I'm pretending I just don't have feelings because it's much easier. I can't have feelings for her because we're temporary. Not to mention, I'm not about to let my heart take over something that will only end up with my son being crushed.

"I'm not sure what my feelings are. We're taking things slow and we're both happy with how things are."

She lifts one brow and laughs. "If that's not the biggest load of bullshit I've ever heard. Grady, you're over there all the time. Every night since you had your night together. You care about her."

"Of course I care about her."

My sister sighs heavily. "You're also the smartest of my brothers so don't play stupid."

"I really am the smartest." I lean back, enjoying this line of the conversation much more. "I think I'm also the best looking, but I'm sure Asher thinks it's him. No, I take that back, definitely Rowan."

"I take back saying you were smart," she mutters.

"If you had to pick the better looking one, it would be me, right?" Brynn just shakes her head. I know she's coming from a place of concern, so I let her off the hook. "I promise, I'm really aware of what I'm doing and I'm being careful."

Although the fact that I went back over last night after saying I wasn't going there sort of proves otherwise.

"Okay. I just had to ask."

I stand, kiss the top of her head. "Thank you, you're a good sister. No matter what Rowan says."

She slaps my stomach and laughs. When I start to walk toward the sink, she grabs my wrist. "I worry about you. I worry about all of you, but you more than the other two. You told me a few weeks ago you never wanted another relationship and now you're dating Addison, who very much wants love again. Are you sure you know what you're doing?"

I should tell her the truth, but I don't. I won't do that to Addison and we have a plan. We leave in days for Rose Canyon. We will have fun, come back, hopefully I'll get the investment, and then we will go back to being friends.

Maybe even friends who fuck.

I give my sister a tight smile. "I'm sure."

And I'm sure I'm full of shit.

twenty-five
ADDISON

"I go first, Jett!" Elodie yells as the two kids rush off to the play area in the back of Brynn's house.

"Me first!" Jett tries to run faster, but Elodie has a little head start.

Grady laughs and takes my hand in his as we follow behind. It's been two days since I saw him. The night he was going to come over, Jett had a nightmare and he stayed. This morning, I had a video call with Blakely about a possible benefactor who wants to give us a lot of money and expand Run to Me in a way both of us never dreamed of.

However, the very sweet text asking me to come once I picked Elodie up because he wanted to see us had me driving right over here.

"How was your day?" I ask as we near the play set.

"Good. I got a call from Mateo, wanting to have a meeting tonight."

"Tonight?"

He nods. "He's in town, wants to talk about possibly investing, and I meet him at seven."

I'm so happy for him. "That's amazing."

"It will be if I get the money."

255

"You will."

Grady squeezes my hand a little. "After the call, I went to the county office for two hours, trying to figure out what the holdup is with the permits, got a vague answer and a promise to get it pushed through in the next week, and thought about you and me getting naked very soon."

"I like that last part," I admit.

"Thought you might." He pulls me to the blanket and cooler over to the left.

"What's this?" I ask as I sit and he hands me a bouquet of flowers.

"A single-parent version of dinner."

I smile. "I see."

"Kids run around, we sit and watch, and eat whatever I could find out of Brynn's kitchen."

"Well the flowers are beautiful, thank you."

"You're beautiful."

I feel the heat rise in my cheeks. I love that he makes me blush. "You're biased, since you're getting some."

"Am I?"

I nod. "You are."

"I don't think so. I thought you were beautiful before I got to do very rude things to you. I'm just smart enough now to say it in the hopes I get to do more of it."

I glance over at the kids, who are climbing up the rock wall, ignoring us completely, and lean in, brushing my lips against his.

"I think I'm a pretty sure thing. Now, what do you have in here?" I ask as I lift the latch to the cooler and laugh at the contents. Inside is a packet of Pop-Tarts, a half-eaten bag of Oreo cookies, a jug of milk, which is always available around here, chips, juice boxes, and string cheese. "I see we have a very good variety."

"As I said, I grabbed what I could."

I pull out the milk and cookies because, how can that combo ever be wrong? He smiles, making me want to kiss him again, but instead I pour the milk and open the cookies.

"To sex in different states and multiple orgasms," Grady says, lifting his Oreo.

"To a man who knows how to do the multiples thing." I tap his cookie with mine and we both take a bite.

"I'm going to miss that part," Grady notes.

"What?"

"The sex, once we end this."

Right. We end this. Duh. I know this, but for a second there I let myself forget. "Well, anytime I need a booty call, I'll text you first."

He laughs. "I'm flattered."

"You should be, I don't make that promise lightly."

"No?"

I shake my head. "Nope. I'm pretty picky on that front."

He leans back on one arm. "I'm glad I made the cut."

"For now. Once I'm forced back into the dating pool, who knows what I'll find."

"Oh, yes, we could always call Dan, he was pretty boastful."

I shudder at that thought. "I'll pass on him."

"What about the first guy, Phil?"

Oh, Phil. "Yes, poor Phil. He was so sad at the meeting last week. He convinced himself we had a connection, and he was thinking of ways to cut back on the video games to make me a priority."

"Very magnanimous of him."

I slap his chest playfully. "Whatever. I'm stuck with you for another week, and you give me nothing."

"I give you orgasms. Lots of them."

"How magnanimous of you," I toss back at him.

"I'm a giver."

I roll my eyes. "Yes, a bleeding heart you are."

Jett and Elodie run over, big smiles on their faces. "Tan I have a cookie, Mommy?" Elodie asks.

"You may have one cookie and then we're going to head home for a real dinner."

"Can I have one too, Daddy?" Jett asks Grady.

He hands him one and the two kids squeal. "Will you push me on the swing?" Elodie asks sweetly.

I start to move, but Grady rests his hand on my arm. "Can I push you instead?" he asks, already getting to his feet.

"Daddy pushes high to the sky!" Jett tells Elodie.

"I like to go high!" Elodie tells Grady.

"Well, then you better hurry so we can fly," Grady says as he starts to move toward the swings.

Her eyes fill with delight and she rushes to the swing, Grady following. I sit here, on the blanket, and something inside of me both aches and lifts. It's crazy how it can be both at the same time, but here is this man, who I really freaking like, playing with my daughter without even a second thought.

A single tear rolls down my cheek as a mix of joy and sadness fills my chest. It's going to hurt when I lose this. I brush it away and promise that will be the only tear I cry because you can't lose something you never had.

And I never had Grady.

Not for real anyway, but I'm going to hate losing him.

"Oh, Addison, darling, this place looks amazing," my mother-in-law says as she looks around the house. The last time she was here was about a year ago and I definitely wasn't settled.

"It's really become a home," I tell her.

She walks over to the side table where there's a picture of Isaac and me holding Elodie the day she was born. It's one of my favorite photos in the world. "He would love this." I don't say anything but a piece of my chest aches. "He would really want you to be happy and living on, even if he can't be here."

He would. Isaac didn't believe in love being selfish and we would laugh often because I would tell him if I died, I didn't want him to be happy for at least a set time. It was only fair. He disagreed and hoped I found love immediately.

I just don't know how he could've ever thought it was possible to do. He was the only man I ever loved. The only man I've ever been with and it took me three years to finally be ready to try again.

I try really hard not to think about the fact that this would not be his idea of moving on, but I think he'd understand.

Maybe.

"I'm trying," I admit to her.

Elodie comes in holding her baby doll that Judy bought her. "I have baby!"

Judy smiles. "I see, did you name her?"

"Baby."

I fight back the laugh sitting in my throat.

"You named the baby, Baby?" Judy asks.

"Her name is Baby," Elodie informs her with pride in her little voice.

"Okay then."

And then my little firecracker is gone and running out the door to find something else to show her.

Judy and I sit in the living room, waiting for her return, and she places her hands in her lap. "Addy?"

"Yes?"

"Are you happy with this new guy?"

I have to hand it to her, she waited a whole lot longer than I thought. I was prepared for this deep conversation in the car on the way here, but nothing, just small talk and about Brielle and Spencer. Then, we got here, settled her in, and still not a word about Grady.

I was just starting to relax. I should've known better.

However, of all the lies I've told, Judy is the one person who doesn't deserve it. She is a second mother to me. All my life, she's supported and loved me. This all ends in a few days if he gets the funding, and I really don't want to see her endure the pain of our falsehood.

I go to open my mouth to tell her the truth, but she beats me to it.

"Don't say anything, please. I debated talking about this with you, and Brielle urged me not to, said that she met him and liked him. That you are finally getting out there and no matter what, it's your choice. I think it's just that, you've always been part mine." She smiles and tilts her head. "You've been coming to my house since you were a little girl with those four boys. There's not a time in Isaac's life that you weren't right at his side. I came because I wanted to meet him. I shouldn't have changed my plans because of that."

"Mom," I say, needing her to stop. "My relationship with Grady is complicated."

"Life is complicated, isn't it?"

That's an understatement.

"It is."

She smiles softly. "Whatever your relationship with Grady is, is yours and his. Complicated or not, I'm sorry I forced you into doing something you might not have been ready for. Or maybe it's that I'm not ready for it."

My throat gets tight at that thought. All this time I was kind of worried about me, but Judy is probably struggling in her own way. I come over to the couch, sitting and taking her hand in mine. "I never wanted to hurt you."

Her eyes widen. "Addy, no. I didn't think that. It wasn't really until I was on the plane coming here that it hit me. It's been three years since he died and some days it feels like yesterday."

"I know what you mean."

"I guess what I'm saying is that maybe I can meet your new boyfriend when you get back from Rose Canyon. If that's all right with you." She pats my hand.

"It is."

"Good." She rises. "Now, I better get in that playroom and soak up every minute I have with Elodie. I want to enjoy every second I have with my granddaughter."

twenty-six

ADDISON

"It'll be fine. This is going to be fine, all will go off without bloodshed," I whisper to myself as Grady and I walk up to Emmett and Blakely Maxwell's house.

While he's met Blakely and Brielle, Emmett, Spencer, and Holden are different. They were Isaac's best friends. They are my best friends. Blakely is in by marriage and as Isaac's baby sister, Brielle was always around.

These guys—they're *my* guys.

The ones who will want to instill the fear of God in Grady, which is funny because I don't think he's afraid of anything.

Grady chuckles and pulls me to a stop. "Relax, dove. I'm perfectly capable of handling them. It will be fine."

He is so sure of this. He has no idea how protective they are . . . it's ridiculous. I've tried to warn him, he claims it'll be no big deal.

I beg to differ.

"You keep saying that, but I'm not buying it."

"Then, we'll just have to prove you wrong." He turns, pulling me to his chest. "What has you so scared?"

"Uhh, they're insane."

"And?"

"They won't like this. They don't even understand a world where I'm with another man. I know it sounds stupid, but I've known them since I was eight. Eight. And I was Isaac's girl from like then on."

"They also know he's gone and that you weren't coming to this wedding alone."

He has a point, but that doesn't really matter to the dummies inside.

"It was theoretical then."

"And now it's reality. Look, we did this arrangement for this exact thing. Nothing they say to me is going to actually be an issue. We both know that. They can be dicks to me, so the next guy who comes along doesn't have to endure it as bad."

"Right. You're right." He is doing this to prepare them for when I meet my forever guy. You know, once I get back to Sugarloaf and back in the dating pool.

"I know I am. Come on, let's go in."

I've never seen anyone excited for their execution, but here we are.

As I lift my hand to knock on the door, it flies open and there are Emmett, Spencer, and Holden, all standing with their chests puffed out and arms crossed.

Dear God, it's literally as I imagined it.

"So, you're with Addison?" Emmett's deep voice, which I'm pretty sure he's trying to make deeper and threatening, asks.

Instead of nerves, I feel anger towards these idiots who are like brothers to me. "Are you three kidding?" I ask.

I glare at Holden first because he's the first who will crack. Which he does. His arms fall and he tilts his head. "Hi, Addy."

I don't reply, I move my eyes to the next jackass who will fall—Spencer. "Do you want me to kick you in the shin?" I ask. "Because I totally will."

His arms drop and then I see him wince as his head dips forward. "Really, Brie? You hit me?"

She pushes through and slaps his chest. "No one can leave you three alone without you being fools. You're lucky I didn't do more. Hey, Addy! Grady, it's great to see you again," my sister-in-law says and then pulls me in for a hug, and then hugs Grady.

"This is Holden, Spencer, and Emmett," I say to Grady.

Grady steps forward, extending his hand to Emmett, who still hasn't moved. "I understand you were an Army Ranger? I was fortunate enough to get to know a few when I was on deployment."

Instantly I see Emmett's stance relax. "Were you army?"

"No, I was a fighter pilot in the navy. I got out a few months ago after my commission was done."

Emmett shakes his hand. "I met a few pilots as well. Where were you stationed?"

The two of them keep talking and I swear I feel like I can breathe for the first time. Then Grady turns to Spencer, shaking his hand before finishing with Holden.

They all talk, very superficially, but the hostility is gone. Brie nudges me with a smile, her voice low so only I can hear. "Seems he even won over the guys in a matter of seconds."

I shake my head in disbelief. "I'm shooketh."

She laughs. "He's a good guy and we all threatened castration."

I let out a loud laugh and hook my arm in my sister's. "Good plan."

"All right, let's all get inside where you can start the interrogation where we will all yell at you and then you guys will become friends," Brie says while ushering them in.

And just like that, I relax because I know these people love me and will always have my back.

"Your friends are great," Grady says as we are unpacking our things at the apartment that Brielle is letting us stay in. Instead of selling it when she married Spencer, they kept it and use it as a guest house when either Elodie and I or Judy come to visit.

"My friends are crazy and took all your money," I note. Tonight was the boys' weekly poker game and they, wanting to make their wives and me happy, asked Grady to play.

They fleeced him.

He comes up behind me, wrapping his arms around my middle, his scruff brushing against my neck. "Have I ever told you that I played poker almost every day when I was overseas?"

I grin, resting my head on his shoulder. "You didn't."

"Well, I did with a few of my buddies. By the end of the deployment, I was about five thousand dollars richer, and it wasn't from bonus pay."

I bite my lower lip as I laugh. "You let them beat you."

"I let them think they beat me."

"Is there a difference?" I ask, turning around to face him. My arms rest on his shoulders and I get lost in his green eyes.

Then a part of me is sad. This will end soon, we'll go back to being friends who don't have moments of touching. Friends who wave as we pass each other at school again or in the diner.

Friends who don't kiss or share moments of intimacy again.

And I want that.

I need it.

If this is the last weekend we might have together, then damn it, I want every possible second to be something I can recall when I'm lonely again.

"Would there be a difference if we had sex and I orgasmed or faked it?"

He pulls me against him so there's no room between our bodies. "You know there is."

I move my finger from the base of his throat down his chest. "Spoiler alert, I never have."

"I would know."

"You would?"

His face moves close, nose brushing against mine, and then his words are a whisper against my skin. "I would, dove. I would know if your moans were fake, the pulsing of your tight pussy wasn't milking my cock the way it does. I'd know."

"I'm not sure I believe you," I say back with a challenge hanging at the end. "I'm a very good actress."

I'm full of shit on that one. I actually suck at acting. Sure, we're both fooling everyone we know, but it's also not hard to like Grady and want more with him.

"Not that good. I would know."

I grin. "Prove it."

Before the last syllable is out, he lifts me in his arms, carrying me to the bed, but he stops before we get there, my feet hitting the floor.

His one arm wraps around my back, the other hand gripping my chin. "Do you know anyone who lives in this building?"

The question confuses me, but I nod. A few of my friends still live here. "Yes. Why?"

"Because tomorrow, you're going to be embarrassed when you see them because tonight, they're going to hear you scream my name as I make you come several fucking times."

"I can be quiet."

His eyes flash and I know I'm in for it. "You won't. Maybe the first, maybe even the second time, but by the third, you won't have the ability to keep quiet."

"Third?" I ask, now wondering if this game was a good idea.

His hand at my chin drops, moving to the back of my head where his fingers tighten in my hair. "The first one, I'm not even going to touch you. You're going to come with my cock in your mouth. Get on your knees, Addison. Let's see how quiet you can stay."

The deep timbre of his voice has my stomach clenching and I want to say no, to deny him, but I can't. I want every perfect orgasm this man will give me.

So I step back and start to lower myself, but he grabs me, pulling me back up. "Strip first."

The command unfurls something inside of me. I really fucking like it when he's bossy this way. Maybe it's because this is the only place it is so prevalent. Maybe because in my entire life, I've never known how sexy it is. Whatever the reason is, my body responds to it—to him.

I lift my shirt over my head, tossing it on the floor, then hook my fingers in my leggings and slide those down.

Grady looks at me and jerks his chin. "The bra and underwear too, dove. I want to see every inch of you as my cock is in your mouth and you're writhing as you fall apart."

I'm not saying I hate sucking dick, but never before have I come while doing it. But I issued this challenge and if he can make me come three times, I might just fall in love with him.

I do as he asks, standing naked in front of him. "You're stunning, Addy. You're so beautiful, every fucking inch of you is perfect. After you're a good girl and come for me once, I'm going to enjoy touching every part of you."

His words alone have me wet. "No one said you couldn't touch me."

"You think you can fake it and I won't know. I'll be able to tell standing here." He lifts his shirt over his head and then starts on his belt and pants. "I'll know. I'll know without feeling the way you grip me like a vise. I'll know without your warmth flooding my cock, bathing it because your body loses control. So here's what I want." Grady steps closer, but not touching me at all. Instead, his hand is wrapped around his cock as he's stroking himself. "I want you on your knees, sucking my cock and touching yourself. I want you to try to fake it and when I call you out on it, you do exactly what I tell you to do. Understand?"

Oh, yeah, I'm so in for it, but not in a bad way.

"I understand."

"Now, baby, suck my dick and make yourself come."

I lower to my knees, my hand trailing from his chest to his dick where his hand falls away, refusing to touch me. Something about that alone has my body tight. I like his touch and want it, but he's keeping it from me, until I orgasm first.

In the last three years, I've gotten pretty good at self-pleasure. I've had no other choice, so making myself come won't be hard, especially because I'll have Grady there, watching and fucking my mouth.

I lick around the tip of his cock, an idea dawning on me. I look up through my lashes at his beautiful face. The strong jawline is tight, green eyes blazing with heat, and his dirty blond hair falling forward. "Are you going to touch me at all?"

He shakes his head. "Not until you come first."

Now it's my turn to grin. "Pity."

It means I can torture him the way he plans to do to me. I take his cock in my hand, pulling it toward my mouth, and run my tongue around the tip slowly. I lick the little bead of moisture and make a humming sound.

"Addison," Grady says my name as both a warning and a plea, but no way am I giving in yet.

Turnabout is fair play.

Plus, I want this night to last as long as it can. I want every one of these next few nights to go on forever.

"Hmm?" I ask as I make another slow loop around the top.

"Suck my cock, dove."

"I'm not sure I know how you want me to do that," I say innocently.

"Fuck," he groans as I take my tongue down the backside. "Lick it again."

I do as he asks. Sliding my tongue back up. "Like that?"

His jaw is clenched. "Yeah, baby, lick it just like an ice cream cone."

I do it more, licking the sides, the tip, the bottom, but not putting it in my mouth fully.

"Now I want you to suck."

"The whole thing?" I keep playing as though I don't know what to do.

"Yes, take my cock in your hand and put it in your mouth."

Okay, maybe I am going to come without him touching me. I do as he asks, loving the way his voice sounds strained as he's trying to command me.

My fingers wrap around his cock and I put just the tip in. His head falls back, a moan escaping his lips. I pull back a little and then he thrusts his hips, forcing me to take more of him.

"Stay like that, dove. I'm going to fuck your mouth and while I do it, I want your hands between your legs, playing with your clit."

I want his hands, his mouth, his touch so bad I'm literally aching for it.

I try to keep steady because he's pumping his hips slowly, his eyes finding mine. "Now, Addy. Move your hand down your chest, touch those beautiful breasts." I do it because honestly, I'm on fire. I need to release. "That's it. If it was my hands, I'd tweak that nipple, twist it between my fingers."

Unsure if that's a command, I do it, imagining it is his touch. Those calloused fingers touching me the exact way I want.

I moan, my eyes closing as he pushes deeper.

"Now, go lower, find your clit, sweetheart. But don't touch it hard, just a little."

My fingers slide through my wetness, and I have to use every ounce of control not to scream, not that I could make any sound with his dick in my mouth.

"Now I want you to play with yourself and convince me you're faking it."

I don't know that I can fake it. I'm so close already. I want to argue, but I'm desperate.

So, I start to whimper, my finger making circles, forcing me higher.

Grady stills. "Give me your eyes, Addison."

I lift my gaze to his, his hips still rhythmically moving as though we have all the time in the world.

He looks down at me. "You look like a fucking goddess on your knees, hand touching your perfect skin, my cock in your mouth as spit drips down your chin."

I moan again. My God, this is happening.

"It feels good, doesn't it? You're such a good girl, sucking my cock like it's your favorite thing."

Yeah, it is my favorite thing. However, I can't speak to tell him that, so I hope my eyes do.

"Now, I want you to orgasm. If you're not there, fake it. I'll tell you if it's real or not."

I circle my clit faster. There's no faking it. The way he's looking at me, talking to me, pushing me higher without him putting a single finger on me.

God, I can't stop.

His dick in my mouth, pumping slowly. I want it faster. I want him to feel this out of control too. It's not fair that it's just me.

I move my head faster, my other hand wrapped around his cock, sucking him deeper in my throat as my orgasm is right at the top.

But he pulls away, leaving my lips, and I cry out. Wanting him back. "Grady!" I scream in frustration, my knees aching, and desperate for an orgasm.

I circle my clit, flicking it harder so I can get there before I die. I part my legs to give myself better access, and then he touches me, just a little. He pulls my chin up so I can look at him. "I want to hear it, dove."

The endearment, the sweet endearment and the connection between us is so intense, I can't hold back. I close my eyes and let the pleasure of it wash over me as my orgasm rocks through me.

Grady pushes my hand aside and sinks his finger in, fucking me with his hand as I fall apart. My head falls forward to his chest as I pant with my heart racing. "That's it, baby, let it go. I have you."

When it finally stops, he smiles at me. "That was real."

"Yeah, no shit," I say with a laugh.

"Now, as promised, we're going to try for two."

He scoops me up, bringing me to the bed, and this time he's on his knees, my legs over his shoulders, and he makes me come again.

It feels weird being here, but when I mentioned to Grady that I wanted to visit Isaac's grave, he asked if he could go with me.

So, we're here, walking hand in hand to the gravesite.

"It's beautiful here," Grady observes. "I've never seen a cemetery like this."

"Do you see that spot over there?" I point to the cliff that juts out to a point. "That's where he proposed to me. This cliff, the fact that you can hear the ocean is why I made this his final resting place." That and really there aren't many cemeteries around here.

Grady squeezes my hand. "I'm sure he's at peace."

Well, if he was, I have no idea if he will be with me bringing a guy to his grave, but I needed to visit him today, and a part of me thinks Isaac would've liked Grady. Minus the sleeping with me thing.

We approach the headstone where Davis is written in big block letters with a football etched in the top corner. "Hi, baby," I say as I sink down to my knees, brushing away the dirt off the bottom. "It's been a while and I brought a friend I wanted you to meet. He met the guys already—and survived, so that's something. I . . . well, he's here as my date for Jenna's wedding. So, you know, awkward me talking out loud about this. Anyway." I adjust a few of the items that are here from the town, making it a little more organized as I ramble. "Elodie is getting so big. She's got a best friend, his name is Jett and he's Grady's son. The two of them are so cute together and I'm sure you'd love watching them."

Grady moves closer behind me, his hand resting on my shoulder. That gesture, that little support makes my chest tighten. I haven't had this. For three years I've been battling this world alone, and he reminded me what it's like to have a pillar behind you, there to lean on when you feel like falling.

I lift my hand, tangling our fingers together. "I told you I thought I was ready to date again, and I kind of am." I look up at Grady and he smiles down at me. "I hope you'll be happy for me if you're listening. I . . . well, I'm happier than I've been since I lost you." I kiss the tips of my fingers and press them to the cold granite. "Until I see you again."

Slowly I rise and Grady wraps his arm around my shoulder, pulling me to his chest. "Are you okay?"

"I am." And that's the truth. I'm alive and happy and working on building the future I want. There are a million possibilities and since meeting Grady, I feel that they're all in reach.

I wrap my arms around his middle as we start to walk back to the car.

"Thank you for letting me be here with you."

"I'm surprised you wanted to come," I admit.

"While I didn't talk aloud, I had some things I wanted to say to him too. As the guy who is in your life."

I stare up at him through my lashes, wondering what he could possibly say to Isaac. We're nearing the end of this relationship. When we get back home, we start the falling apart, but then I wonder if he wasn't explaining that?

Still, it's not my business, even if I'm dying to know.

"I'm sure he would've appreciated it. He was a guy who always did the right thing. He was giving to a fault and selfless. More than anything, he was just honest. Isaac would tell someone the truth no matter what and accept the consequences of his words."

"That is admirable."

I laugh once. "It was annoying too, but you never had to guess with him. He told it like it was and you always knew you'd get the truth."

We reach the car and Grady turns me so my back is against the car and brushes my hair back. "He would've hated our arrangement."

"Yes, but probably for more reasons than the deceit part," I say with a grin.

"Like the fact that we're sleeping together."

"That would definitely not weigh in your favor."

Grady lets out a heavy breath and his warm hand cups my neck. "What would he think if we weren't pretending? Do you think he would've been happy for us?"

I close my eyes, hating that the image of that reality is all I want.

"I think . . . if this was real . . . Isaac would be rooting for us because you make me smile and you're good to Elodie."

He rests his forehead to mine. "You deserve to smile, Addy."

"And so do you."

He presses his lips to mine, just briefly. "I wish just the thought of you didn't make my whole day brighter, it would make us walking away so much easier."

I got news today that will take me much farther away than he realizes.

twenty-seven

GRADY

We're lying in bed, her head resting on my chest, and I really wish I could find something about her that I dislike.

But I can't.

She's sweet. She's intelligent. She makes me laugh and she lets me boss her around in the bedroom. Everything I want in a woman is wrapped around my body right now and yet . . . I am going to give it all up when I get my investment.

I'll have to find a way to see her and not want to pin her to the wall and make us both forget the world.

I'm not quite sure how I'm going to do it, but I will. For Jett.

Because I can't upheave his life again. I can't risk him loving Addison and losing her. For the fact that my son can't love a mother figure and lose her. He's already lost one. And I know the pain of losing a wife, so it's better this way.

More than that, I can't put him through another change in his living environment. I've already taken him from Oklahoma to Sugarloaf and away from his grandparents who raised him while I finished my commission. I have to do what's best for him, no matter what.

Addison lifts her head to look at me. "I got some news when we got here," she says a little hesitantly.

"What news?"

"Do you remember I told you we had a benefactor come in and want to expand Run to Me to be a global operation?"

I nod. "You seemed cautiously happy."

"I was. I mean, the idea of taking this issue globally is amazing. The meeting went really well, at least I thought so. There were so many ideas and things they wanted to do."

I look into her blue eyes, seeing the confliction and worry there. "But?"

"But . . . they will require me to move back here."

"Why?" I ask, trying to squash the immediate desire to tell her not to go. Which is selfish since we're going to break up anyway.

Also, it might be better this way. If I don't have to see her every day, maybe I won't regret it as much.

"They want a headquarters and that'll be run by me and Blakely. We'd have to be ready to expand very quickly, to have a five-year roll-out plan within the first six months. The amount of work it will take can't be done with us on opposite coasts."

"What's holding you back?"

Addison tucks her hair behind her ear, a tell I know is her trying to assemble her next words. "I don't want to leave Sugarloaf."

"Your family is here, Addy. You have friends, your sister-in-law, and a chance to make a real difference in the world, why wouldn't you jump at it?"

I see the hurt flash in her eyes for a second and then it's gone. "I left here because it was hard to be in the shadow of Isaac's ghost. No one here will ever date me, I want things in my life that I can't get in Rose Canyon. You know this."

I do. She wants a family, more kids, to love a man who is her world again.

"And what if you lost all that again? Doesn't that scare you too?"

Addison sits up, pulling the sheet with her. "Of course it does. I don't want to endure that kind of heartbreak again, but I don't want to let life pass me by either."

I'd rather it pass me by than be run over by it. Still, I know

Addison has different wants than I do. "I'm just saying that this seems like a chance to change the world and that's really worth considering."

She goes quiet for a moment. "It means giving up a lot. Giving up things I wasn't ready to just yet."

I open my arm again. "Come here." Addison nestles into my side, her head on my shoulder. "I know how hard it is to give something you love up. When I left Jett with Lisa's parents, I never thought I'd survive it. I kept saying, it's just six months. It's no different than if Lisa was alive. Then, when I got back, I realized how settled he was with them. He knew them, loved them, and I would be leaving and training which would mean him going back to Oklahoma every few weeks. Then, I knew I couldn't do it anymore and I gave up my career to do what was best for my son, I understand what you're feeling. In your case, though . . ." I kiss the top of her head, willing the words not to hurt. "I think coming back to Rose Canyon gives you both. You get the career and your family."

"Right."

"Right."

Although it feels incredibly wrong.

I'm sitting in one of the front pews on the bride's side. I was directed to sit here with the other spouses.

I tried not to flinch when they said that.

However, I'm next to her three best guy friends who have welcomed me into the fold, exactly like I knew they would. Once they realized I wasn't a piece of shit, they backed off. This morning Addison kissed me, informed me Emmett and Blakely would pick me up, and then ran off with her friends to help the bride get ready.

"I hate weddings," Emmett grumbles, pulling at his throat. "Seriously, does anyone else feel like they're being choked in these tuxes?"

"Just you," Spencer says, adjusting his cufflinks. "My wife thinks I look hot and that's all I need."

Blakely snorts. "Your wife thinks the sun shines out of your ass."

"Jealous?"

She raises one brow. "Not at all. I like fighting with Emmett. Hate fucking is the best."

Someone behind us gasps and I can't stop my laugh.

Then Holden pipes in. "I can't express my level of discomfort."

I learned today that Jenna is his ex-wife. And his wife is a bridesmaid. Go figure that one.

I swear, all small towns have some weird shit.

Spencer shifts in his seat to face Holden who is in the row behind us. "I keep forgetting you were married to her."

"Yeah, super easy to forget." He shakes his head. "Anyway, I'm happy for Jenna, but I could've skipped this and been fine."

"Well, other than the fact that you married the nicest human on the planet and Sophie befriended Jenna since she started working with her."

"Don't remind me."

I turn to him. "I'm with you, it's weird."

"See, the new guy gets it." Holden clasps my shoulder. "I knew I liked you."

"I'm touched," I say with sarcasm, which has the other guys smiling.

They are seriously just like my brothers. Full of sarcasm, humor, and a deep bond that they treasure. I imagine if I didn't have my brothers, I would've wanted to find my family the way they did.

My phone buzzes in my chest pocket and I fish it out to see an email from Mateo Kopaskey.

Grady,

I know you're traveling, but I wanted to inform you that I've come to a decision regarding the four-million-dollar investment. After a lot of consideration, and the proposal that we discussed regarding leasing of the

plane and the payment restructure, I would like to move forward with the
investment when you return. I'll have the paperwork drawn up and then
you can have your lawyers review it. Enjoy your time this weekend and I
hope this brings you even more happiness.

    Best,
    Mateo Kopaskey

I read it four more times to make sure it says what I think it says. I can't believe this. I got the money. I got the investment. I can buy a new plane and my company can finally get off the ground —literally.

I shift in my seat, looking to see if I can find Addison in the back. All I want to do is tell her the good news. I'm so fucking happy.

When I look around, I see Brielle standing toward the front, but no Addy.

The music keys up and then the bridal party starts. First, Brielle comes down, smiling, and then when her eyes find her husband, her entire face lights up.

Then comes some girl I don't know, then Sophie.

And then it's Addy.

It's strange, my eyes don't take in anything else. All I see is her and my chest fills with joy. Her gaze finds mine and there I see the look. The one that I saw each of her friends give their husbands. Where that one person they found makes them feel joy.

I wink at her, which causes her to look away while biting her lower lip. The music shifts to "The Wedding March" and we all stand to watch her enter.

Instead of watching her, I look at the groom. The guy who is about to marry the woman he loves with his whole heart. He stands there, hands in front of him, trying to fight back the tears.

I remember feeling all the same things, hopeful that it was the start of our happy life.

And if I'm honest, we did have a happy life.

While it wasn't as long as I hoped, what we did share was wonderful.

When we turn to face the altar, I find Addison's gaze again. The two of us stay connected and I feel my chest tightening because while this couple is beginning, Addison and I are coming to an end.

One where she'll probably move back here, and I now have my funding.

There's no reason to continue our fake dating once we get back, and now we have the perfect reason.

She lifts her fingers in a small wave, and I give her a nod.

Then I pray for a way to stop time so this day never ends, and I can pretend for just a little while longer.

twenty-eight
ADDISON

"Can I have this dance?" Grady asks with his hand extended.

I lean back in my seat. "Hmm, I'm not sure. Do you have any qualifications you can present?"

"What exactly are you looking for?"

I tap my lips with my pointer finger. "A tall man."

He stands straight. "I'm six-foot-two."

"That will work. Are you a smart man?"

"I can fly planes. Not just any plane either, a fighter jet."

"Wow, that's impressive." My eyes widen as though I've never heard it before. "What about gentle and good with kids?"

"I'm a single father to a three-year-old boy for whom I would burn the world down if he was ever hurt."

"Oh, and protective. My, my, this is sort of exciting. What else do you think would make you more appealing?" I ask playfully.

"I'm an exceptional lover. I can give you references if you like."

I laugh through my nose, not expecting that. "If memory serves you, I'm not impressed by that."

He leans in, a devilish grin on his handsome face. "Dance with me and find out." Once again he extends his hand.

I place my hand in his, letting him lead me to the dance floor.

My arms rest on his shoulders, his fingers splay against my back, and we sway.

"The last time we danced we ended up dating," he reminds me of our first dance in Sugarloaf.

"We did? I don't remember that."

Grady's chuckle warms me. "I remember it."

My eyes lift to his, searching for some sign that he doesn't want this to end. That the fake is real and he wants something more.

But I don't see it.

I force a smile. "I must have been pretty memorable then."

"You absolutely are."

Ask me to stay. Ask me to try.

But he doesn't. Just like he didn't last night. I silently begged him to but then he urged me to go.

"I have something I need to tell you," he says with eyes shining.

Maybe he is going to ask me or tell me his feelings are deeper than whatever this arrangement is.

"What?"

"I got an email from Mateo."

"Oh," I say, taken aback. "What did it say?"

"He's going to give me the investment. They're drawing the paperwork up now."

"Grady! This is amazing," I say, genuinely happy for him. I know how much he wanted this and how hard he's worked to show them whatever they were looking for in regards to his plan.

"I honestly can't believe it."

"I can. You're so smart and I knew you would do this."

He leans in and gives me a sweet kiss. I pull back, a little shocked since we really haven't had any affection other than holding hands here.

"Thank you, Addy. You helped a lot. If it weren't for you approaching them on our first date, I don't know that I would've gotten a second look."

I shake my head. "No, no way. You were going to get this money. I was just by your side, that's all. This is all you."

"I think you played a part, but I appreciate you saying that."

I smile. "So much good news all around. I swear, weddings are magical. I don't know if it's the hope that two souls have found their other half and will find happiness forever or if it's just that they're surrounded in love, but I love them."

Grady smiles. "You look so beautiful when you smile like that."

"Like what?"

"Like everything is going to be okay."

My eyes soften. "Aren't we living proof of that? We're alive after feeling pain. We've endured grief that many can't fathom. We've learned to laugh again, smile, and live. It's not perfect, but it's life."

And God, I wish he would open himself up enough to share it with me. We could be so good together. This investment and my possibly moving back to Oregon changes everything, though. He is going to be starting a company as a single father, building the house on his land, and he's made it abundantly clear that he doesn't want a relationship and wants this time with Jett to be just them as they navigate living together for the first time since he was born.

Then there's this idea of taking our grassroots foundation and it becoming something none of us dreamed of. Which is exciting, but also terrifying.

"I just wish I could feel it the way you do."

"I wish you could too," I confess. "I want nothing more than for you to feel it."

"I do when I'm with you."

"That was very sweet."

Grady turns us and his thumb makes swirls on my back. "What are you going to do about moving back to Oregon?"

"I don't know," I admit, not sure what the right move is.

I want to stay in Sugarloaf. I've built a life there and I love my home. Then there's this really stupid part of me that's considering him, but now, he has the money and there's no reason to stay together.

"Grady?" He stares at me as we sway. "Is there a reason I should stay in Sugarloaf? Any reason?"

Like you want to try?

He looks to the side and then back to me. "I'm sure there are lots, but those aren't for me to tell you. You need to follow your heart."

Right.

No, he's right. He's made it very clear what we are, and I agreed to it. It's not his fault that I want to change things. However, my heart wants something very different than my head knows I should.

"Hopefully my heart will give me some answers."

As though he can read my mind, see into my soul, he shakes his head and then pulls me close. After a few seconds, he leans in, our foreheads touching. "I wish I was a different man."

"If you were, I wouldn't be here right now."

I would be alone or trying my hand at more bad dates, but I'm not. I'm in *his* arms. With *this* man who has so much love to give if he'd just try.

"That would be a travesty. God, Addy, I'm going to miss this when we get back. I'm going to miss you."

I put my finger to his lips, not wanting him to talk about when we end. Not wanting to think about what's to come.

"Right now, you don't have to miss me. I'm right here. Just dance with me and we'll deal with the future when we get back."

This weekend may be our last and I'm going to soak up every freaking minute. It'll be what I hold onto at night when I no longer have him.

And it makes me coming back here just a little more appealing.

"You look happy, Addy," Blakely says as she hands me a glass of wine. "You know we can still walk away from this deal, if you want to stay in Sugarloaf..."

Grady is at the table with Emmett, talking about military life, the things they've done, and Blakely pulled me here because neither of us cared to hear their stories. Not that Blakely doesn't have enough of her own as a former combat medic. It's how she met Emmett, she was assigned to his Ranger unit, and they met, became friends, and then got married—both claiming not to have feelings for each other.

Which was total shit.

Sort of familiar now that I think about it.

"I just need to think about it. Moving Elodie isn't an easy decision."

"It's back home, though. You'd have us and we're family. I know going to Sugarloaf after Isaac died was the right move for you, but we miss you and this is a great opportunity."

It is, but it's also a lot. "It just kind of changes the entire point of what we did. You know that I worked doing corporate mergers before I got pregnant, and it's not cut and dry. They're going to want huge changes. Us having one main office here in Rose Canyon is just the beginning. They'll change everything. Everything we do will have a policy in place and it's just not as easy as me moving back. It would change the entire charity."

It's one of the things that worries me. The company that wants to come in is actually a really good one. It's probably the only reason we're entertaining it, but it still leaves us in a very different reality than we are now.

We've spent the last few years building a community around Run to Me. It's a place where people get personal attention and their needs met on a level that corporations aren't going to want to fund.

"Maybe we need that, though. The amount of people we can help will just be a million times bigger than we can do with our grassroots operation."

"I know."

Blakely rests her hand on mine. "But even with that said, I'll support turning it down. While our mission is important to both of us for many reasons, it's not the *most* important thing."

I smile at my friend, loving her even more than I already do. "I appreciate that."

"I mean it, Addy. I know what it feels like to walk away from the man I love for work. I did it with Emmett. I spent years hating myself for it, trying to come up with some bullshit reason to excuse it. Then, he served me with divorce papers, and it was like I couldn't breathe. The thought of closing that door had me on a plane weeks later and . . . well, we know the outcome of that." She looks over at her husband with soft eyes. "Just know I'll deny this if you ever repeat it, but there's nothing more important in life than him and if you feel even an inkling of that for Grady, then we turn this down."

My vision blurs as the tears start to form. Damn it. I don't want to cry. However, the thought of a daily life without Grady breaks my heart, and it shouldn't, because we aren't real. All of this, every damn minute of our entire relationship has been a lie.

It's a fabrication to achieve two goals that now have happened.

"I don't think I feel that for him," I tell her.

"No?"

I shake my head, the tear falling, and I turn my head to wipe it. What a lie that is. I steel myself, refusing to shed another one. "I don't think he's really ready to build a life with someone else. He has a lot of guilt and ideas of what the future looks like, I'm not sure I'm in them."

"Oh."

I nod. "Yeah, he just says things sometimes and . . . I don't know. I wanted things to work, but I can't force them, you know?"

Her smile is sad. "I understand. Still, we can push this off a few weeks, give you time to figure that out."

"Okay. Let me see what happens when we get back to Sugarloaf. I'll know in a few days, but I'm leaning more towards making Run to Me what we never could've dreamed of."

She lifts her glass. "To dreams coming true."

To broken dreams. "To dreams," I say, clinking our glasses together and feeling my heart ache.

This night has been such a dichotomy of emotions. One minute we were laughing, having fun, and the next I wanted to weep.

Tonight is almost over.

It's our last night here.

Our last night together, most likely.

The more I think about a daily life without him, the more I don't want it. If I have to be miserable, then I might as well do that while building something that will help people. Blakely and I spoke before I left, and I told her I was leaning more towards coming back here. Which made her both happy and sad.

Probably because she knew that if I was coming here, it's because my relationship with Grady wasn't what I hoped.

First seed planted toward our breakup has happened.

Grady opens the door and we enter the apartment, heading to the bedroom. I toss my shoes over by the suitcase and feel my entire frame wilt a little.

Neither of us have spoken much. I haven't had the words to express my thoughts, and even if I did, I don't know that I could say them.

Not because I'm afraid, but because I'm smart enough to know when they don't make a difference.

However, if I had a superpower, it would be the ability to freeze time, to steal a few extra minutes of whatever I wanted, and I would use this one.

Grady turns, tie hanging in his hand, top button undone, and his green eyes flash with emotions. "Come here, dove."

My feet move as though they are at his command and I stand in front of him. "I'm here, now what?"

His arm snakes around my middle, pulling me against him, and slowly his mouth inches towards mine. "Now, I'm going to kiss you for a very long time."

There are no complaints about that.

I rise to meet him, equally as slowly, savoring each breath we share together before the pressure of his lips meets mine.

This kiss is different than every other one we've shared. There's a longing between us that causes an ache in my chest.

I want this man. I want this man to want me—forever.

I push that desire away and cling to the physical. To the way he makes my body come to life and how good I know the sex will be. Because with him, I'm free. There are no expectations to be perfect or sweet, he takes me how he wants, how I didn't even know I wanted.

His hands frame my face, tilting my head to the side, and then I feel his tongue slide against my lips. I open for him, inhaling everything that is Grady.

The kiss deepens and he moves me back, my knees hitting the bed. His one hand moves down my neck as his lips leave mine. "Tonight, we're going to go slow. I want to savor every second, every touch, every kiss."

"Grady," I say his name softly. I don't have anything else to say, I just want him to know I'm here—with him.

He steps back just a little and the loss of his heat is immediate. He turns me slowly and brushes his lips down the column of my neck. "You're stunning, Addison. When I see you, there is no one else that can even get me to glance their way. Don't ever doubt your beauty, your heart. You're worth the world and deserve a man who will give it to you."

"What if I don't want the world?" I toss back as his lips go to my shoulder as my zipper drags down.

"You should."

But I don't. I had that before. I know what the world gives, and I just want him to give me him. That's all. I don't need anything else, but he won't give me that, and I can't handle him saying it any clearer than he has.

When my dress drops to the floor, he turns me back and then lifts me up in his arms, placing me on the bed.

I lie back, lifting up on my elbows to watch as he unbuttons. "I love watching this."

"What?"

"You, undressing. You may think I'm beautiful, but you are incredibly hot."

He smiles and that dimple appears. "I'm glad you think so."

"I very much do." When his last button is undone, I decide I want to remove it. I want to touch his muscles as his shirt slides off his body. "Stop," I say quickly. I rise up onto my knees as his hand stills. Our eyes meet and I crawl toward him. "You always tell me I need to ask for what I want."

"I do."

"Well, I want to undress you."

His eyes turn molten. "Then by all means."

I do exactly what I wanted, letting the shirt flutter to the ground, my fingers moving over his taut skin. He's so perfect. Like a freaking dream of the exact man I would be attracted to.

And tonight . . . he's mine.

Grady's hand moves to my neck, his fingers on the back of my head as he pulls me to him. "I want your mouth, dove."

I give it to him. Kissing him, needing the same thing he does. The connection we share will be gone soon and if I never get to kiss him again, then I want now.

twenty-nine
GRADY

I take Addison's hand as we enter Sugarloaf.

I don't feel happy about being back and getting to see the kids. I feel sad and pissed off because we have no reason to fake our relationship anymore.

I could be selfish and ask for more, but I'm not what she needs in this world. She deserves love, a man who will marry her, give her more kids.

I can't lose another wife. I can't raise another baby on my own and it was her pregnancy that killed Lisa.

When Addison asked me if there was a reason to stay, I wanted to tell her me and Jett. That I would try, but I remembered how I swore I would never let Jett get hurt, which means I need to focus on him.

"Thank you for going with me," Addy says as we pull onto her street.

"I promised you I would. It was our deal."

She nods. "It was. And you got your money now too."

Yeah, I do. I can't even use that to keep this going. "Which is all thanks to you."

"We've been over this, Grady."

I smile. "We have. I'm sorry."

295

"I forgive you," she jokes.

I park the car, my heart in my throat as I know the next part of the conversation we have to have. "So what now?"

Her lips become a flat line as she releases a breath through her nose. "I guess we break up?"

"Are you going to move back to Rose Canyon?"

"I think I have to do what's best for the charity. It's a lot of money . . . I . . . don't know what to do. Would it change anything if I stayed?" Addison asks, and I know that I cannot stand in her way.

No matter my million reasons that I have, it wouldn't be fair to her. "I care about you. I care about you more than I ever thought I would. I think about you all the fucking time. I ache for you when you're not with me, and that terrifies me. When I moved here, it was to give Jett and me a chance to have a new life. One where he was surrounded by his family, my siblings, and grow up in a small town. I can't move again. I can't move across the country when I have a business I'm building, a house that's about to start construction. I can't do that to him, Addy. No matter how much I want things, I have to do what's right for my son. I also can't do that to you. I can't ask you to love a man who is half broken."

There. I've said it.

I laid it out on the table.

Addison looks down at our clasped hands. "You aren't half broken, you're half healed, but I understand your reasons around Jett. I really do."

I let out a heavy breath. "I'm not ready to let this end."

She gives me a sad smile. "I'm afraid I can't let this go on. I'm going to fall in love with you, I'm already halfway there."

"Addison . . ."

Her hand releases from mine. "We had an agreement, and I was aware of the risks. I worried this would happen, and I tried to convince myself not to let my heart open to you and Jett, but it did. You're so easy to love, Grady. That said, I know that you don't want what I do. A family, more kids, a life like I once dreamed of before it was broken. I want that . . . and you don't."

"I can't do it."

"Can you at least tell me why?" she asks, hesitancy in her voice.

"I already have. I can't understand how after everything you went through how you can be willing to risk your heart again. How can you allow it for Elodie?"

Her head pulls back. "Elodie?"

"Yes. What if you and I were to fall in love and get married, merge our families together and build a life, only to have some horrible thing happen? What if you got pregnant and had an aneurysm? I went to sleep after Lisa was nursing Jett, she went downstairs, and never opened her eyes again." I snap my fingers. "Just like that. Every dream. Every hope. Every fucking promise of a future was gone. Not just for me though, I could've handled it, but for Jett. He'll never have the life we planned for him, and in a way, I thank God every day that he never truly knew Lisa and loved her. He doesn't remember how it felt to be loved by her, so he doesn't experience that level of pain. I experienced the loss, which was bad, but then I had to give Jett up for three years. I was a part-time dad, and I will hate myself forever for that. Now, I will give him every part of me because he deserves nothing less."

"So for Jett, you'll keep yourself closed off?"

I wish. "I'm not closed off, Addison. I feel far too fucking much. Things I swore I never would. I was perfectly fine not dating or remembering how much life was better when you had someone to share it with. But you, you were just so easy to care about with your kind heart and beautiful smile. None of that matters, does it? We both have different dreams now. Mine isn't for another family. It's to give Jett the best I can with a stable job, life, home, and then . . . what if it doesn't work? What if we get to a point where we realize that we aren't right for each other?"

The words are coming out so fast, but I can't hold them back. This is what I worry about. This is who I am now. Life experiences change people, and I will never be the same again.

"I don't have an answer for that. I don't know what my future holds, but that's the point of life. We don't get the answers. We don't know what lies ahead, but we go on the journey. Am I scared of all of those things? Of course I am. I would be lying if I said I wasn't. Not just for Elodie, but for me. I don't want to bury another husband. I don't want to lose everything, but I don't want to stay behind a wall where I live a half existence either." She lets out a heavy sigh, a defeated one. "I respect your decision. I do. I wish it was different, but that's not what either of us signed up for. We agreed to fake date until the wedding and you got the investment. Both have been satisfied, and a deal is a deal. So, maybe we just cool off for a few days, let the town think we had a fight?"

Why does it feel so fucking wrong agreeing to this?

Yeah, because I did fall for her. Because I want to spend as many more nights as I can with her. Because if she's leaving, I want every goddamn night so I can remember them once she's gone.

And that's the part she isn't talking about. Addison is going to move to Oregon. She's going to run an empire, and I can't go. I can't force Jett to move across the country for a woman I don't even know if I have a future with.

He is what matters.

When I took him from Oklahoma, I vowed that I will sacrifice everything for him. I guess this is the first time I'm learning how hard keeping that promise is.

"Okay. If that's what you think." The words taste like acid on my tongue, burning down my throat and straight to my heart. "If we can at least try to keep this up until the deal with Mateo is done, that would be helpful."

She nods. "Sure. We'll just . . . be busy the next few days and he'll never know."

"There's a dinner party on Saturday," I remind her.

"Shit. Of course, I'll still go with you."

I force a thin-lipped smile, wanting to say something, but Addison's front door opens and Elodie runs out. "Mommy! Grady!"

Addison looks to me, panic in her eyes, but I'll never do anything to hurt her. "Come on, let's see her and your mother-in-law, then I'll go."

"Thank you."

I nod and exit the car, scooping up Elodie and hating that this could've been a future for us.

"Hello, Grady, don't you look dapper this Tuesday morning," Mrs. Cooke says from behind me as I'm paying for my coffee and bagel at the register at Sugarlips Diner.

"Thank you, and you look beautiful."

She smiles, her head tipping to the side. "Aren't you just like your brother, Rowan. He's a sweet talker, that boy, but I've seen him with the ladies. A heartbreaker at the core of it all."

Oh, she doesn't know the half of it.

"Well, I'll let him know you said that." I slip my credit card in my wallet and start to move, but she places her hand on my chest.

"You know, I haven't seen you with Addison since you got back two days ago," Mrs. Cooke notes.

"She's been busy and I've been flying, trying to catch up on things." Not that it's any of her business.

"Oh, I'm sure you're both very busy, but love takes effort."

My breathing stops for a second and I stare at her. I'm not sure what the hell she's talking about. No one in the town thinks we're in love. It's only been over a month for heaven's sake. "Of course it does, but Addison and I are just dating and taking things slow."

I don't know why I explained that to her . . .

"Yes, but I just see you both so happy together and Addison is a wonderful girl. A heart of gold, that one. I would hate to see you screw it up."

Of course it'll be my fault. No matter what she says about our breakup reason.

For two days, I've stayed away. The first day I took Jett to school late, knowing I would miss her. I had Brynn drop him off yesterday and then I picked him up at lunch just to avoid seeing her. Jett was none too happy since he wanted to play with his friends, but I let him ride the horse for an hour and that placated him.

It wasn't until today, when I had to rearrange my schedule again to bring him first thing, that I realized just how much I've allowed Addison in my daily life. How much she's penetrated my world and how hard it's going to be going forward without her.

Instead of saying any of that to Mrs. Cooke, I just give her my best Whitlock smile and tip my head. "I appreciate the advice. Truly."

"Addison!" Mrs. Cooke beams and my body locks when I hear her sweet voice.

"Hi, Mrs. Cooke. Hey, Grady, I missed you this morning."

I turn to her, keeping my emotions in check, and smile. "Hey, I meant to call to tell you I'd be taking him early. I have a flight today and I wanted to get there to check on something."

I'm a fucking liar. I have no flight today. Tomorrow I'm meeting Mateo to go over the paperwork, but today . . . nothing.

"Well, don't let me hold you up."

Mrs. Cooke rests her hand on my arm. "You're flying today? Jimmy said there were no flights today. He keeps track of the logs to make sure the farmers can tend their crops. He told me this morning you didn't have one."

This town could win a gold medal for meddling.

"He must've looked at the wrong date," I try to smooth over.

"Hmm, Jimmy!" she yells across the diner.

"What?"

"Grady says he has a flight today!" she screeches and I seriously want to crawl in a hole.

"No flights today."

"Are you sure? He says he has one and it's why he can't have breakfast with Addison."

"Oh God," I hear Addison mutter.

She turns to us. "Sometimes, he doesn't read the right days."

"Mrs. Cooke," Addison steps in. "Grady and I are having dinner tonight, so breakfast doesn't work for us. Thank you so much for trying to help though."

"Oh," she says, placing her hand on her chest. "Dinner? How wonderful. With the kids?"

Addison looks to me, eyes pleading to save her. "Yes."

"Not very romantic," she says and nudges me with her elbow. "However, you're both single parents and you do what you must. Well, I should get back to my breakfast. You both have a great day!"

Mrs. Cooke heads off, and Addison stands here, her lips between her teeth, clearly trying not to laugh.

"Don't even," I warn.

"Oh, come on, you have to admit it was funny," she laughs a little. "The town is definitely invested in us."

That much is clear, but what will happen when she leaves and the distance between us isn't the town, but an entire country?

"Speaking of invested, I'm flying tomorrow to meet with Mateo. He mentioned I should bring you. I was going to call you, but . . ."

Addison's eyes are wide, excitement swimming in them. "I can go. That's fine."

"You don't have to."

"I know, but . . ." Addison looks around the room, rolling her eyes. "We'll talk tonight. I'll call you."

I guess we're not doing dinner then. "Sure. I'll be home."

She smiles. "Okay. I'll call once I get Elodie to bed."

"Talk then."

"Bye, Grady."

I lean in and kiss her cheek, inhaling her scent and wishing I could drown in it. Her hand rests on my chest and I'm sure she can feel my heart pounding. It's been days since I've been near her, talked to her, seen her face, and my body aches for her.

"Bye, Addy." As I walk away, I feel her loss immediately.

thirty

ADDISON

Devney is sitting in my office, talking about Christmas plans while I'm fretting about this flight tonight. "Are you and Grady going to do anything?"

"We haven't talked about it," I admit.

"No? It's only a month away."

"We're both busy, Dev. We had his parties, the wedding, and we weren't really sure if our relationship was going to last."

Also, we won't be together in a month, but I don't mention that.

"Well, now you know. Make plans."

I sigh. "Have I mentioned just how much I love it when you're back home?"

She grins. "You have."

"You're welcome for being such a good friend."

"The best," Devney agrees. "I'm only here for another day, so get your fill while you can. I want to talk about your trip back to Oregon. How was it? Did you and Grady . . . you know . . ."

I've done my absolute best to keep any details of our relationship private. Especially the intimate parts. My friends are great, but if they know we're sleeping together, they'll lose their minds.

"Grady and I are taking things one day at a time. And now, with this company wanting to give us all this money and merge into their organization, it just changes everything. How am I supposed to build a life with a man three thousand miles away?"

The worst part of this conversation is that none of it is a lie. Yes, we have been fake dating. Yes, we planned to break up, but this wasn't supposed to be how I really feel.

And I do. I want this life with him. I want to stay here and forget all the lies we told ourselves and others because the reality is that none of it was really fake. Not the kisses, or touches, or smiles, or days and nights where we opened ourselves up. The only part of our fake relationship was thinking it was fake.

At least for me.

"I don't know. It definitely changes things."

"It changes everything," I say, feeling the sadness wash over me. "We're going to talk soon."

"Good." Devney rests her hand on mine. "No matter what, you guys will figure it out. You know, even if it doesn't work out, this experience was good for you. Not only did you put yourself out there, but you allowed yourself a chance at something great."

"I'm scared, Dev. I'm scared that I'm going to lose it all."

"Then don't."

She says it as though it's the easiest statement in the world. "I'm not sure it's that simple."

"It never is, but if he's worth it. If you feel like this man is the one you could build a life with, then what kind of life will you have if you let it go?"

"Mommy, is Jett coming here?" Elodie asks as she puts the plates on the table. She loves to "help" me with this part.

"I don't think so, sweetheart."

"I like Jett."

I smile at that. "I do too. He's a very nice boy."

"His mommy is in heaven with my daddy."

I nearly drop the plate I was holding and look at her. "She is?"

Elodie nods. "In the sky!"

I crouch down in front of her. "I bet your daddy and Jett's mommy are looking down and smiling when they see you two. You're both the best kids in the whole world."

Elodie wraps her arms around my neck and squeezes. "I lub you, Mommy."

"I love you, Elodie Grace."

"I lub Aunt Debknee, Aunt Chloe, Jett, Grady, Miss Michelle and Uncle Sean. He tickles me." Her sing-song voice has my heart so full. And I don't miss that she loves Grady.

Please let tonight shed some light on what to do.

My phone rings and I see Blakely's name. This is the last call I need to take, but it could be something not about the merger, so I answer.

"Hey, I only have five minutes," I warn her as I answer.

"I'm happy to take even less if you have an answer."

I sigh. "I'm not ready to say yet."

"Addy, we have to tell them something." I can hear how frustrated she is, but she's not the one giving everything up.

"Tell them I want another web meeting tomorrow. I want to know everything before I decide."

She is silent for a moment and I know she's trying to keep her anger in check. "I get that this is a big deal, but we can't keep stringing them along."

"That's all well and good, but I have a life here. Elodie is happy, she's settled, and so am I. Yes, we can do amazing things if we take this, but we are doing amazing things now. If I'm going to leave Sugarloaf, I need to hear more about the future plans from them, okay?"

I need to know exactly what their vision is.

"I get that. I have reservations too."

Well, that's good to know now. "Like what?"

"A lot, if I'm being honest. I don't know how all of this will work. What if they completely change our company mission? We're going to have staff, a corporate office, and have to worry about having more locations than we ever planned. I'm also excited about all of that though. Run to Me was to help girls avoid trafficking. It was to honor Isaac and heal all of us after the hell we endured because of what happened to him. This community was rocked by it and this center really gave us something to hold onto. Imagine all the people we could help avoid this kind of pain by expanding."

It's the exact reason I haven't just turned it down.

But then I think about the fact that I'm giving up my home.

I'm walking away from a place I love and . . . Grady.

I know we're nothing, but what if we could be more? What if I went to him and asked him? Would he turn me away? I don't know, but I know I can't go without at least trying.

"Set up the meeting and let's go over these concerns and see what they say," I tell her, feeling resolved and sad.

"Okay. I'll let you know when and we'll get all our questions answered."

"Thanks, Blakely."

"Of course. I love you and want this to be good for you too. This was your dream, too."

It was, but I don't know that this dream won't become a nightmare.

"Love you too."

I look over at Elodie who is drawing on a piece of paper, legs swinging in the chair, and murmuring to herself. I walk over to see what she's coloring and smile.

"What's that, El?"

"It's a picture for Grady and Jett."

My stomach clenches and I grip the back of her chair. There is a sun and something that looks like wings, and four figures on the wings, but one never knows what she's thinking. "What is it, baby?"

"That's me, Jett, you, and Grady on the plane."

"Where are we going?"

She looks up. "Home."

thirty-one
GRADY

"You're being a dick," Rowan says as he tosses a card down on the table.

"Seriously, more so than usual," Brynn unhelpfully adds on.

I huff, looking at my cards to see if I can make another set if I draw from the discard pile, but there's a king and a jack in there that I really don't want. My family's runs for Rummy are very different than anyone I've ever played with. I swear Brynn created it so she could win each time.

"I'm fine," I say as I draw a card instead. "Why do I have to get two sets again?"

"Because that's the Whitlock rules," Brynlee explains. "Now, tell us why you haven't gone sneaking off to Addison's house in days. Did something happen in Rose Canyon?"

"It's none of your business, Brynn."

Dinner last night was fine. We talked as much as two people can with two three-year-olds running around and refusing to give us any privacy. Jett was in a terrible mood and I had to leave before we could talk about anything significant.

While I wanted to go back over later, I passed out with Jett on my chest after his massive crying fit.

Then this morning, she sent me a fucking email detailing what she could agree to this week. An email.

Like we're a business arrangement.

And I only have myself to blame.

Rowan pulls from the discard pile and rearranges his hand. "That's evasive. Is it my business, since I'm partially your boss and all?"

I glare at him. "Definitely not and you're not my boss, asshole."

"Well, technically, I am. You work with *my* horse on *my* part of the farm. So, why don't you take a load off your mind, son, and tell me what's weighing you down," my brother says with a smirk.

"Fuck off."

"Yeah, totally not an asshole," Brynn says with a laugh. "Grady, you can talk to us."

No, I really can't. The deal isn't done, I can't talk to Addison because I have nothing I can actually say to change things, and I fucking miss her.

I miss her and I hate that I miss her.

Explaining all of this in half-truths to my siblings isn't going to make sense, so it's best I just fester in the ever-remaining pain of my life when it comes to women.

Brynn picks up a card and places it back on the discard pile. "I heard that her company got a pretty amazing offer . . ."

I keep my eyes on my card. "Did they?" I feign ignorance.

"Yeah, when she was back home . . . you didn't hear about it?" Brynlee asks, probably already knowing the answer.

"I heard something about it."

"So what are you going to do?"

I lift my gaze to meet hers. "I'm not doing anything. It's not my decision."

She scoffs. "Please. If you let her go, that's you deciding."

I place my cards face down on the table and stare into my sister's blue eyes that aren't filled with mischief, but pity, and that pity is what has me pushing my chair out, throwing on my sweat-shirt, and going out the back door.

"Grady!" She calls after me, but I keep going. Right to the barn. "Grady, stop!" My sister runs up behind me, hand touching my back. "I'm sorry. I just . . . I wish you'd talk to me. Talk to any of us."

"And say what, Brynn? That again, I'm going to lose someone I care about? That the woman I was absolutely not going to fall in love with somehow managed to get under my skin and I can't figure out what the hell I should do? She's got the offer of a lifetime. A chance to take her charity and make real changes in the world. To help more people than she ever imagined, and I'd be the worst asshole that ever lived to ask her to give it up. Is that what you want me to say?" My chest is heaving at the end of my rant.

Brynlee tilts her head and smiles. "That's a start."

"And that isn't even the half of it!"

"What's the half?"

I stare at my sister who gave up her home, her comfortable life, for me and Jett. So loving, so caring to everyone, and I wish to God I had a sliver of the heart she does.

"All of it was fake, Brynn. The dating, the dinners, the whole damn thing. Addison and I were pretending so I could get the investment and she needed a date for the wedding. The entire fucking relationship was a show," I confess it and wait for her censure.

Instead of that, she bursts out laughing. "Oh, you're an idiot."

"What?"

"You're so stupid!" She laughs harder, tears starting to come out of the corners of her eyes. "You think . . . it was fake?"

"It was," I tell her.

She lets out a huge breath, collecting herself a bit. "Grady, stop it. You weren't pretend. Or the only thing you were pretending is that it was pretend. You don't sneak over in the middle of the night to see a woman you're fake dating. You guys became friends, and whether or not it started that way, it's sure as hell not that way now."

"I know."

She crosses her arms over her chest. "You do?"

"Yes, and that's the issue."

Brynn's eyes narrow. "What is? That you have feelings for her?"

"Yes, because I didn't want this. I didn't want a woman who could break my fucking heart again. I needed to protect myself and Jett."

"Whoever told you that was possible?"

I look up at the sky and groan. "What is with the women in my life?"

"We love you, that's what. You can't protect Jett from love any more than you can ensure you'll never die. Losing Lisa . . . well, it was a tragedy. One that you have spent the last three years doing a good job at grieving. You have also lived in the shadow of her death until Addison."

My head jerks back and I feel as though she punched me. "What?"

"You were trying so hard to make up for the fact that you weren't able to care for Jett after her death that you basically rebuilt your life with Lisa when you got here. You took her furniture from Oklahoma, put photos everywhere, just like it was at her parents' house, and you read the book she wanted every day. Then, two weeks ago, you picked a book about planes. I don't even know if you were aware you did it, but you did." Brynn takes a step to me. "Your heart still beats, and your eyes have come back to life since you've been . . . *fake dating* . . . Addison." She air quotes the fake dating part.

I shake my head, moving backwards. "And how do I handle her leaving me? How do I let someone like her go? I can't fucking breathe thinking it's a possibility. I wasn't supposed to feel this. I was closed off, and that woman broke through. What kind of a man would I be to take her dreams from her when she's already lost so much?"

"Look, I can't answer those questions for you, and the best part is, neither can you."

"What the hell does that even mean?"

She sighs. "It means that the only person who can answer those questions is Addison. And you, big brother, have two choices. You can try to pretend you're a mind reader and give her exactly what she might not want, or you can go to her, and . . . you know . . . communicate."

"That's what I was doing until you stopped me."

Brynn rocks back on her heels. "Oh. Good."

"Now, can you watch Jett?"

She rests her hand on my chest. "Of course. Go show her the man you are and give her every reason to stay. No matter how much it scares you."

"I'm not scared."

"If you say so."

I chuckle and take a step back. "Thank you, Brynn."

"Go."

I turn, head to the barn, and saddle up Brutus. I stand in front of him, petting his neck. "I need you to behave and take me to Addison. I'm taking a huge risk and I could really use your help, big guy." He raises his nose and drops it. I take it as a yes. "All right."

I grab the horn, step in the stirrup, and mount. Brutus shuffles a bit and then I kick my feet and we head to her.

This is pretty much my plan.

Show up.

Tell her that my feelings for her are more than I admitted, and see where we go.

I can't leave here. I can't beg her to stay.

So, I'm not really sure where the hell that leaves us, but . . . I'll figure out something.

I make my way to her barn that isn't used, but there's a stall I can leave Brutus in for the night. Again, didn't really think this through.

I left my phone at my sister's house, which means I can't call or text. There's no way I'm ringing the doorbell, and I have her spare key still, so back door it is. I also have to avoid a nosey neighbor who probably has a night vision camera on her house.

The back door is locked and the downstairs level is dark.

Great.

Well, it is past midnight.

There's one light on off the side of the house, which is her window. "Addison!" I whisper and then wait.

She's never going to hear me. I'm really starting to doubt my brilliant idea here.

I need to get her attention.

Pebbles. That's what I need.

I look around, grabbing a few that won't damage a window, and start tossing them.

First one goes, hits the side of the house. Awesome.

Second one hits the wrong window.

Third finally hits the window. "Ha!"

I throw another. Miss again. This is ridiculous. I grab a handful of small pebbles and toss them all, chances are I'll hit the window.

Sure enough, a bunch of pebbles land and the curtain is pulled back. There she stands with the light behind her, like a goddamn angel.

The window slides up and she pops her head out. "Grady?"

"Hey."

"Hey? What the hell are you doing? It's freezing out."

Yeah, I'm running off adrenaline and pretending the cold isn't really happening. But it's late November and it's definitely freaking cold.

"I need to talk to you," I tell her.

Addison leans further out. "Now? And why are you throwing rocks instead of calling me?"

"Long story. Can you let me in?"

She rocks back and then tucks her hair behind her ear. "I'll be right down."

The window closes and I go to the back door, waiting for her. When the kitchen light goes on, my heart starts to race. All of this is a risk and while I can't predict the outcome, I know I'll regret not laying it all out there.

The door opens and she has her robe wrapped tight around her, the steam from our breath floating toward the sky.

"Do you want to come in?" she asks.

More than anything. "Please."

She steps back, and I enter, wondering what the next move should be.

I turn to face her, and the need to kiss her is so great, I can't fucking think. She's so beautiful. Her blue eyes are trained on mine, her hair pulled to the side of her shoulder, and then she runs her tongue along her lips as she stares back at me.

"Grady . . ."

Her voice. The ache in it. The way those two syllables fall from her lips makes me so goddamn insane with desire.

It's not a want.

She's a need.

I take two steps and her hands grab my face, pulling me to her.

Like two planets, we collide and I kiss her deeply. The moment her tongue touches mine, I'm lost to her. My hands are at her back, clutching her tight to me as she kisses me hard.

"Bedroom," Addison gets that one word out and I sink down, pulling her into my arms. She doesn't stop kissing me as I try to carry her. We reach the stairs and I push her against the wall, needing to anchor us.

"Fuck, Addy," I moan as her hand is in my hair, fisting it as she moves her hips to ride me a bit. "We need to talk," I manage to say as my thoughts are scattering when she rocks again.

"No talking, just fuck me."

I groan as I take her mouth again, my fingers under her ass, digging into the flesh.

I turn her so her back is against the stairs and she's a few above me.

Thank God she's wearing just a T-shirt.

I pull it up and slide her panties down, tucking them in my pocket.

"One orgasm and then we talk," I say, as I spread her legs apart and lick her. I feast on her, licking, sucking, and flicking my tongue.

CORINNE MICHAELS

She writhes against my mouth and I fucking love it. I love tasting her pleasure, knowing it's me giving it to her.

She whimpers as she tries to keep quiet. I like pushing her. Making her take risks because the reward is so much sweeter.

"I'm so close. Oh, God. How?" she says, her head thrashing. I watch her face as I move my tongue in different directions against her clit. "So. Good. Grady, don't stop."

Her fingers slide into my hair, holding my mouth right where she needs me. I love when she takes what she wants. If I could do nothing but watch her fall apart, I'd be a happy man.

She bucks forward, fighting the pleasure that's begging to be released. I take my hand, moving it to her ass, rubbing the rim, just teasing her with the possibility of sliding it in.

"Oh. Oh. Oh." Addison pants, her eyes closing, and I know it's close. I wiggle my finger, just breaching her hole, and suck hard on her clit. She lets out a long, incredibly low moan that almost sounds pained as I drink her in, her thighs tighten around my head, and I could drown in her.

After a few moments, she releases her grip on my hair and my face, and she goes limp.

One orgasm down, and as many more as I can drag out of her to come. I know we need to talk but right now, I need her more.

I scoop her up and carry her to the bedroom. I close the door, push the lock, and lay her on the bed.

She scoots onto her knees. "I want you to stay right there."

I raise one brow. "Do you?"

"Yes."

I slide my boots off, tossing them to the side, unbuckle my belt and place it on the bed in case I want to use it later. Then I undo my button. "Why is that, dove?"

Her eyes flash with something and then she grins. "I want to suck your dick."

"If that isn't the hottest thing you've ever said to me, I don't know what is."

"Get naked."

"Yes, ma'am." I pull my sweatshirt off, lose the jeans, and stand before her completely naked. "Well, now what is your plan? Are you going to stay on that bed or are you going to get on your knees and do what you promised?"

Addison slides off the bed, her hand pressing against my chest before running it slowly over my abs. Her delicate hand wraps around my cock, as much of it as she can, and strokes. "I'm going to make you lie down, and I'm going to straddle your face, so you can look at how wet I get doing what I want."

I grin. Weeks ago, that would've never come out of her mouth. She was timid about this, and now she's ready to take what she wants, knowing I'll give her anything.

I do as she asks, lying on the bed, hands tucked behind my head. "If you want me to touch you, you're going to have to move your body to where you want."

"What?"

"I'm not moving a muscle, dove. If you want that pretty pussy to get licked, you better put it on my mouth and ride my fucking face. If you want my cock to fill you the way I know you want to be filled, then you better climb on me and fuck me how you want it. However, if you want my hands somewhere, you tell me and I'll do it."

The confident girl a few moments ago is gone and she nods.

"And what do you want?" Addison asks, her eyes filled with desire.

"I want you to suck my cock and love every second of it."

She moves her leg over me, dangling her pussy in my face. I now see the small error in my plan. All I want is to lift my head and lick her again.

I want to taste her excitement as she blows my fucking mind.

But I have to stay still, watch it hang above me like a ripe apple I can't pick.

Fuck, this was a bad move.

She takes me deep and I feel every muscle in my body go taut.

This is going to be torture. The best kind, but still torture. Addison sucks my dick like it's her favorite thing in the world.

"That's it, baby, don't stop," I tell her, urging her on more. "God, your mouth feels so good wrapped around my cock. I'm so fucking hard. Keep going. That's my good girl." I like talking to her and by the way she's moving, she likes it too. "Take it deep, dove. I want to feel the back of your throat." She does what I ask, and I have to fight hard not to blow my load. "Fuck, Addy, I want to lick you until you come again on my tongue, letting me taste your release. Sit on my face, baby, and let me make you choke on my dick."

Then, she sinks down on my face and rocks. I move my tongue against her, licking along her seam, and then when she moves back, I push inside of her. She moans while she takes me deep again.

I know I said I wasn't going to move my hands, but I can't stop myself. I grab her hips, holding her right where I want it. I move my hands to her ass, squeezing, wanting to drown in her. Then I slap it hard, wishing I could see it turn red.

She gasps, causing her to stop sucking my cock. I spank her again, knowing how much she likes it. "I didn't tell you to stop," I say as she's panting, rocking her hips against my face. "Suck my dick, Addison."

Immediately, her mouth is back around me and I reward her, flicking her clit again. "That's it, good girl, suck it deep." I move my other hand up, shoving a finger deep in her pussy as she does what I tell her.

Then I slap her ass again, harder than before. She clenches around me, and I can't wait until my cock is buried inside her.

I feel my own release coming and there's not a chance in hell I'm going to spend this soon. I want every fucking minute I can get.

"Addy, stop." She lifts her head and the second she's off, I roll us and climb on top of her. "I want to be inside of you when I come. I want to feel your muscles contracting around my cock while I make you scream my name."

She smiles, her hand moving to my face. "I look forward to it, but I thought you said if I wanted your cock, I have to ride you."

"You will ride me, but first I'm going to fuck you." Addison's face heats as she stares at me. "I want to watch you fall apart again. You are exquisite when my cock is in you as you come."

"Good to know."

I smile at her. "You're exquisite all the time."

As I line up, something flashes in her eyes, and then her finger strokes my cheek. "Thank you."

"For what?"

"For everything. I didn't know this side of myself, and you allowed me to show it. I'm pretty sure you've ruined me."

I lean down, kissing her softly. "You'll never be ruined, Addison. You're everything good in this world, if anyone is ruined . . . it's me."

Instead of giving her a chance to say anything, I kiss her roughly and slide deep inside of her. When I feel her around me, I fight for control.

She feels like fucking home.

And she can't be.

She's not home.

She's going to leave Sugarloaf and I'm going to have to watch her walk away.

We rock back and forth, neither of us saying a word, but our eyes are connected. I know she feels it and I both love it and hate it.

"Addy," I say her name, moving my hips with hers. "God, Addison."

"Don't let me go," she says as she clings to me. Her legs around my hips, arms tight around my neck. "Just hold on, please, I'm falling apart."

"No, dove, I'm here. I have you," I promise.

And you'll have to kill me before I let her go.

thirty-two
ADDISON

G rady is lying in my bed, and my chickenshit ass is in the bathroom, having a minor—okay, major anxiety attack.

I'm not sure how the hell we ended up here.

How did I go from reading my book in bed to doing very dirty things with him, negating the fact that he came here in the middle of the night to talk?

Oh, I remember. I didn't want to talk.

I didn't want to hear him tell me to go. I wasn't ready to have my heart broken again.

So I kissed him.

And then we . . . well, did what we do.

But now what?

Now I have to tell him that this has to stop. He can't come here, we can't do this, not when I have to make a decision in six hours.

Six hours and I don't know what to choose because I really don't want to leave, but I don't think I can stay and live a life without him.

I exhale, stare at the woman in the mirror, and buck up because I need to handle my shit.

More like this is my house and I can't exactly move into the bathroom, but . . . semantics.

I open the door and Grady is there, sitting with his back against the headboard, ankles crossed.

"I came here to talk," he says, one brow raised, with a grin.

I lean against the doorjamb. "We tend to forget to do that when we're too close."

"Is that why you're staying over there?"

"I think it might be best."

He chuckles. "You might be right."

"What did you want to talk about?"

He shifts, his legs coming off the side of the bed, and he makes his way to me, slowly. "I realized something. Something that warranted me riding Brutus here in the middle of the night because it matters—you matter."

My stomach drops and I stay still as he approaches. "I matter?"

"You do, very much to me."

"And you wanted to tell me that because . . .?"

"Because I think you should know all your options before you move. I'd like to lay my cards out on the table if that's all right with you?"

I should tell him no. I should remind him that he has made it clear that he has no plans for a family, but my traitorous heart can't say the words, so I nod.

Grady's rough hands take mine, squeezing gently. "I've been good at pretending about us. I've convinced myself so well that I failed to notice when it stopped being a lie. I know we had a plan, I know *I* had a plan, and it's bullshit, dove. I don't want you to leave thinking that this wasn't real for me. That how I feel about you isn't real, because it is."

"And what do you feel?"

He lifts his hands to my face, cradling me like I'm precious and delicate. "I'm falling in love with you. Against every attempt to stop it, I couldn't and I don't want you to go, but I love you enough to let you if that's what you want."

He loves me? Did that really come out of his mouth? "You love me?"

"Yes."

"You love me?" I ask again.

Grady smiles then brings our faces close, rubbing his nose against mine. "More than I ever knew I could. More than I ever wanted to. I love you, Addison, and I was a fool to ever think I could stop myself because you are incredibly lovable."

I feel the tear slide down my cheek, my heart bursting into a million pieces but from happiness. "You have really good timing," I tell him, my fingers wrapped around his wrist.

"Why?"

"Six more hours and it might have been too late."

He pulls back, his eyes finding mine. "Why?"

"I have to give my answer."

"Well, here's mine. No matter what you decide, I can't lose you. If you go to Rose Canyon, I'll follow you," he admits.

And that confession, those three words tell me everything I needed to know. He would've fought for me, for us.

"You can't move there."

His thumb wipes away the tear that falls. "You can't stop me, Addison. If you leave, we're going too. We'll figure out how to make it work until I can get things settled here. I can fly back and forth easily and then when I have a plan in place, Jett and I will come there. I just need time. I need to make sure Jett is okay."

I shake my head. "No. You're not moving to Oregon. Not without me at least."

Grady sits back, his eyes wide. "What?"

"I'm not going to take the deal."

"Why?" Grady asks quickly.

I release his wrists and his hands drop. "I'm not someone who has a hard time making decisions. I'm kind of the opposite most times. My gut doesn't fail me, and I trust it. The only reason I was considering taking this deal was because of you."

"What about me?"

I scoot forward, taking his hands in mine. "I love you, Grady Whitlock. And just the idea of knowing what loving you feels like and then having to lose you was too much for me. To be in Sugar-loaf, see you and Jett, but not ever feel your touch again—broke my heart."

He lifts his hand, running the back of his fingers down my cheek. "I couldn't imagine a day where I couldn't do this." He leans in, kissing me softly. "Or that." He pushes me down on the bed, hovering above me. "Or feel you beneath me again."

I smile. "That last one would've been a tragedy."

"No, dove, the tragedy would've been never getting to love you. Now that I do, now that I've had you in my life, I'm not ready to let go."

I play with the back of his hair, twirling the silky ends through my fingers. "So what are you asking me to do?"

He smiles down at me, and my heartbeat accelerates. "Addison Davis, will you be my real, honest-to-God girlfriend and date me?"

I pretend to think about it for a second.

"Addy, are you contemplating this?"

I laugh and then take his beautiful face in my hands. "I'm already halfway in love with you, I want to fall all the way."

"You don't have to fall, dove, I'll hold your hand as we soar together."

"Date me. Love me. Just don't break my heart," I say as I lean up to press my lips to his.

"Doves mate for life and I think that's why I called you that. Not just because you gave me peace, but because I could envision the future with you—always."

"Always? What about all the other things?" I ask, not really knowing if I want the answer or not because while I want nothing more than to jump with him, I'm not sure we have the same idea of the landing.

"What other things?"

"I want a family again, Grady. I want more kids and you don't."

He kisses the tip of my nose. "I've always wanted it, I'm just afraid to reach for it. Can you give me time? Let me settle into this with you and then we can figure out a plan? I'm not saying no, I'm just saying I need a little time."

My chest feels as though it could burst right now. "Really? You want that? You want to think about it?"

"Addison, there's nothing more I would love than to see you pregnant with our child. It's the after part that has me fucking terrified. I can't endure the idea of losing you. I'm warning you now that I'll be a crazy person when you do get pregnant. I want us to build a life together, I just know I'm not ready right now to have a baby. We have so much to overcome, let's just give us a little time."

I laugh softly and lift my head to kiss him. "I can handle that. I didn't want that tomorrow, just to know that it wasn't off the table. And . . . when I close my eyes, it's always you I see, Grady. You, me, Jett, Elodie, and a family we make of our own. I promise if we have another baby, I'll understand you being crazy, and I promise not to fuss about it."

At least I won't fuss too much.

"Good because I will go back to heaven and drag you back if you try to ever leave me."

"Same. No being a hero and all that," I warn him. "I need you on this Earth, not in the ground, because you're a good man. Work on being a shittier person, would you?"

"How about I'm only the hero with you, Elodie, and Jett?"

The lie makes me smile. "I would appreciate that."

He kisses me again, this time deeper, and I swear, I can feel his love wrapping around me and it is the best thing in the world, and now it's mine.

Grady is sitting beside me on the couch as I dial Blakely's number.

She answers on the second ring. "Hey. Do you have a decision?"

Leave it to Blakely to skip the small talk.

"Good morning to you too, I'm good. I slept . . . very little." My cheeks burn as I look at the reason I didn't sleep. "However, it was a good night regardless. How are you?"

"Addy, I love you, but I wasn't up because I was being ravaged by my husband. I had a kid puke on me twice and the dog got sprayed by a skunk this morning. I'm ready to run away."

"We can talk later," I tell her.

"Nope. I'm not waiting. Spill it."

"I can't take the deal."

She sighs and I can't tell if it's a good sigh or a bad one. Considering I just shit on her already terrible morning, I'm going with the second.

"Thank God," Blakely says. "I was so worried this was what you really wanted, and we'd give up our vision because after the last call, it's clear they want to completely reshape Run to Me into something neither of us want. I love our charity, and I want to help more people, but I really don't want to be in a stuffy office dealing with corporate rules."

I smile and huff out a laugh. "Are you serious?"

"Totally. I mean, it would've been amazing to have you back here. Everyone misses you, but Emmett even said that he hasn't seen you so happy as you were when you came for the wedding. He likes Grady and said he was someone he wouldn't hate having in our lives, which is high praise."

It is. Emmett is a tough nut to crack and I'm so happy he likes Grady. "Well, Grady and I would've moved there, but our kids are happy here."

"Ohhh, you both would've moved?" she asks and I can totally picture her shit-eating grin.

"We would."

"I figured it was serious since you brought him here, but . . . this makes me so damn happy."

I look over at him as he watches me. "I'm happy too."

"Then this is the best choice."

It really was. "I think so too."

"Love you, Addy," Blakely says with a hitch in her voice.

"Love you too."

"Now, go kiss your man, do all the things I can't do because I have a sick kid and Emmett is going to smell for a week as he's bathing the dog. I'll send an email tonight informing them that we're going to pass and appreciate their offer."

"Okay. Thanks, Blakely."

"Don't thank me, babe. Thank God for giving you a second chance at finding an incredible man."

Every day I do and now I can thank him for so much more.

thirty-three
GRADY

"Hello, Mrs. Symonds," I say as I open the door to Sugarlips, allowing her to exit.

She glares at me a little. Seems a few months isn't enough time to forgive me for not naming her as the winner of the chili cookoff. "Mr. Whitlock, have a wonderful day."

I laugh under my breath. "You too." As she passes, an idea strikes me. "Mrs. Symonds, I have a question."

"Yes?"

"Do you happen to have any chili still? I know Mrs. Parker froze her batch for when I regained use of my tongue and I was thinking maybe you, her, and Mrs. Cooke could bring some over soon?"

Her eyes widen. "Of course I have some, you don't just throw away award-winning chili. I won six years in a row before Lynn came in with those fancy spices she got from overseas." She leans in close. "If you ask me, that should be grounds for disqualification since they're not authentic. But far be it from me to suggest such a thing."

I think she did just suggest it, but whatever. "I feel as though I missed out by not getting to enjoy it."

"You did."

I fight back a laugh. "Maybe we can do a tasting at the tree-

329

lighting ceremony?" My plan is also to make Asher eat it since he went on and on about my mishap. "I'm sure my brother would make a great judge as well."

She grins so wide it could crack her cheeks. "I think that's wonderful! Oh, I think we could have the winner of this year face-off with us too. That way we can really see if that Sullivan family has the best chili."

I would rather eat snails, but this will put me back in the good graces of the three women who run this town.

While dating Addison has given me some clout, it hasn't been enough to recover from upsetting them.

"That sounds great. I'm sure Charlotte will be up for the challenge."

Her lips turn up slowly as though she's rather enjoying the idea of it. Apparently, I not only pissed off the three of them, but Rowan was even more unbearable. The fact that I chose Charlotte Sullivan, his archenemy in everything, was a dagger to his heart.

Brynlee enjoyed it, as did the rest of us because anything to piss Rowan off is always a good time.

Mrs. Symonds leans in, pulling my arm down, and kisses my cheek before patting it. "You are definitely not a jackass like the rest of them say."

And then she walks off, leaving me a little unsettled with that last comment.

I look around for Addy, spotting her in the same booth she sat in that night I saved her from the dickhead who wanted to sleep with her. I walk to her, my entire day feeling better just because I get to look at her.

"Hi, dove."

"Hello. I see you have done something to make Mrs. Symonds happy?"

I laugh. "We're going to taste their chili."

"No."

I raise one brow with a smirk. "No?"

"No, I am not. I endure it once a year, I'm not signing up to do it again."

I slide in next to her, kiss her pouty lips, and then kick my feet up on the bench across from her. "Well, I didn't say you were. I've volunteered Asher. Since he is doing the tree-lighting ceremony, it works perfect next week."

She laughs. "He's going to kill you."

"He can try."

"Well, I'm sure the old ladies of Sugarloaf are going to spoil you the next two weeks."

"All part of my plan. The women love me, I just have this way with the ladies."

Addison scoffs. "Please."

"Hey, look who you're in love with . . ."

"A fool."

I shrug. "We are all fools in love."

She laughs loudly. "Oh, you're in a mood. Did you talk to the permit office?"

I swear to God, someone there hates me. Once again, my permit was denied. This time claiming the drainage will be an issue, creating runoff into another farm. How the fuck that's even possible is beyond me since there are about thirty acres to the closest farm on either side.

"I'm never going to get out of my sister's house at this rate."

Addison lets out a sigh through her nose and turns to face me. "Move in with me."

"What?"

"You and Jett, move in with me. I know it's fast. I know we said we'd take things slow, and I know this is the opposite, but you're sneaking over every night anyway. I have a four-bedroom house that's built, and . . . I want you there when I wake up in the mornings. I want us to have dinners together, the kids can play. All of it would make our lives easier. Of course you can say no, but . . ."

"Yes," I answer without even thinking. All I know is that after her first sentence, I could see nothing else but a life with her. The two of us getting the kids ready for bed, tucking them in, then going back to our room. I can see the dinners where Addison and I work as a team, laughing and making a mess as we navigate in the tiny kitchen. Late nights where I make love to her until she collapses and mornings filled with kisses.

All of it is what I want.

"Yes?" Addison asks hesitantly. "You said yes?"

"I did. I want every day with you, Addy. I want to create a home for our kids and . . . well, I'm not doing that with Brynn. You're my future, baby. You're my days and nights, and fuck if I want to miss any more of them."

Addison leans in, pressing her lips to mine. "I love you, Grady Whitlock."

"And I love you."

More than I knew I ever could again.

"Can you put that over in the corner?" Addison asks as she's trying to set up Jett's room in an airplane theme.

And when I say theme, I mean it's fucking ridiculous. She has what looks like the front of a plane coming out of the ceiling and it's the ceiling fan.

Then, the bed is more like a cockpit with buttons and levers. "You know he's never going to sleep when we put him to bed."

She shrugs. "He loves this room, Grady. He loves it. He is moving again, and I refuse to let that boy feel anything less than loved."

I walk up behind her, wrapping my arms around her middle, and kiss her neck. "He knows you love him, dove."

"I do, and I want him to be happy in his home."

I turn her to face me. "He is happy. He's living with his best friend and a woman who made his room into a damn airplane heaven."

She sighs and steps back. "I just want him to love it here. I need him to feel like this is his home."

"Addy, it's his home because we make it a home."

I know that better than anyone. A house is just a house, but a home is what you make it. It's the people, not the location. Addison and I are building a home together. Two people who love each other and are merging a family.

"I know you're right."

"I know I am too. Jett is beyond happy to be living here with us. All he talks about is how he can't wait to move in with his Elodie and his Addison. His. Not mine. His."

She smiles at that. "He's my heart too."

"And me?" I ask playfully.

"You're getting there."

I step forward, grabbing her, and she giggles as I tickle her. "Getting there?"

She pushes back, her eyes full of humor. "Fine. You're my whole world."

"That's better."

"And what about me? What am I?"

The humor in the mood leaves me as I want her to know the words I'm going to say are the truth in every way. "You are the reason I breathe. You're the stars, the sky, the moon, the planets, and what we don't even know exists. You gave me a reason to open myself to love again and instead of running away . . ." I take her hips in my hands, pulling her close to me. "You gave me something to run to."

Tears fill her eyes, but her lips turn into a smile. "That . . . was beautiful."

"No, baby, you're beautiful and what you're trying to do for Jett is beautiful, but he is going to love you no matter what his room looks like because you love him."

She lets out a sigh. "Okay."

"Okay."

Addison kisses me softly. "Now, go move the dresser so I can get the room perfect."

I shake my head, knowing this is a battle I won't win.

We work for the next fifteen minutes, arranging, rearranging, and then re-rearranging again until Addison is happy.

"Daddy!" Jett barrels into the room. "I have an airplane in my new room!"

I scoop him up and nod. "You do."

"I sleep here all da time?"

"You do. This is your room," Addison says, coming up behind us, her hand resting on his back. "Do you like it?"

"I lub it!" He practically leaps out of my arms into hers. He wraps his arms around her neck and buries his face there.

She looks over at me, her smile bright, and she squeezes him. "I think he likes it."

I chuckle. "I think so too."

Addison closes her eyes and kisses the top of his head, and my heart becomes hers just a little bit more.

"Oh, this is good," I lie as I try to choke down the chili. This has to be the worst thing I've ever tasted.

"Yes, great," Asher says, nearly gagging as he does. I don't know how the hell Mrs. Parker won last time because this is terrible. Addison must've been drunk or just lost all her tastebuds by then.

"The other two weren't that bad, definitely better than this one," I whisper to my brother.

"Jesus, I can't even breathe after that."

"Last one is Charlotte's," I say as we walk toward her table. "I'm picking her no matter what."

"Your funeral," Asher says with a laugh.

Not only did Addison pretty much warn me that not picking one of those three was going to be my demise, but Rowan threatened to cut my balls off. Seriously, one day he'll realize threatening me only makes me want to do it more.

We walk up, Charlotte has her bowls assembled, and she smiles at both of us. "Hello to the only handsome Whitlock brothers that reside in Sugarloaf."

"Flattery will get you everywhere, Charlotte," Asher says as he lifts the bowl. "Same recipe?"

She nods. "Yup. I know it's a winner so I wouldn't alter it."

I smile and lift the spoon. When I take a bite, I remember why I chose her. It's good, really good. It's got some heat, but not to the point that your eyes tear like the others we've had. It's chili that I would eat again, which I can't say about the others.

Asher and I both take another taste and place the bowls down, like we did with the others.

"Thank you," I say. "We'll announce the winner soon."

Asher and I walk over to the table and he huffs. "You know we can't pick Charlotte, even though she's definitely the best one and it is always fun to piss off Rowan. However, pissing off those three is at your own peril."

"I know, Addy basically warned me of the same thing."

In fact, she basically threatened to kill me if I did anything different than picking them when we were lying in bed last night.

Our bed.

The bed we share in the house we share.

"So, I think we pick Mrs. Cooke. It was the best of the worst."

"All of these are rigged, aren't they?" I ask.

"Yup."

"And the dance-off?"

He shakes his head. "No, Phoebe wins that fair and square."

"Sure she does."

Asher rolls his eyes. "Okay, so we're prepared to pick Mrs. Cooke, get in their good graces, and have the Sullivans hate Rowan more than they do already?"

I nod. "Sounds like a plan."

We head back to the area where the town is standing around, waiting for the results. Addy is there in the front row with Elodie and Jett in the wagon with blankets bundling them up. I stare at her, wondering how in the world I found someone I can love again. She smiles up at me, her hair pulled to the side in some braid thing that's peeking out of her hat.

She winks at me, and I grin back before Asher huffs and elbows me. "You're announcing this."

"Oh, right." I clear my throat. "Welcome, everyone, to the second judging of the chili competition. Due to my allergic reaction, we didn't have a chance to taste all the competitors and I felt it was necessary. My brother, Asher, has deemed the winner and it's Mrs. Cooke. Congratulations."

"You son of a bitch," Asher says beneath his breath.

"For me, it was a tie between everyone. So to me, you're all winners."

I smile at everyone, clasp Asher on the back, and walk to Addison who I lift up and kiss.

"That was smooth," she says as she wipes lipstick from my lips.

"Well, you told me not to pick anyone, so I made Asher do it."

"He's going to kill you."

I shrug. "He's been threatening it since we were five. I like my odds."

"And I just like you."

"I like you too!" Elodie adds and I look down at the two kids, snug in the wagon, watching us.

I lift her up, squeezing her tight. "I like you more."

"No way!" She giggles as I rock her side to side.

"I promise."

"What about me, Daddy?" Jett asks.

"You? I like you more too!" He stands and I take him in my arms too, holding both kids close. "I love you both." I look to Addison. "I love you all."

And I want to spend the rest of my life loving them.

thirty-four

ADDISON

"On your hands and knees, dove," Grady commands as he leans against the wall, just staring at me.

I had to undress slowly as he sat in the chair in the corner, not touching me, not moving other than to stroke his cock.

I wanted to go to him so bad, to feel him, kiss him, but he wouldn't let me. I've missed this side of him. Since we've moved in, it's been constant lovemaking, which I have enjoyed, but I also love the domineering man sitting here now.

"Grady," I call his name, begging him to come to me.

"Stay like that, Addison. Face the wall and don't look."

Looking is the only damn thing I've been able to do and now he's taken that. "I need you."

"Are you wet?"

"Yes," I moan.

"Good. Are you aching for me?"

"Yes!"

"Good. I ache for you every fucking day. I leave this house, with you in bed, thinking of your skin, your scent, your perfect body that I have to imagine." His voice is getting a little closer. "I have to dream of the things I would do to you. Do you know how filthy my fucking dreams are with you?"

Probably about as filthy as mine are, so I can guess. "Tell me," I urge him.

He chuckles low, this time the sound coming from a different spot. "I think of taking you in every room, watching you bounce on my cock as I angle deeper so you get every inch of me. I lick your pussy until you come and still don't stop after, making you hurt because it feels so good. The good dreams, the ones I never want to stop, are when I slap your ass so hard my hand is there, marking your perfect skin before I fuck your ass. I want to own every part of you, Addison."

I groan, actually groan, and then rub my legs together to try to help the throbbing. "You already do."

He owns my heart, my soul, my body, my whole world, and I never knew I could love like this. I didn't think I could ever feel something similar if not more intense, but I do with Grady. It's been a month of us living together and seeing him love Elodie has changed me in a way I can't explain.

We didn't have any hiccups becoming a family of four. It was as though it was meant to be this way and once we stopped fighting it —it clicked.

Grady's hand slides against my ass cheek and I nearly jump from the unexpected touch. His voice is low and soothing. "I want more. I'm greedy for you. Lean on your elbows."

I do as he says, my ass moving higher in the air. "Like this?"

"Yes, love, just like that."

Then I feel him bite at my thigh before his tongue slides against the skin and up higher. I rest my head on my forearms as he licks me, sliding his tongue deep inside of me. "God," I say as I rock my hips toward him.

"Mmm, my favorite taste." Then he does it again, moving his tongue in and out before flicking my clit. "Stay just like that."

I both love and hate this, when I'm at his mercy, having to hope he'll give me all I want.

"Grady, I need you."

"I know." His voice has hints of pleasure in those two words.

He likes this. He likes being the one who controls my pleasure and who deems when I'm allowed to have it.

I feel his tongue again at my entrance, sliding against the wetness as he moans. Then his hand slaps down hard. I buck forward from the force and also the pleasure of it. God, I love this. I never thought being spanked would turn me on, but I fucking love it.

"Again," I beg.

He doesn't make me wait, his hand slaps against my ass while driving a finger deep inside of me. "That's it, fuck my hand, dove. Imagine it's my cock."

They're not the same, but I don't care right now, I just want him. Any part of him.

He pulls his fingers out and I feel him rim my asshole. This is the one part I'm still not completely comfortable with, but it feels so damn good, my inhibitions usually take a backseat.

"Do you want this?" Grady asks. "Do you want me to claim your ass, baby?"

I whimper a little as he pushes in a bit. "Grady," I say his name, still not all the way comfortable with things.

"Say it, Addy. Tell me you want it and I'll give it to you."

He knows when to push me out of my shell. "I want it."

"Damn fucking right you do." Then he gives it to me, pushing his finger in and moving it back and forth. "One day, I'm going to take your ass with my cock. I'm going to fill you up and fuck you while I spank your ass for being a bad girl."

I'm on fire and can't find the strength to be embarrassed by his words. "Only with you."

"That's right. This is mine," he says as he pushes deeper. Then I feel his other hand at my pussy. "And this is mine." He shoves deep at the same time.

"Yes!"

He pulls out and turns my head to the side, shoving his finger between my lips as I taste myself. "This is mine."

I try to nod as his finger moves against my tongue.

341

"You're mine."

"I am. Always."

When he removes his finger from my lips, he takes the other out of my ass and before I can say anything, he slams deep inside of me, filling me until I can barely breathe.

"Fuck, Addy. Fuck, you feel so goddamn good."

I had my IUD put back in until we're ready to have kids, which I promised Grady I am fine with waiting. Now we can completely stop using condoms.

All I feel is Grady and it's absolute bliss.

"Harder," I tell him and he rears back, slamming into me again.

He keeps up his pace, the sound of slapping skin and sex fills the air. His hand is on my lower back, pushing me down so he gets the angle he wants. "You look so hot like this. My cock filling you, your red ass in the air. I want to fuck you until you can't walk without thinking of me."

"I always think of you," I say as I toss my head to the side.

Grady grips my hair, wrapping it around his hand, and pulls. "I'm going to own you, Addison. I'm going to ride you so hard you can't stop thinking of me."

There is a balance of pleasure and pain that he walks perfectly. The bite of him pulling my hair is just coupled with the intense pleasure of his other hand at my clit.

"I'm close," I warn him.

"I know. I feel your cunt clutching me. I've been too gentle with you the last few weeks, you've missed it rough."

"Yes," I hiss.

I've missed it. Not that making love to him slow and gentle hasn't been perfect, because it has, but I like this too. I like when he's bossy and doesn't treat me with kid gloves.

"Yes, what?"

"Yes, baby."

He pulls on my hair harder. "That's not what I want, and you know it."

"I like it when your hard cock is fucking me. I like when you're rough and make me feel good when I'm bad."

His grip loosens and he rewards me with a deep thrust. "That's my good girl."

We don't talk again. Grady focuses on fucking me hard and deep. My orgasm crashes through me without warning and I fall apart, grateful for the pillow close to my face.

I scream into it, biting the fabric as he doesn't slow.

As the last moments of my orgasm are pulsing, he moans and finishes. The two of us crumple to the bed and he stays inside of me, arm wrapped around my middle, holding my back to his chest.

I close my eyes and lie here, my emotions scattering like broken glass. I feel so much when we're together. As though a simple emotion is more than it was before and it's because of him.

He makes me feel alive in a way I wasn't before. It's amazing on some levels and terrifying on others.

There are days I feel weak because I miss him when he's traveling or working late. I worry about him all the damn time, which I've been getting better at. I also think about him all the time, I wake up and it's Grady. I eat food and I think about Grady. When I'm going to sleep, again—Grady. It's sort of annoying.

Then at the same time, I feel stronger, more confident, and as much as the arrangement we had wasn't what I wanted, it was what I needed. He's what I needed, and I love him so damn much.

"What are you thinking, my love?" Grady asks against my ear.

"That I love you."

I can feel his smile. "It's a good thing because I love you."

My hand moves to his hip, wanting him to stay connected to me. "I wish that love didn't come with all the worries."

"What do you worry about? Let me carry those for you."

I smile, loving him even more. "I just never want to lose this. Lose us."

"I'm glad you feel that way."

I look back at him, well, what little I can see. "Why is that?"

"Because I have no intention of ever losing you, dove."

Sometimes he says the sweetest freaking things.

"Good."

His scruff rubs against my neck. "Good. Now," his voice changes back into that silky rasp. "I think I want to seal that promise with my favorite thing."

"What?" He doesn't answer with words, his finger moves to my clit, and he answers it with something much better—an orgasm.

"Who wants to take pictures with Mickey?" Grady asks the two kids who are damn near bouncing with excitement.

We came down to Orlando for the ribbon cutting of the newest center of Run to Me. It has been a whirlwind two weeks and after my second breakdown from missing Elodie and Jett, I woke up the next day to the three of them ringing the doorbell.

My amazing boyfriend didn't hesitate, even though I was coming home in four days to pack them up and bring them here.

To celebrate the end of this hellish journey, we are at the magical place where no one can be sad, other than your wallet.

"Me first!" Jett yells.

"I go first, Jett! I'm four now!"

"I'm four too!" he retorts, arms crossed and an attitude befitting a four-year-old.

To which my daughter returns the gesture and sighs. "You always go first."

"How about neither of you go first?" Grady jumps in before it gets heated. "Addy and I will go first."

"You can't do that!" Elodie scolds him and I have to turn my head to hide the smile.

Grady squats down. "And why not, Els?"

"Because you're too big."

"Too big?"

She nods. "You and Mommy are grown-ups. You don't see Mickey."

"Hmm," he says, eyes narrowing as though he's contemplating that. "Are you sure?"

One head bob.

"But what if I want to see him first?"

She shakes her head vehemently. "No way, Daddy. You can't go now. Jett and I go to see Mickey first."

The two of us freeze, Grady's gaze meets mine and my heart is pounding. She hasn't called him Daddy before, and while we aren't married or even engaged, Grady has become a father to her since we've been dating.

We've been together for over six months and have been living together for about three now. He picks her up from school, reads her bedtime stories, and takes her to see the animals every Saturday morning, just the two of them.

I get my time with Jett where we usually ride on the side by side out to the river, and he stomps around in the mud with me.

I'm not at all surprised she thinks of him like a dad.

I crouch down beside Grady, my hand taking Elodie's. "Els, why did you call Grady, Daddy?" I ask sweetly, so she doesn't think she's in trouble.

"Because I love him."

I smile. "He's very lovable."

"Is he my daddy too?"

Grady clears his throat. "I would love to be your other daddy if you want, but you can call me anything you want. It can be Grady or Daddy or Mr. Fuzzypants."

She giggles and I work hard at keeping my tears at bay. "Jett calls you Daddy."

"He does."

"So you can be my daddy too!"

Elodie wraps her arms around his neck and squeezes tight. Grady wipes at his face and I know he's emotional too.

Jett comes to my side, taking my hand. "Can we go first, pwease, Addison?"

Grady pops up, pulling Elodie up into his arms. "Not this time, my sweet Elodie gets to go first."

She claps loudly and I hoist Jett up with a plan to let my sweet boy get his turn. "While we'd love to give you two this moment, I'm afraid we can't do that."

"No?" Grady asks with a little confusion.

"No, instead, I think we're going to race."

And the four of us take off towards the last sighting, laughing as we dodge people trying to get to Mickey as one happy family.

epilogue

GRADY

~Two months later~

I'm out in the spot that would've been where my house was going to go, for the first time grateful for stupid red tape and issues at the county that delayed it all.

One thing could've altered the life I have now.

One decision going the other way would mean no Addison or Elodie.

The four of us have found each other, built a foundation, and now I want all the walls to go up and our home to be secured around us.

Today I'm going to ask Addison to be my wife. To allow me to spend the rest of my days with her, giving her the life she's dreamed of.

I want everything with her, a home, marriage, more kids, and to love the ones we have now. Both of our businesses are doing great, we're happy, and I'm not afraid anymore. Not of a future, but more of not having one.

I hear the side by side approach right on time. We are going to let the past go so we can start our futures.

"Hey, baby," Addy's soft voice says a minute later.

I turn to see her wearing a flowing sundress, with her sweater on, the kids holding her hands.

"Daddy!" They both run to me, and I laugh as each grabs a leg.

"Hey, guys, I missed you too."

Addy approaches, a wide smile on her lip. "How was your trip?"

"It was good."

I flew to Rose Canyon five days ago where I went to Isaac's grave, talked to him about my plans, as well as Spencer, Emmett, and Holden. I brought them back here, where they've been hiding out at my brothers' and sister's houses. After that, I flew down to Oklahoma to sit beside Lisa's headstone, see her parents again, and explain my intentions to them.

Now that I have everyone's blessings, I feel, more than ever, this is the right time.

The kids release my legs and I pull her into my arms, kissing her softly. "I missed you."

"I missed you. Also, you missed Jett teaching Elodie how boys can pee without a potty in the backyard."

I laugh once and try to choke down the others that follow. "I'm sure she learned a lot."

Addy rolls her eyes. "I believe I had the same lesson from the three dipshits in Oregon."

"It is a very important life lesson."

"Sure it is. However, the kids missed you terribly. We spent yesterday with Phoebe, Olivia, and the baby, and they decided they liked her enough to keep her since she doesn't cry as much anymore."

"How very kind of them."

"I thought so," Addy says with a brow raised. "Olivia has them both doing better with sign language too."

Addison and I have been taking lessons to be able to communicate more with Olivia. Of course, Addy has done better than me because she seems to be better at everything, but I'm nearly as proficient as she is.

The kids, though, pick it up so damn fast. Jett and Elodie sit with Olivia and sign back and forth with Phoebe helping when they stumble. It's been really amazing watching them all, and frustrating as fuck when I try.

Which make Olivia laugh at my poor attempts.

"I'm glad everyone is learning, I know it means a lot to Asher."

Addison shakes her head. "She's your niece and I love her. It's a great skill to have and I wish I had learned when I moved here so Olivia never had to try to communicate with me another way."

I lean in and kiss her. "I love you."

"I love you too. Now. Tell me why you had us meet you out here instead of at home?"

I grin. "So impatient."

"More like, so cold."

"Well no one told you to wear a sweater with holes in it."

Addison huffs. "Yes, well, I didn't know what the hell the point of this trip was, so . . . can we get on with it?"

I almost laugh because she clearly has no idea what's coming. "Sure, I brought you here because I wanted to do something special with the kids."

"Oh?"

The two of us look over to see Jett lifting a rock and Elodie scrunching her face as he digs.

Great.

"Jett, put the rock down and don't dig!" I call over.

"He found a bug! It's gross!" Elodie informs us.

Of course he did. "You guys come here, I need your help."

They rush over, eager with no idea what they're going to be helping with. "I help first, Daddy," Jett says, always the same fight with these two.

"We're all going to do it together." The four of us make our way to the blanket laid out where there are four paper lanterns. "We are going to send these up into the sky. We can put any message we want to your papa or momma."

"Oh, Grady," Addison says as she kneels on the blanket. "This is perfect."

It's about to get more perfect.

I help Elodie write a message to her dad and Addison does the same with Jett. Four-year-old messages aren't very eloquent, but the kids had fun painting their handprints and sticking it all over the lanterns.

"I think Momma will like this!" Jett says as he holds it up.

"I think she'll love it," Addison tells him.

"Mommy, can you write a letter to Momma?" he asks. Addison is Mommy for him, and Lisa is now Momma.

Elodie calls me Daddy and refers to Isaac as Papa.

It happened really easily. They both just started calling us by the names the other does, and we decided they should have a way to distinguish who they meant.

"What should I tell her?" Addison asks.

"Tell her about me!" Jett laughs with his huge smile.

"Okay." Addison writes some words down, explaining them and what they mean as Jett listens attentively.

"Are you ready to send it up to the sky?" I ask. The kids clap as we open it up, Addison holding the top as I light it. "Come hold onto this part." Each take their lanterns. "Now let it go and it'll fly up in the sky."

They both do it, laughing and watching with wide eyes.

Then I turn to Addison, facing her to me. I see behind her, our friends making their way to us. I grab my lantern and smile at her.

"I made this for us to put into the sky."

"Oh?"

"It has a note from me to Isaac."

Addison's brows rise. "What?"

"Well, he loved you first. He loved you with his whole heart, and I think that he would've hoped that you'd find a man who would try to do that and more."

She smiles softly. "Are you that man?"

"I am."

"Aunt Brielle! Uncle Emmett!" Elodie screams and Addison

turns to see our friends and family around.

"What are you . . .? Why are you all here?" Addy's voice cracks and I sink to one knee, waiting for her to turn back to me. "Grady?" Then I see her entire face change. Tears fill her eyes, and her hands cover her lips. "Oh God."

"Addison Elizabeth Davis, when we met, I remember thinking you were the most beautiful woman I had ever seen. You saved me the first day we met, helping me with Jett, and you've saved me every day after that. I was the one who didn't even realize when I asked you to pretend to be my girlfriend, that you'd be more than that. You'd be my best friend, my love, my light, and the reason I smiled again. You're the only woman I ever want to laugh with, fight with, smile, and pretend with. I may not have had the honor of loving you first, but I want to be the man who loves you last." I pull the ring from my pocket, holding it between my fingers. "Will you—"

"Yes!" she yells and drops to her knees. "Yes. Yes. Yes, and more yes!"

"I didn't even ask you anything," I say with a grin.

"Oh!" She laughs. "Please, go on and ask your question."

"Thank you. Addison Elizabeth Davis, will you do me the great honor of becoming my wife?"

"Yes!" she screams and then launches herself into my arms. "I love you."

I pull her tight and call over her shoulder. "She said yes!"

The group laughs and some are wiping their eyes. Addison kisses me and rests her forehead on mine. "Nothing about us has ever been pretend, Grady Whitlock. I loved you before I knew I could, and I will love you forever."

"Good, because I plan on forever lasting a really long time."

Ready for more of the Whitlock Family?
Rowan & Charlotte are up next!

The next page has access to an EXCLUSIVE Bonus Scene!

Dear Reader,

I hope you enjoyed Broken Dreams! I had a hard time saying goodbye to Grady & Addison. I wanted to give just a little more of a glimpse into their lives, so ... I wrote a super fun scene.

Since giving you a link would be a pain in the ... you know what ... I have an easy QR code you can scan, sign up, and you'll get and email giving you access! Or you can always type in the URL!

https://geni.us/BD_signup

If you'd like to just keep up with my sales and new releases, you can follow me on BookBub or sign up for text alerts!
BookBub: https://www.bookbub.com/authors/corinne-michaels

Join my Facebook group!
https://www.facebook.com/groups/corinnemichaelsbooks

V.

books by corinne michaels

Want a downloadable reading order?

https://geni.us/CM_ReadingGuide

The Salvation Series

Beloved

Beholden

Consolation

Conviction

Defenseless

E ermore: A 1001 Dark Night Novella

Indefinite

Infinite

The Hennington Brothers

Say You'll Stay

Say You Want Me

Say I'm Yours

Say You Won't Let Go: A Return to Me/Masters and Mercenaries Novella

Second Time Around Series

We Own Tonight

One Last Time

Not Until You

If I Only Knew

The Arrowood Brothers

Come Back for Me

Fight for Me

The One for Me

Stay for Me

Willow Creek Valley Series

Return to Us

Could Have Been Us

A Moment for Us

A Chance for Us

Rose Canyon Series

Help Me Remember

Give Me Love

Keep This Promise

Whitlock Family Series

(Coming 2023-2024)

Forbidden Hearts

Broken Dreams

Tempting Promises

Forgotten Desires

Co-Written with Melanie Harlow

Hold You Close

Imperfect Match

Standalone Novels

You Loved Me Once

acknowledgments

My husband and children. I love you all so much. Your love and support is why I get to even have an acknowledgment section.

My assistant, Christy Peckham, you always have my back and I can't imagine working with anyone else. I love your face.

Melanie Harlow, you have no idea how much I cherish our friendship. You are truly one of my best friends in the world and I don't know what I would do without you.

My publicist, Nina Grinstead, you're stuck with me forever at this point. You are more than a publicist, you're a friend, a cheerleader, a shoulder to lean on, and so much more.

The entire team at Valentine PR who support me, rally behind me, and keep me smiling.

Nancy Smay, my editor for taking such great care with my story. My cover designer who deals with my craziness, Sommer Stein. My proofreaders: Julia, and ReGina.

Samaiya, thank you for drawing that lock so perfectly!

Every influencer who picked this book up, made a post, video, phoned a friend ... whatever it was. Thank you for making the book world a better place.

about the author

Corinne Michaels is a *New York Times, USA Today, and Wall Street Journal* bestselling author of romance novels. Her stories are chock full of emotion, humor, and unrelenting love, and she enjoys putting her characters through intense heartbreak before finding a way to heal them through their struggles.

Corinne is a former Navy wife and happily married to the man of her dreams. She began her writing career after spending months away from her husband while he was deployed—reading and writing were her escape from the loneliness. Corinne now lives in Virginia with her husband and is the emotional, witty, sarcastic, and fun-loving mom of two beautiful children.